# STRINGS

Turner Publishing Company
Nashville, Tennessee
www.turnerpublishing.com

Strings

This is a work of fiction. All the characters and events portrayed in this book
are either products of the author's imagination or are used fictitiously.

Cover design: Callie Lawson
Book design: Karen Sheets de Gracia

Library of Congress Cataloging-in-Publication Data Upon Request

9781684423408  Hardcover
9781684423392  Paperback
9781684423415  eBook

Printed in the United States of America

19  20  21  22      10  9  8  7  6  5  4  3  2  1

# STRINGS

## THE ABLES ⚡ BOOK TWO

TURNER
PUBLISHING COMPANY

This book is dedicated to

## YOU,

*the person reading this right now.*

## YOU ARE ABLE!

# THE FIRST STEP

*Bong.*

"Ladies and gentleman, this is your captain speaking. We are curr-ently cruising at an altitude of twenty-eight thousand feet, mostly clear skies ahead, on target to beat our expected arrival time by five minutes. Sit back and enjoy the ride, and we'll be in Chicago before you know it."

"And then a two-hour drive from there to Freepoint," Bentley added.

Henry sighed. "It's times like these I really miss James," he said.

"That's not funny," I replied flatly.

"I wasn't saying it to be funny. I'm just saying . . . airline travel is expensive and takes time and . . ."

"And you're afraid of flying," Bentley chimed in, completing Henry's thought for him.

"Well, I am. And it's just a hassle, man. James made a lot of headaches disappear is all I'm saying."

"I'm not ready to talk about it, okay?" That was an understatement, but it effectively ended that line of discussion for the time being.

Henry's hands went up in defense. "Okay, okay, I'm sorry, Phillip. I just wish we were home already."

"We all do, Henry," Bentley agreed, attempting to stamp out the disagreement before it began. "Any good movies on this flight?"

We were traveling first class, courtesy of Bentley's ridiculously rich family, and we were finally headed home. We'd spent two weeks in Orlando, seeing every theme park possible and riding every ride we could find, and frankly I was exhausted from the vacation. Even Henry was tired, having been surprised to find so many rides these days were wheelchair-friendly.

Dad had insisted that we boys take some time out before the new school year for youthful, non-crime-fighting fun. And granted, we'd grown up faster than most fifteen-year-olds, mostly owing to an adolescence spent fighting crime. Perhaps we'd skipped some key "kid" moments along the way. And with the new government crackdown on custodian activity, a vacation seemed like the perfect way for us to be kids again, forgetting the very adult world we lived in, if only for a handful of days.

Bentley was already sixteen, though all three of us had faced enough evil in our lives to give our parents confidence in our ability to keep ourselves safe. Who worries about a trio of kids traveling on their own who had already defeated two of the biggest threats to mankind in recorded history?

Relaxed and rejuvenated, the three of us were flying back to Chicago. There we'd catch a custodian-run car service out to the countryside and our home of Freepoint.

While Freepoint continued to operate as a custodian city, tensions between custodial negotiators and American government officials were at an all-time high, with the Senate formally passing a bill decrying any and all "superhero" vigilante acts by custodians. The Department of

Homeland Security's powers had been strengthened, with an entirely new Custodial Detection unit. Most of this was pushed through by Senator Luder, a high-ranking member of Congress and member of several key committees. He was the most vocal anticustodian politician in Washington, and his rhetoric of fear and security had brought him many supporters both in and out of government office.

He stoked the fears of the American public by highlighting the little-known "victims" of custodial activity—the injured, those with property damage, folks with PTSD. His media team was quite talented, and he'd begun to turn the public discourse regarding custodians toward the negative. A recent poll suggested an even 50 percent of the country had questions or doubts about the custodians' motives.

Crime still existed, and we still fought it, but things had never been more dangerous for custodians. Nearly every custodian who had been spotted in public committing an act of heroism in the last year had disappeared shortly thereafter. Speculation ran rampant about a secret government prison for custodians, while others spoke frantically of an underground network of hidden heroes who were on the run but still doing custodial work.

There'd been, officially at least, twenty-eight documented custodial acts caught on camera by witnesses, news crews, or DHS agents. Each of the custodians involved in these acts was gone, including one of Bentley's older brothers, Brendan. He was a flier, and he had swooped in to grab a college girl falling over Niagara Falls. He'd been there vacationing with his wife and kids at the time, but they hadn't seen him since.

I tried not to think about it. I had plenty to occupy my mind anyway; her name was Emmaline.

Due to my persistent blindness, I'd "seen" her face only a handful of times, at events outside of school, but her voice and personality had already won me over. She was a teleporter, like Mom, and also had epilepsy along with a balance disorder. She'd come to Freepoint last year and had taken up residence in my thoughts since pretty much the moment of her arrival, though she'd yet to say more than three words to me. I was smitten, in a way that I'd never been before. Plenty of my free time ended up being spent thinking about this girl and conversations I would have with her if we were dating. In fact, I decided to spend the remainder of the flight with my eyes closed, pretending to sleep while I daydreamed about a future where Emmaline not only knew I existed, but liked me back.

Henry opted to watch the latest "giant fighting robots" movie. Bentley, as usual, devoted his free time to learning—this time diving deep into an index of superpowers by year, searching for patterns in the appearance and disappearance of certain powers, such as the suddenly now virtually extinct no power zone ability.

Everything was going according to plan, and we were an hour away from landing and returning for our sophomore year in custodian high school . . . when one of the plane's engines decided to quit working. Henry happened to glance out the window as the incident began to unfold.

"That doesn't look good," Henry stated flatly.

We all looked. Smoke billowed out of the engine, creating a dark line in the sky behind us, as tiny flames flickered about the front of the wing-mounted contraption.

"That airplane engine is smoking," Bentley replied, mild concern in his voice.

"Relax," I assured them. "Planes have more than one engine."

"Ladies and gentlemen," the captain intoned, punctuating my point, "we have lost power in one of our engines, as many of you may have noticed. Please be assured that the plane has a second, fully-functioning engine that has more than enough power to get us to our destination."

The cabin filled with the murmurs of concerned passengers while Bentley started doing calculations in his head. "He's right," my friend declared. "We'll be alright as long as the other engine—"

The right-side engine of the jet exploded in a ball of flame and smoke. "Well, shit," Bentley said at the futility of his calculations.

The plane was now coasting. With no functioning engines, it would be forced to coast and float, leaving its landing spot mostly to chance. Would any kind of highway or long paved roadway exist near the stall-out zone to support a gliding landing?

"Henry, can you tell me what the pilots are saying?" I urged, tucking my tray table into the upright position and pulling out a custom pair of glasses.

"Mayday, Mayday, Patriot Air 902 has lost both engines," Henry repeated. "Going down over northwestern Indiana. Need intel on possible landing sites, over."

"Jesus," Bentley breathed.

"Is this plane going to crash?" I whisper-yelled.

Henry shrugged, but Bentley was more specific. "Statistics suggest that a gliding plane with no engines typically ends up landing in places that aren't airports."

Henry and I jerked our heads toward Bentley.

"Streets, fields . . . places like that."

I sighed. "Well, we can't let that happen."

"We can't do this, Phillip. They're going to know a custodian was on this plane."

"Not necessarily. Maybe someone on the ground at the airport did it?" I smiled.

"They'll arrest us," Bentley said flatly.

"Only if they know it was us," I said. "Open a three-way channel." I tapped the earpiece on the glasses I was wearing.

"I've got a bad feeling about this," Henry said while following my instructions.

Turning my attention back to Bentley, I said, "Besides, what are we supposed to do? Let the plane crash and kill everyone on board, which happens to include us?"

"We don't *know* it's going to crash-land. Maybe it'll just be . . . bumpy."

I cocked my head at him skeptically, just as the plane hit a patch of turbulence that rocked the cabin. A loose piece of engine debris flew off the left wing.

"Okay," Bentley finally agreed.

"Henry, can you give me the view of one of the pilots?" I asked.

"I can, but it'll be useless. They're not steadily looking out the windows. They're looking at the controls, each other . . . It's utter panic in there."

I sighed.

The plane lurched with a rapid descent as the passengers gasped. One of the flight attendants made her way up the aisle, so we switched from whispers to thoughts while she struggled past.

*Okay, Bentley, I'll need to be able to see. Aren't there cameras on these modern planes?*

*Yeah*, he responded in silent thought through Henry. *Actually, this model has a camera on the nose and the tail.*

*Gimme the tail*, I thought before standing up. *Henry, you know what to do.* Bentley had invented a set of eyeglasses for Henry to wear in the field as well. They projected a feed from my camera onto the lenses in a way that allowed Henry to see those images and still have his own natural vision at the same time. Bentley had created some kind of "woven display" that he called Subconscious Video. I called it Typical Bentley Wizardry.

*Gotcha*, Henry responded silently. *We're so going to die.*

*Thanks for the confidence, Henry.*

*Can you even control something this large?*

*Remember the train?* I countered, which pretty much ended that debate.

*Okay, okay*, he giggled, remembering. *Just let me know when you're in position.*

Henry used his favorite new trick to slip into Bentley's mind, grab his vision of the aisle, and send that viewpoint to me. We were in first class, so I didn't have far to go. I ran to the front lavatory and locked myself inside. The ride was bumpy, and standing upright was difficult. Finding my balance, I lifted my hands into the air, feeling myself grab hold of the plane itself with my powers. I'd learned how to control my abilities enough to "lock on" to an object without taking immediate firm hold of it. "Okay, Henry, where am I going?" I asked into the radio.

"Just a second," Bentley advised. And then suddenly—visuals.

I was seeing the view from the perspective of the giant airliner's nose. It was intense and amazing, but not remotely helpful to me at the moment. "Bentley, you gotta give me the tail view, man. I can't see anything but air from this angle!"

"Sorry, they're not well labeled and this thing's code is kinda janky," he responded. Seconds later, the view changed to that of the tail camera.

"Okay, perfect," I said. "Now, I'm just going to gradually slow this thing down so that I'm holding it firmly without just grabbing it outright and shaking everyone around like lottery balls."

"Sounds good," Henry said. "I'm in favor of any approach that avoids me facing physical pain."

"You'd feel only half of it," I shot back. I'd gotten pretty good at paraplegic jokes over the years.

"Touché," he chuckled. Over the last few years we'd gotten pretty comfortable joking about our own disabilities, and each other's. Maybe too comfortable.

Gradually I began applying my version of the brakes, and the aircraft began to slow.

"You should totally be hearing these pilots, man." Henry laughed. "They are freaking the heck out right now."

I smiled at the thought of their confusion. Engines go out, but the plane suddenly begins flying itself. It had to be a shocking experience. "Bentley, see what you can do about shutting down their controls so they don't do anything stupid that counteracts what I'm doing."

"On it." I could hear him typing away on his laptop for a few seconds while I continued killing the jet's momentum and slowly lowering it. "Okay, Phillip, they're dead in the water in there. She's all yours."

I smiled to myself. I was almost sixteen years old, and I was about to safely land a plane using my brainpowers. Every now and then, just for a moment, I allowed myself to enjoy my life. Then my ears picked up the muffled panic of the passengers through the lavatory door, and I was jolted out of my pride. "Man, I wish there was a way to shut those people up, or, you know, let 'em know it's going to be okay."

"I could stand up and make an announcement if you think it'll help," Henry jabbed.

"You're going to stand up?"

"Well, you'd have to help with that, of course."

A sudden patch of clouds enveloped us and completely killed my view. We were somewhere over the northwest corner of Indiana, not far from two major airports in Chicago, which meant that lots of planes and other aircraft were in the sky. And now I was blind again.

"Um . . . Bentley?"

"I see it, Phillip, but I don't know what you want me to do about it. Penelope's the one who controls the weather."

"Funny," I said in a way that suggested it was not. "Just . . . think! Find me a way to see!"

He started thinking, while I just sat there waiting.

"Man, you'd think eventually these things would clear, right," Henry said, amazed. "This is a big-ass cloud!"

"Bentley? I don't want to rush you but—"

The clouds parted as suddenly as they'd arrived. "Aha!" I breathed a sigh of relief.

"There you go," Henry added.

"Great. Now what do I do if we run into more clouds?"

"You're the one driving, dude. Just . . . avoid 'em."

"Oh, okay, Henry," I said sarcastically. "That sounds easy."

There were patches of clouds everywhere, and dodging them all as well as the other planes in the sky, while descending, would be tricky. I decided to try anyway, because I didn't really have any other options.

"Can't you hack a satellite or something?"

Bentley replied, "Maybe, but you'd still have to deal with the clouds there as well."

He was right. I slowly guided the jet to its left to avoid a large cluster of clouds just in front of us. We clipped the corner and lost visuals for a second but then floated gently around and below as we continued dropping.

"Nice!" Henry was giggling. "It's like a video game. Dodge the Clouds!"

"I'd play that," Bentley added, a smile in his voice.

The cheerful moment was harshly interrupted when a piece of the damaged right-wing engine broke off and, because I'd tilted the plane, flew straight into the tail—destroying the camera as well as adding further difficulty to the smooth flight of the aircraft.

The passengers all gasped and continued crying and screaming. The jet was moving in ways that were unnatural, so you could hardly blame them for fearing the worst. But they weren't helping my concentration.

"Well crap," I said. "What do I do now?"

There was a long silence. "I think the pilot's viewpoint is the only option," Bentley finally said.

"Wonderful," I said.

Henry just cackled. I think he was a little punch-drunk at this point, and he was finding the entire affair hilarious. "This is gonna be good."

Suddenly I had the view of one of the two pilots, the one on the left. He was, indeed, freaking out. His eyes darted everywhere—controls, meters, gauges, window, other pilot, controls.

"Oh, man, I think I'm gonna throw up." I was getting dizzy already. "I wish you knew how to control people by now, Henry."

"There is no evidence I ever will, my friend. Just be thankful I didn't give you the audio too."

It did look like there was a lot of shouting going on.

Bentley offered a thought. "Maybe he doesn't have to literally control him to get him to sit still and look out the window?"

"Am I supposed to just ask him?" Henry asked.

After a slight pause, Bentley replied, "Yeah, why not?"

"Hey, mister pilot man, I'm a dude on this plane reading your mind. Could you please look out the front window so I can see where we're going?"

"Yeah, something like that."

"We are wasting time debating the wording," I scolded. "I don't care how you do it, Henry, but you gotta get this guy settled down!" How much longer could we drop and drift before hitting another plane . . . or the ground?

Henry let us listen in while he gave the pilot the shock of his life. *Captain, I need you to look out the window. Um . . . this is . . . God.*

Now *I* was giggling.

*Um. I'm going to land this plane for you, but I need your help.*

The pilot had already stopped darting his glance around and turned it toward the window subconsciously, probably out of shock because there was a voice in his head. Then he snapped out of it and looked at the copilot, then the radio operator, then back at the controls.

*No no*, Henry urged. *That wasn't a figment of your imagination. I'm real. I'm still here. I still need you to lift your head a tiny bit and let me see out of the window.*

He did.

"Landing gear?" I asked.

"I'm on it," Bentley replied.

We were very near the airport now and low enough to the ground to likely avoid any other aircraft. I brought us even lower, just above the rooftops of the strip malls and apartment complexes.

The pilot's gaze tilted to the right. I initially thought it was a curious cocking of the head. But then, after a pause, his entire body slumped to the right and his view went dark.

"Son of a—"

I was cut off by Henry's new view, out his own window. "We're almost there, Phillip. Just spin the plane ninety degrees so you can see where you're landing!"

He was right, of course, and there was no longer any reason to fume over the series of obstacles we'd faced. Just land the darn plane.

To people in their homes and cars below, it had to be a pretty insane sight. A jumbo jet airliner doing a quarter turn midair on a nearly level approach to the runway, hovering over them and flying wing-first. But it gave me the perfect angle to see. We were only a few hundred yards away now. The passengers had quieted down. They were probably in shock, though they could also now clearly see they were going to be safe.

I felt a small jolt in the plane.

"Landing gear is out, Phillip," Bentley said cheerily.

I guided the plane toward an empty gate, spun it back to the original orientation, and gently set her down. The passengers erupted in cheers as I stumbled out of the lavatory and threw up.

# 2

# ON THE RADAR

There was a massive DHS presence as we deplaned, as expected. Everyone was interviewed, photographed, fingerprinted, and then released. Those inside the airport, and even some from local businesses, were given the same treatment.

"What were you doing on the plane?" I was asked by a guy obviously trying too hard to seem intimidating.

"Coming home from a vacation with my friends."

"Did you land the plane?"

"Ha ha ha ha, yeah. I used my superpowers," I mocked. "I'm a superhero with . . . jet-flying capabilities. All while blind," I ended, laughing out loud. It was absolutely ludicrous to think that a young teen like me was a custodian with superpowers—even though I was. I knew from Dad's training that one of my best tactics would be to scoff and agree sarcastically with the accusations. Sure enough, a few more moments of scornful guffaws later, I was released. Bentley and Henry had also been trained for this sort of encounter. Adults weren't primed to suspect kids anyway.

Perhaps most importantly, Henry had fogged up the interrogators. Another of his favorite new tricks involved "fogging" a target, which used his mind-entering abilities to basically distract a person and keep them from being alert and focused for a few minutes.

"Well this is just wonderful," Bentley groaned. "Do you have any idea how mad my father is going to be?"

While we were relieved to go free, this was a very bad development. We were now first-stepped; we were on record as having been present during a custodial act. If it ever happened again, we'd be flagged and detained and would face not just questioning, but interrogation.

"I don't know what the alternative was, Bent," I said defending myself.

"I'm not mad at you," he allowed. "I'm mad at the situation."

"Well, I think we all are," I agreed.

Just then, my mobile device beeped out the ringtone signifying my father as the caller. "Well, here we go," I said before answering. "Dad, I didn't have any choice."

"Phillip!" he nearly shouted.

"Both engines went out," I protested, "and debris damaged the tail!"

"Are you okay?" he said deliberately, as though that had been his original question anyway.

"Yes. Yeah, we're all fine."

"Did they question you?"

"Yes, we all did just like you trained us to."

"Did they photograph you?"

I sighed. "Yeah, and fingerprints too."

"Dammit," I heard him mutter.

"I'm sorry, Dad. I really don't think we had any other options. That plane was going to have to try and land in a freaking parking lot or something."

"I know, son, I know. I'm just"—he paused, his mind racing—"considering the implications. You guys are headed back now?"

"Yeah, we're in the car." The car service was one based out of Freepoint, run by members of the human-support community, so we were free to talk about custodian business in front of the driver.

"Okay," Dad said. "Look, I'm really proud of you. I mean . . . I saw the news video and what you did is just . . . I'm so proud that you're my son. I'm concerned for your safety after this, but . . . good job, my boy. You did good."

"Thanks, Dad."

"I'm in London, but I'll be home around seven. There's cash on the counter so you can order pizza. Your brother's still at Jason's house for another day, okay?"

"Okay, Dad. See you tonight."

"I love you."

I hung up.

"Doesn't sound like he's very mad," Henry offered.

"He's not. I mean, he is, but he isn't. Even is a bit proud."

"Well that will definitely not be my father's reaction," Bentley lamented.

"Sorry, man," I said sincerely.

"At least your father will bother to even ask how the trip went, or even realize you've been gone for two weeks," Henry said, further depressing everyone.

"Just think, guys," I said, trying to lighten the mood, "we get to start school in three days!"

They both smiled and laughed weakly.

"Maybe this year you'll have the guts to talk to your girlfriend," Henry poked.

"I've talked to her! Casually . . . I said 'Hi' at least . . . once! And she's not my girlfriend," I objected.

"Okay, okay. I just hope you talk to her some this year. You don't want some suave senior stealing her out from under you or anything."

"I was actually thinking of asking her to join our SuperSim team. Sure could use a teleporter, no?"

Henry and Bentley both paused. Henry finally said, "Doesn't she have, like, dizzy spells and stuff?"

"Yeah," I allowed.

"Wouldn't you think teleporting would aggravate that kind of condition?"

"I actually don't know. I'll ask her . . . sometime after I introduce myself and shake her hand. You're getting ahead of things. I'm just saying, we could use a teleporter now. And she is one, and she's even in our class. And we don't have even *one* of those on *any* of our teams."

The special education class was roughly triple its original size due to all the students disabled during the attack by Thomas Sallinger (a.k.a. Finch) three years ago. The Ables as a SuperSim team had never been more popular, and had grown beyond the classroom. Able-bodied students were jockeying to join our squad ever since our beatdown of Finch in the schoolyard—which, of course, had really been all Donnie's work. Currently, the Ables fielded five to six full teams for each SuperSim, three of which had claimed victory at least once. The entire group was composed of about 65 percent disabled kids and 35 percent able-bodied kids.

We arrived at my house a short while later, still debating the makeup of our teams for the year's first SuperSim. "Remember," Bentley advised as I unlocked the front door, "there may be new students this year that we're not yet aware of who may be part of our teams."

I turned on the foyer and kitchen lights. "So what you're saying is we should hold off discussing team assignments?"

"Indeed."

"I agree. I'm just suggesting we formally invite Emmaline to be part of one of this year's teams. I don't think that's jumping the gun."

Bentley seemed somewhat skeptical. "We may have to make sure you two are on different teams."

"Why? Sexual harassment?" I was incredulous.

"No," Bentley countered, "focus. If she's on your team, I'm worried about your focus."

"Jeez, guys, do I really think or talk about her that much?" I was pretty sure I didn't, but Henry and Bentley's collective laughter told me how wrong I was. "Dang, I didn't realize I was that fixated."

I heard the touch-tone sounds of the phone being dialed. "The usual, I imagine?" Henry asked.

"Yeah," Bentley and I both agreed.

"Hello, Jacks?"

"I still can't believe you landed a freaking plane sideways," Bentley admitted. "And like a hovercraft! Slow and low!"

Henry used his power to project his vision into my mind so we could watch the footage of the landing on the news. We'd seen it several times now, each time laughing and recounting particular moments.

"I haven't laughed this much in a single day in ages," Henry said. "I can't believe you puked in the aisle!"

We all laughed, our bellies full of pizza and our heads full of great memories of the trip and the rescue at the end of it.

There was a long pause.

"Still," Henry ventured, "we're kind of screwed now, though, right?"

"Only if we're caught hanging around any public custodian activity . . . which I'm not sure any of us are ready to give up . . . so . . ."

"Yes," I finished Bentley's answer for him and then sighed. "I'm sorry, guys. I mean, I still don't think we had any choice."

"We didn't, and you don't need to be sorry," Bentley assured me.

"Still sucks," Henry added.

"So our options are to either stop fighting crime," I said, summarizing the situation, "or make sure we're invisible when we do. Do we even know anyone with invisibility?"

"I don't think so," Henry replied.

"Maybe there's an option you haven't considered," Bentley teased, the way he always did.

"What's that?" I asked, not expecting a good idea—which, given Bentley's history, was a dumb position to take.

"Costumes," he said simply. "We don't have to be invisible. We just have to be unrecognizable."

"Oh, man, I don't know, Bent," I wavered. "Costumes? That's so corny."

"At least masks to hide our faces then," he allowed.

"Great," Henry said. "We'll look like a group of Mexican wrestlers."

"They don't have to be Mexican wrestling masks," Bentley said. "They can be any kind of mask or way of obscuring our faces."

"I wish Henry was just a whole lot better at fogging people," I teased.

"Ha ha, yeah," he laughed. "I'll just advance my abilities a decade in a few short weeks. Also, you're welcome for my help back at the airport, by the way. You should thank your stars I can fog at all."

"I really don't want to wear a mask," I moaned.

"Let me talk to Haywood tomorrow and see what ideas he has," Bentley suggested. "There's gotta be a way to hide our identities that isn't corny."

Haywood Barnett was a teacher at school. He taught science. After he got inadvertently mixed up in our ordeal last spring, he and Bentley had formed a friendship. They had the same ability, and he acted as a bit of a mentor to Bentley. He also helped out with gadgets for the Ables crew from time to time. He'd created the skin cream Penelope now wears that allows her to go outside anytime she wants without fear of a reaction from the sun. He also invented the soundproofing gel we sometimes used in audio-sensitive missions.

"Well, I hope there is," I said. "I'm picturing Zorro and Batman and—"

"Mexican wrestlers," Henry said again.

"Yeah," I agreed.

Just then I heard the sound of Dad arriving home to his office via teleportation—*ooph!* There was a muffled goodbye, another *ooph!* as the teleporter left, and then Dad stepped out into the main house. He stopped in the doorway across the living room a moment and looked at us sitting there at the kitchen table.

"Hey, Mr. Sallinger," Bentley offered.

Dad kind of looked a little intense. "First things first," he barked, stomping over to the table. It felt like a rebuke of some kind was imminent. At the end of the table he stopped, clapped his shoes together, and bent down, still scowling. Then, as he slowly brought his hands up toward his face, palms out, he grinned ear to ear. "Gimme some. Gimme some! Come on, right now. High fives all around!"

We all smiled and exhaled, playfully volleying high fives back at Dad for a few seconds. Then he pulled the fourth chair away from the table, sat down, and sighed. "I have *never* seen anyone do what you three did today, and certainly not at your age. I am just . . . I'm stunned and impressed with you all for even thinking to do that."

He'd been giving us special hero coaching here and there ever since Freepoint's mental protector, Weatherby, had died and things had become more dangerous for custodians. And this was not a father-son moment, but a proud and loving coach moment.

We all beamed appropriately.

"Now, next thing is . . . the board wants to talk to you guys about what happened." Our smiles faded.

"Great," Henry muttered.

"What do you mean 'talk' to us?" I asked.

"Informal. I'll be present, and your parents can be there too," he added to Henry and Bentley. "Mostly they'd like to know what went down so they can be proactive about protecting you guys should the government ever come sniffing around."

I was still nervous, and Dad could obviously tell. "Relax, Phillip, it'll be fine. The board is there to help us. Heck, Bentley's father is the director!"

"That doesn't necessarily mean good things for us," Bentley said flatly. He and Dad exchanged looks. "Let's just say I'm not looking forward to going home tonight." Then, after a pause, he added, "I'm sure I'll get an earful."

Dad gave that a beat while he processed, but then he recovered quickly and said, "Well, you guys are always welcome to spend the night, as usual."

"Thanks, Mr. Sallinger," Bentley said. "I think I'd better go home and get it over with."

"I would stay over," Henry lamented, "but I have too much to do to get ready for school on Monday."

A few short moments later and the guys had gone, and it was just Dad and me.

"I want to hear all about it," he said. "You know that to this day I've never gotten to control a 747," he gushed jealously.

I spent the next few minutes telling him about the entire ordeal, how we kept gaining then losing a good viewpoint of the plane as it went down. He asked lots of questions and made note of several moments in the story he enjoyed.

Dad had changed a lot in the last three years. For the first year after Mom's death, he'd been distant and robotic. But then a couple years ago something snapped in him, and he'd turned into the coolest dad ever. These days, it wasn't uncommon for him to revel as much as we did in the things we boys enjoyed. It was actually fun being around him, and his enthusiasm for our endeavors grew only stronger. In some weird, twisted way, it was almost as though his widower status allowed him to embrace his inner boy again and be one of the guys in ways he wasn't able to as a husband.

As we both rose to go get ready for bed, he paused. "Son, is everything okay with Bentley?"

"What do you mean?"

"I don't know. The way he talked about his dad, I just wondered if there were any issues he was going through that you might know about."

I shrugged. "I mean, I know they don't get along. Bentley doesn't get to see his dad much, and kind of lives in the shadow of his older brothers."

"Yeah," Dad agreed, no doubt already familiar with the three older, decorated Crittendon sons. "Okay. Just thought I'd ask."

As I went through the bedtime ritual of brushing my teeth, showering, and climbing into bed, I couldn't help but wonder about Bentley. I'd always known his relationship with his father was strained, but had Dad spotted something I hadn't, some signal that perhaps it was worse than I assumed? Surely Bentley would tell me if that were the case, right?

The subject kept me tossing and turning late into the night, enough to give me one of the more fitful nights of sleep in recent memory. I made a note to talk to Henry about it and see if he'd picked up anything unspoken from Bentley that might shed light on any possible issue.

# 3

# NEW RULES

There was one major change this year at the still-pretty-new Freepoint High, and that was the absence of a school "no power zone" provider. As NPZ abilities diminished among custodians, their importance on the true battlefields eventually outweighed the need to keep schools powers-free. There were still custodians in the world who acted selfishly, even evilly, including the mysterious new Maestro character we kept hearing rumors about.

So all three American custodian cities had recently lost their school NPZ officers to field assignments, which meant that for the first time in over one hundred years, students could use powers in school.

There was a lengthy PA announcement detailing all the reasons students shouldn't use their powers in school, including strict punishments if caught, but none of that would truly stamp out power usage at Freepoint High. Henry's power, for instance, was basically impossible for any teacher or hall monitor to catch, since it was entirely mental.

*This is awesome*, Henry projected to us before the principal had even finished the announcement.

*Just be sure to keep your "Phil-O-Vision" turned on and we'll be fine*, I added. Bentley had helped Henry practice and hone his vision-sending ability to the point of it being a nearly subconscious act for him. And with the help of the new glasses, he could send me a view of what my eyes would be seeing—picked up from the camera in my glasses— without disrupting his own personal vision or even really thinking about it much. Bentley said it was a basic human evolution of our version of the rearview mirror's night mode in an average automobile.

If he was reading my mind right now, Henry would surely know that the no-NPZ announcement had led my brain instantly to Emmaline. Now I'd be able to actually see her during school as well as outside the classroom!

A redhead with brown eyes and a dozen freckles on her face, Emmaline was adorable. She sat directly in front of me, which meant that this school year promised to hold lots of distraction and daydreaming for me personally. My grades would surely suffer, but I can't tell you how little I cared about my grades at this point in life.

Our class was now taught by Mr. Collins, who everyone adored. As much as we missed Mrs. Crouch, we'd progressed far enough in grade to move on to more advanced subjects and learning. She probably had her hands full enough with the latest batch of younger disabled students, some of whom I'd be getting to know soon on the Ables practice field.

Mr. Collins was jovial and generally good-tempered. He seemed to genuinely enjoy the subjects and facts he was teaching and had an uncanny memory for students' names and historical details. He went out of his way to ensure every student felt personally attended to and was all-around the best teacher I'd ever had.

We spent the morning doing the usual go-around-the-room-and-introduce-yourself thing, which I decided not to be annoyed by if only because it would give me three minutes to listen to Emmaline talk about herself. Mr. Collins struggled at first to contain the energy of the students, who all wanted firsthand accounts from Henry, Bentley, and me about the airplane incident—word traveled fast in the custodian world.

Next we broke down the year's syllabus, as Mr. Collins wanted us to be aware up front of how much material he intended to cover throughout the school year. It was an overwhelming document to flip through, though I took comfort in knowing that Bentley would help me through if I struggled with any subjects.

At lunch, Bentley suggested we use the unsupervised time to slip away and visit Haywood, who seemingly never left his classroom. Sure enough, there he was, tinkering with a couple flasks and gently humming to himself. "Oh, hello, boys," he said jovially.

"Hey, Mr. Barnett," I said.

"What are you working on?" Bentley asked excitedly.

"Oh, just some last-minute tinkering with this year's senior lab projects."

"Just spare them the sulfur, okay?" Henry cracked.

"You bet," Haywood laughed. He swiveled in his chair to face us at the side of his desk. "Well, I sure hope it's a challenge."

We looked at each other. Henry was first to speak, of course. "You hope what's a challenge?"

"Whatever you've brought for me," he said grinning. "I can't imagine three growing teenage boys like yourselves would skip out on lunch on the very first day of school if it wasn't about something important. And if I'm going to"—he threw his hands up dramatically—"risk my career, yet again, for you rascals . . . I, at least, hope it's a challenge."

Bentley produced a blue folder, seemingly out of thin air since I hadn't noticed it until now, and handed it to Haywood. "Masks."

Haywood flipped through the folder, which was more like a full dossier. Bentley was nothing if not thorough. He'd included sketches, photos, lists, and text documents and even a few suggestions on possible solutions. Mr. Barnett looked at the materials for a few moments and then closed the folder and looked back up at us with a much more serious face. "You guys realize what you're asking me to do constitutes a crime, right?"

We all nodded. "Wouldn't be the first time," Henry offered sheepishly—and accurately.

"Let's cut the jokes, guys." He set the file on the desk and folded his hands together in consternation. "This is serious. You're on their radar now. What you're asking me to do indicates that you plan to continue your late-night crime-fighting efforts at full speed, when what I think you should be doing is taking a nice long break. Maybe train and practice . . . learn a new skill. Now is not the time for hitting the gas, kids."

"You don't think we're going to stop, do you?" I thought he'd figured us out by now.

After a breath, he grinned widely again and waved his hand. "Nah, I just feel some moral responsibility to at least say something a good adult role model would say before I violate most of my principles. Alright, I've got a class soon, so just give me the bullet points."

"We need a way to hide or conceal our faces and identities when out in the field," Bentley answered. "You know, so we can't be ID'd."

Henry chimed in, "And it can't look stupid or be anything that is already out there and, like, trademarked and established and stuff. No Batman cowls."

I turned toward Henry. "How cool would it be, though, to—"

"No! No Batman, no Spider-Man, no Zorro! No Mexican wrestlers! Something new, cool, and awesome."

"I just don't want to get recognized by people or cameras. That's really my only concern," I said, trying to find the meat of our dilemma.

Another long sigh from the science teacher. "You guys are going to keep going anyway, even if you don't have masks, aren't you?" He pretended to be exacerbated by our requests for help, but we knew he secretly enjoyed it.

Bentley just flipped his hands over and brought them up a bit, as if to say, "Do you really need to ask?"

"I'll see what I can come up with," he finally exhaled. "I don't know why I risk my tenure for you little punks."

"Because we're so charming," Henry said, winking.

Just then the bell rang.

"Go, go, you know what that means. Be gone, you pestering teenage miscreants with criminal requests!" he shouted in mock anger.

We thanked him and scampered off into the hallway to return to our classroom.

The only day of the school year the hallway is more chaotic than the last day of school is the first day. The hall today was jammed, and it seemed nearly every student was talking at the same time.

I just wanted to get the heck out of there and get home. I had a lot to process, and we still had that visit with the board looming.

But apparently I was the only one in a pensive mood.

*Are you gonna ask her? Are you gonna ask her? Are you gonna ask her?*

Henry was often pestering, and sometimes a full-on pest. Today was one such day. When he really wanted to badger me into something I was reluctant to do, he'd just overwhelm my brain with incessant repetitive thoughts; this was basically the friend version of how he fogged up the minds of our foes. And today he'd decided I should talk to Emmaline and invite her to join our team.

*Dude, it's the first day of school. Relax. I have months to talk to her.*

*Chicken. You should totally talk to her. Chicken. Bawk bawk.*

*Man, I really hate you sometimes.*

*And yet hate doesn't stop my powers,* he laughed out loud. *So . . . are you gonna talk to her? Do I have to do everything myself?*

*Shut up*, I pleaded.

*Tell you what*, he teased, *I'll shut up if you talk to her. Just say hi. Just extend an invitation to join our SuperSim team. Just ask if she got the homework assignment, what's her favorite color, anything! Just talk to her, talk to her, talk to her, talk to—*

"Emmaline!" Henry's tactic had worked. Mostly on instinct, I'd shouted her name in order to quiet the noise in my brain more than out of any actual readiness to speak to this girl. I heard a faint chuckle in my brain and then, *Okay, I'm out. My work here is done.*

Emmaline had, of course, heard her name and turned around, and now I was committed to a conversation with her. Henry slunk off to God-knows-where to spy on the conversation and provide me visuals, which I needed, as much as I hated him potentially eavesdropping on the event.

Finally, and well before I was ready, I'd reached Emmaline's spot in the hallway, and now it was time to talk. But I wasn't sure what to say first, so there was a nervous pause long enough to probably let this girl know I had a crush on her.

"Hey," I said quietly.

"Hey," she said back.

"Do you need to go to your locker or something, or are you headed outside?"

"Outside." She smiled.

"Can I . . . walk and talk with you?"

"Sure," she said.

Despite my own nervousness and general lack of ability to keep myself together in front of girls, they seemed to be nice to me on a fairly regular basis. I chalked this up to one or two events I'd been involved in that had grown my fame to levels my actual personality didn't deserve. That Emmaline knew who I was and what I had done in the past was not a question—which made this encounter only more nerve-racking for me.

"So, I noticed last year you didn't participate in the SuperSim," I said, trying to focus on the floor and not get caught blind-staring at her while we walked.

"Yeah," she said simply.

"I was wondering if you'd given any thought to joining up this year."

Other students buzzed around us, emptying lockers and celebrating the end of a school day. All I heard was Emmaline—her breathing, her footsteps, the way her arm made a short scratchy noise every time it brushed up against her backpack.

"My parents aren't really into the whole thing," she said. "They're worried about my health and stuff, I guess."

"Right," I said, not having to try too hard to understand what she meant. "You get dizzy, right?"

"I do, yep. And I lose my balance a lot." She clapped her hands together a few times as she spoke, swinging her arms casually. "And sometimes I throw up."

"Does using your teleportation ability make that stuff worse?" We reached the exit doors, and I knew enough to push and hold it open for her. Part of me wanted to use my telekinesis to open the door as a way of showing off, but I figured that would probably come off too strong. I used my regular old hands instead.

"Actually, no," she replied as she passed through the doorway. "But running does. Even jogging, or fast walking." Just then, as if to underline her point, she wavered slightly. It was a small moment of imbalance, but

I still shot out my hand and grabbed her elbow to steady her. She looked at me with a grateful smile, even as she shook off my hand. In my brain, I heard Henry giggling.

"Are you okay?"

"Yeah, thanks," she said. A car horn beeped nearby. "That's my dad. I should go."

"Okay, yeah. Sure. Well, listen," I called as she walked away, "you should think about coming out to Charles Field Saturday. We're holding SuperSim practice, and I think you could be really useful to one of our teams."

She twirled and walked backward a few steps. "We'll see. I'll talk to my parents. I'd like to," she added earnestly.

"We can take steps to make sure you don't have to run or jog . . . or even walk fast," I shouted, a bit too late and slightly too desperate sounding. Emmaline smiled and then got into the SUV and disappeared down the street.

"Very smooth," Henry said, laughing as he wheeled up behind me.

"Like you could have done any better," I responded.

"Hey, I'm not saying I could," he allowed. "But that doesn't mean I'm not going to make fun of you."

"First you push me to talk to her, then you make fun of me for it," I chided.

"Yeah," he admitted. "What are friends for?"

Dad was working late again, which was common lately, so Patrick and I were left to fend for ourselves for dinner. There were frozen TV dinners, leftover lasagna that was leftover for a reason, and cold cereal.

I microwaved a TV dinner and listened to the news, while Patrick opted for a dinner of his own creation consisting of junk food and snacks. As an older brother, I'd decided to make sure he didn't get himself killed, but generally I didn't care much about his actual day-to-day activities beyond that.

These days it was common for the nightly news to include something about custodians, whether it was a recent sighting and rescue or just another rumor or more political grandstanding. Tonight they were still discussing and dissecting the miraculous airplane landing. Three of the four pundits talking thought it represented a case to get aggressive on custodian registration and identification, while the fourth held out in the lonely position of thinking perhaps custodians were good-hearted people just trying to help. Most of it was just all four of them shouting over each other, but since I had been directly involved in the event being debated, I couldn't help but pay attention.

"I don't know how you watch that stuff," Patrick said from the kitchen table.

"That 'stuff,'" I said with emphasis, "is going to directly impact your life one day, way before you're ready for it to."

"Eh, just a bunch of windbags," he said. Patrick was only eleven months younger than me, though I often felt eleven *years* more mature. He was dismissive of politics and most custodian affairs, preferring to focus on using his superspeed to stage and film pranks on his friends and classmates. Everyone loved his prank videos until they became a victim of one; my turn had come early in his hobby, as he filmed me walking into objects in our home that he'd purposefully moved to new positions in order to trip up his blind brother. Ingenious, hilarious stuff.

"You know, for someone less than a year younger than me, you sure act like a kid sometimes." Just then the phone rang, and Patrick and I both turned our heads toward it. I heard the distinct sound of him activating his powers to move quickly across the room. Unfortunately for him, my own abilities were faster this time. The phone snapped up off the base station and into my hand just as Patrick's superspeed brought him to the counter where the phone stand was located.

"Hello, Sallingers," I said in a cheery tone, letting Patrick know his superspeed had been beaten by my telekinesis yet again—he got the best of me only about 20 percent of the time. "Oh, hey, Dad. Yeah, we both ate. No, I'm watching TV and Patrick is at the kitchen table. Okay. Okay. Love you too." Dad hung up at that point, but I pretended he didn't. "Yeah, Patrick is being a hyperactive weirdo, as usual. I know . . . what a nuisance!"

"Hey," I heard Pat yell in defense.

"If he gets too bad, yeah, I'll use my powers on him." I finally pulled the phone away from my ear and clicked the receiver to hang up. "Dad says don't be naughty."

Patrick stood up from the table, zipped over to my location, and interrogated me. "Yeah, but he meant that for both of us, right? Didn't he? Didn't he?"

"Yes," I admitted, if only to get him out of my face. Pat zipped back over to the table and continued eating. "I'm going to my room."

"Don't do anything I wouldn't do," Pat shouted after me.

"You don't even know what that means," I scolded him before pushing open my bedroom door.

I plopped down on my bed and turned on my DHS scanner. Bentley had rigged up a device that, when I cared to listen, would broadcast all active DHS radio chatter related to custodian activity. Tonight it was nothing but static. I turned it back off and went to sleep.

# 4

# AUDITIONS

"Please describe the events that led to your use of your powers aboard a Patriot Air flight from Orlando to Chicago."

The room was very dark. The only lights sat in front of each member of the board and on the table in front of us. The light on our table was bright enough to make it difficult to make out each individual board member's face. Deep-blue curtains hung along the walls, and a large window let in the faint light of the night sky. The A/C was cranked up high, giving the room a slight chill. Dad had said the purpose of this inquiry was ultimately to help protect us, but everything about the design of the room itself said otherwise.

Henry, Bentley, and I exchanged glances before I decided to handle this first question. "Well, the left engine started smoking and then lost power," I began. "But we knew one engine would be fine. Then seconds later, the right engine exploded." There was a small murmur among board members. "Henry listened in to the cockpit, and it sounded like the pilots were predicting a crash landing in a field or parking lot, so . . ." I paused, not sure how to phrase it. "We did what we thought was best and used our powers to land the plane safely at the airport."

A few moments passed as the members whispered to each other. Dad patted me on the shoulder from behind me.

"How confident are you the plane's landing would have produced casualties without your interference?" The voice was male, and it came with the sort of nasally tone you might expect from the type of person who would ask such a question.

Bentley took this one. "On board, sir, I calculated an 87.2 percent chance of casualties if we were to do nothing. Sir."

Another minute or two of quiet debate.

"And did anyone see you using your abilities?"

It had been a female voice, though I wasn't sure which board member had spoken. "No, ma'am. I went into the plane's bathroom—lavatory—and used my abilities from inside there. And Bentley's and Henry's powers aren't observable to the naked eye. Not to mention the passengers were all panicking and freaking out anyway. I don't think anyone would have noticed even if I'd stayed at my seat."

More internal board chatter.

*Well, this is exciting*, Henry mentally projected to Bentley and me. *Least they could do is leave a magazine or a Rubik's Cube or something on the table for us to keep ourselves occupied.*

I stifled a chuckle.

Eventually there came another question, this time from a male voice to the right. "Were you questioned afterward?"

Bentley handled this one. "Yes, sir. Each of us was questioned briefly, photographed, and fingerprinted, as were all the other passengers on the plane and every single person in the airport's A-terminal at the time of the event, even the café workers."

More whispering followed. This was part questioning, part meeting, and the downtime between questions was beginning to aggravate me.

"Did they take any physical samples like hair? Was your blood drawn?"

"What?" I asked, taken aback.

"Was your blood drawn?" the voice repeated slowly, with phony patience.

"No, sir," I said, shaking my head. "Why would they take our blood?"

My question went unanswered as the board again discussed the issue internally.

*Why* would *they take our blood?* Henry wondered silently.

*DNA*, Bentley answered almost immediately. *If they get our blood or hair, they could, at least in theory, begin researching our DNA, and eventually even discover a way to identify custodians by DNA sample alone.*

*Okay then*, I thought, *that sounds completely frightening.*

*Well, at least it makes sense why they're asking about it*, Bentley answered. *Doesn't sound like it's something the DHS is thinking about yet anyway.*

Our silent dialogue was interrupted by a board member who had no idea we were having it. "Have any of you been contacted by persons unknown to you since your return to Freepoint?"

I was utterly perplexed at this point, as almost none of these questions followed the line of logic I'd expected. "No," I said in surprise. I turned to Henry and Bentley.

"No," Bentley said.

"Nope," Henry added.

*What in the heck is going on?*

*I don't know, Phillip, but it seems like maybe there's more to this than we realized*, Bentley offered.

*Or maybe the shit has hit the fan with the government talks, and we set off some kind of international incident*, Henry guessed.

*You always fear the worst*, I chided.

Another question jarred us from our conversation, this time from the far left side of the table. "Do any of you remember seeing anyone or anything . . . suspicious?"

"What?" I had spoken before really thinking but had at least spoken honestly. I had no idea why they would ask such a thing, and it caught me by surprise. I just sat there stammering for a moment in confusion.

"Did you see anyone behaving or talking in a strange way, or doing anything suspicious?"

"On the airplane? No," I answered immediately, baffled as to who or what they thought I might have seen.

*What the heck?*

*I don't know, Phillip,* Henry answered. *That's a weird one. I got nothing.*

Finally Bentley's father—Jurrious, the chairman of the board—spoke. "Boys, you are free to go. We'll let you know if we need you again in the future." He slammed down his gavel, the sound echoing throughout the large hall.

On our way to the car, we finally broke our stunned silence.

"What the heck was that last question about?" I asked aloud.

"Yeah," Henry agreed. "That was weird."

"I don't know," Dad responded. "Maybe they're just covering all their bases. Wait here. I'll go get the car." Dad was always awesome about not making Bentley and Henry travel any farther to the car than necessary.

"Do they not believe that it was us that landed the plane?" I wondered aloud.

"Maybe," Bentley said, obviously still chewing on it himself.

"That whole thing was the weirdest super-important-but-not-really-all-that-eventful hearing I've ever attended," Henry blurted out in frustration. "What was the point of any of that? Did they learn one thing they couldn't have found out from other sources?"

"I think there are a couple conclusions we can draw from tonight's line of questioning," Bentley teased. "First, it's possible they think that plane was brought to safety by someone other than us. Either that or they think someone caused those plane engines to fail on purpose, which admittedly is pretty far-fetched. But why else would they ask us about seeing anything suspicious?"

Henry and I pondered that fairly deep thought while Bentley continued. "Second, the DHS currently has no idea our DNA is unique, or how to spot or track it. But the board is worried about it, hence the question about the blood and hair." No one could put together the clues of a mystery faster than my friend Bentley.

"If they figure out how to spot our DNA signature . . ." I trailed off, not wanting to complete the sentence.

"Crap," Henry muttered.

"Listen," Bentley offered, "if they were onto the DNA link, they'd have taken our blood at O'Hare. That's the takeaway here. The humans don't yet realize we have a unique genetic identifier. That's good news . . . right?"

"Then why don't I feel very good?" Henry asked.

I was suddenly sick at the idea of a near future reality where the government hunted down custodians based on their DNA markers.

"Until they start taking blood, they have only facial recognition to go on," Bentley said flatly as Dad pulled the car up to the curb. "And Haywood's gonna find us a way around that, so buck up, guys. This is not a bad night. It's a good one!"

Henry and I smiled and each returned Bentley's fist bump, but neither of us was particularly enthusiastic about it.

"Okay, if you're a first-year student at Freepoint, no matter the grade, move over here to my right and form a group." This was my third year directing Ables tryouts, but I still felt like a complete novice.

About a dozen kids ended up on my right, while thirty or so gravitated to my left side. These were the returning students and non-rookies.

"Alright. Welcome," I said to the newcomers. "My name is Phillip, and I promise we're gonna find a place for you." The Ables had grown considerably since its inception, in part because of an influx of students disabled during Finch's attack on Freepoint three years ago. We'd decided long ago to be the most open and accepting SuperSim team in existence, which had led to a pretty high annual number of recruits.

Emmaline had not shown up, much to my disappointment, but I managed to shove that aside and play the role of mentor and trainer for the evening.

We split into groups and ran some basic hero simulation scenarios for a while, before breaking for dinner around a roaring campfire. It was only a few hours in on the first night, but already I was beginning to get an idea of what this year's Ables teams would look like for the first SuperSim.

Bentley, Henry, and I were on the first team as a given. In addition to being Ables founding members, we were also the most experienced. We left two spots open for now: one we planned to fill with either Patrick or another recruit with a versatile power like superspeed, and one spot I was setting aside in case my crush decided to join our team. Bentley thought we should fill the slot now, at least until she showed up, but I argued strongly enough that he backed down. I was absolutely sure Emmaline would be a part of our team at some point, though I was probably too close to the issue to be objective.

We wanted to seed the remaining Ables teams with a mix of newcomers and veterans. Freddie took the leadership role on squad two, which was filled out entirely with a raucous group of rookies who called themselves the Smash Squad. I liked them instantly. Bentley had worked with Haywood last year to develop a special device for Freddie. It's a mouthpiece he can activate by biting in a specific way, which then shoots a megadose of his asthma medicine into his lungs. Freddie activates it the instant he turns on his powers, and the dose is enough to keep him from having an asthma attack even at his full giant size.

Penelope had been a part of our first team in recent years, in part because of her relationship with Bentley, but this year she'd decided to branch out and lead a team of her own. Greta joined her, as they'd become fast friends, and the rest of their team was filled out by second-year students and rookies.

Trevor, a transfer last year from Goodspeed, took up the leader's role on squad four. Trevor was a flier, and about as hilarious as any human or custodian teenager could ever hope to be. He was the class clown yet a phenomenal tactical commander in battle. I think everyone wanted to be on Trevor's squad, including me.

We were in Charles Field, a memorial park built on the land Luther Charles had formerly farmed as a Freepoint citizen. His heroic acts during the showdown with Finch had led to this land being converted into a public park, which the Ables continued to use as practice space in honor of the man who had hosted us long before we'd been accepted.

Most everyone was finished eating, and multiple conversations were happening at once. "Alright, alright," I said loudly. Everyone quieted down. "Since this is the first practice, and we don't want to push too hard . . . how about some soccer?" A happy roar went up around the fire, and several kids started running for the soccer field immediately.

Soccer was a long-standing Ables practice ritual, mostly because we played Super Soccer, where power use was encouraged. And even if they didn't realize it, the games provided the young heroes with a chance to sharpen reflexes, think on the fly, and work as a team. If a little fun was had along the way, who was I to complain?

I watched the game, courtesy of Henry's subconscious stream. I was always the referee, since my powers were deemed too strong to make the game fair if I were to play. I stood along the sideline near the one set of small bleachers where those choosing not to play tonight sat and cheered on the others. Bentley typically stood next to me to keep score and provide play-by-play, mostly for his own amusement, but tonight he was sitting with the others on the first row of bleachers. I wondered if his ataxic cerebral palsy was acting up and his legs were giving him trouble.

My brother Patrick was absolutely lethal on the soccer field. It helped immensely that he'd played a lot of soccer as a boy before developing superspeed. He scored the game's first goal before the first minute of gameplay was up.

The other team was ready for him on the second run, as Freddie ran and slid into Patrick's path while simultaneously growing to his full three-story-tall size, effectively causing an instant wall. Patrick spun off at the last second, and the ball careened to the other side of the field, where Trevor grabbed it between his feet and flew up twenty feet into the air heading for the goal.

"Sorry I'm late," I heard behind me. I knew right away that it was Emmaline, and I smiled.

"You made it," I said while turning, genuinely happy to see her.

Penelope used her weather-controlling ability to stop Trevor at the last moment by enveloping him in a small, focused tornado, and the ball flew out of bounds.

"I don't know what you said at that board hearing, but my father has completely changed his tune about me being in the SuperSim."

"Wait, your father's on the board?"

"Yeah, that's why we moved here." She shook her head. "He said the world is changing and I need to know how to use my powers to defend myself. It was basically the exact opposite of the reaction I got when I asked about the SuperSim last year."

"I didn't know that about your dad. I guess you heard about what happened last week then?"

"Oh, not from Dad. He doesn't tell me anything about hero government stuff. But yeah, I heard about it at school like everyone else." Patrick zipped by us with an audible swoosh as Emmaline continued. "It must be weird to know everyone at school is talking about you and, like, revering you and stuff."

"Well, I . . . I didn't. Everyone? I didn't really realize people talked about me much at all."

"I find that hard to believe," she said, not convinced of my humility.

"Do they at least like me?"

At that she laughed out loud for several seconds. "You really have no idea how famous you are, do you?" She was shocked.

"Well, I am blind," I offered. "And until this year I wasn't ever able to use Henry's vision inside school."

One of the Smash Squad kids with superstrength, Owen, stopped right in front of us. "Hey, Phillip, watch this," he bragged, hoping to impress me.

He tossed the ball in the air and started a leaping aerial kick, his leg turning to iron as it swung. When it made contact with the ball there was a dull thud; the ball easily traveled five miles before it came down. Everyone groaned and gave Owen some playful grief over losing the game ball. Fortunately, when you play Super Soccer for any length of time, you learn to bring plenty of spares.

I tossed a new ball to Owen, and he smiled at me a moment and then scampered back out onto the field.

"See," Emmaline said.

"What?"

"That kid already worships you. Are you telling me you can't see that?"

"I think worship is a little strong. He just knows I'm one of the leaders here and wants to make a good impression."

Just then Patrick's friend Jason, an eye-beamer, shot a laser toward the ball to knock it away from a lunging Freddie, but he accidentally burned the ball to a crisp instead. I jogged the three steps to the spare balls and tossed another one in. "Too hot, Jay, too hot. Dial it down a little, no?"

"Sure thing, sir," he said, catching the ball and returning to the game.

"He just called you sir," Emmaline exclaimed. "I mean, I can't decide if your obliviousness to your own celebrity is adorable or annoying."

"I'm pretty sure it's adorable," I said with mock certainty.

"I'm pretty sure it's kind of both," she said giggling.

"Okay, okay," I allowed. "As long as there's at least a little adorable in there."

"I think so, yeah," she said, holding up her thumb and forefinger an inch apart. "At least . . . that much."

Henry never missed a chance to play soccer, and was maybe the dirtiest player on the team, often overwhelming another player's brain with so many thoughts and images that they get distracted or fall down. He wheeled up to us for a breather. "Did you see me just throttle that kid? I think he broke his legs trying to figure out which way to go! Oh, hey, Emmaline, glad you could make it!"

"Thanks, Henry." Just then the ball whizzed toward us and was about to hit Henry in the back of the head until—

*Ooph! Ooph! Smack!*

Emmaline hopped five feet in a nanosecond by teleporting and grabbed the ball with both hands. She looked at me and smiled. "I think I'm gonna get out there before the game's over."

"Fine by me," I said as she disappeared and then reappeared near the center of the pitch.

Henry wheeled closer. "You sly dog, I saw you flirting with her!"

"I wasn't flirting!"

"If you're fifteen and you're talking to a girl about something other than schoolwork . . . you're flirting."

"Whatever."

"So, how's it going?"

I had never had a girlfriend—I hadn't even been on a date—so I had no idea how well I was doing at this point. "She showed up, didn't she?"

"She did, yes." Henry held out his fist, which I reciprocated. "I'm going back in," he said, before turning and immediately shouting at the other players, "Hey, no fair! No fireballs!"

There was so much potential this year for me—with Emmaline, a promising squad of Ables teammates, and even the ability to see during school hours.

If it wasn't for that pesky first-stepping from the airplane incident, I would have been, for the first time in a long time, 100 percent optimistic about the future.

Eh, I was close enough to enjoy it.

# 5

# NIGHT OPS

Two weeks later, thirty-six miles north of Freepoint, a car raced south-bound along a lonely, dark state highway. Inside were three men, each armed. In the trunk was Celia Winters, recent kidnapping victim and teenage daughter of a wealthy Chicago real estate developer. Her hands and feet were bound and her mouth was taped, but she was otherwise unharmed.

The kidnapping had been planned for months, and the abduction had gone off without a hitch. The crew was traveling at night, zigzagging around the northern part of the state, holing up each day to hide. The latest ransom call, a few moments earlier, had indicated they planned to kill Celia if the money wasn't paid in twenty-four hours.

They would have been less bold and stupid if they'd had any idea how close behind them the state police were—or what hung in the air just above them.

Hovering overhead, my abilities kept everyone in the air with me as we discussed the best plan of attack.

"I just don't wanna get shot," Henry repeated for the third time.

"Okay. Fine. No one shoot Henry," I said to shut him up. "Now,

Freddie, you could probably take this car out no problem, but I'd be worried about the girl's safety."

"I could try smashing only the front," he offered.

"That didn't work so well last time," I reminded him. "Man, that kid with the iron foot would come in handy right now, I bet."

"Owen," Bentley added.

"Owen, yeah. Thank you. Man, I've got to find a way to get better with names."

"Well," he offered, "in your defense, there are an awful lot of them this year."

"Aren't there!" The Ables, as a SuperSim outfit, had grown in number every year since its inception, but this year's jump was the largest yet.

"I could try messing with his head like that pilot," Henry suggested, getting us back on track.

I mulled it over a moment. "I'm too worried about what they'll do, man. The pilot was, presumably at least, just a normal guy. These three are unpredictable criminals low on sleep and high on drugs."

The options were limited. The car was too old a model for Bentley to hack in and stop the engine. We needed a way to slow and stop the car, disarm the kidnappers, and get the girl out of the trunk without harming her. And all in the next seven minutes, since Bentley had already notified authorities anonymously of the girl's location.

We knew about this crime because of Bentley's extensive criminal behavior search engine, which he'd built from scratch. It included police and FBI scanners as well as his own unique algorithm for prediction and detection of criminal behavior. We'd actually known of Celia's kidnapping prior to her parents receiving the ransom call because we were already monitoring these guys' communications after the software flagged them last month.

Tonight we had a limited skill set, since we still kept this real-life nighttime crime-fighting unit limited to the most experienced team members. The last thing I wanted to do was get a rookie hurt by bringing him or her out into the field for real hero work, and that seemed like a policy that was unlikely to ever change, though I'd desperately wanted to invite my new crush along. Instead Bentley, Henry, Freddie, and I were joined by only Patrick and Penelope.

*Penelope*! I had a revelation.

"Penelope, give us a nice, thick layer of fog to slow him down," I said.

"Okeydokey," she said. Penelope was always cheerful, even on the battlefield. It was easy to see why Bentley had been drawn to her.

Seconds later a low fog began rolling in from the south, rushing up to meet the speeding vehicle. Just as it completely enveloped the car, we could see the brake lights, signaling the car was slowing down in reaction.

"Great," Henry moaned immediately. "Now *we* can't see anything!"

"Everyone, switch to thermal," I barked at the group. Then I barked at Henry, "Just shut up and do your job, man."

One of Bentley's best ideas over the last few years had been standardizing the team's video and comms. Everyone wore the same kind of glasses Henry and I did, with video sending and receiving capabilities as well as our team's radio system. Thermal vision was one of the most recent upgrades Bentley had given the units.

I flipped the appropriate switch, and Henry's vision of my camera feed changed instantly to thermal. The car and all four occupants immediately stood out.

"Excellent," I said. "Okay, Patrick, you and Freddie and I are going to do this together."

"Okay," he said. Patrick and I still had our quarreling moments as brothers at home and at school, but in the field, he was one of the most reliable and responsible soldiers I had.

"You'll need to take the keys out of the ignition and unlock the trunk and pull the girl out . . . all in about a second. Can you handle that?"

"Who do you think you're talking to?" he bragged.

"Freddie, your job then is to stop, smash, crush, or otherwise incapacitate that vehicle."

"Got it, boss," Freddie said.

"And I'll disarm the men myself as soon as Patrick is clear," I added. In all honesty, I probably could have stopped these criminals without any assistance. And while stopping real crime was certainly the general idea of these late-night excursions, there was still an element of team and confidence building I saw in them. If I handled the entire affair on my own, it would be a completely wasted evening for the rest of the gang. I'd get to show off, but no one would learn anything or gain any experience.

I glided us all closer to the car, lowering our position so we'd be a mere twenty yards above the car. I whispered. "One . . . two . . . three!"

Faster than I could follow visually, Patrick took off, turned off the ignition, took the keys, and unlocked the trunk. It all happened in less than half a second. Before the kidnappers even realized the car's engine had stopped, they'd lost their victim. Patrick pulled Celia out of the trunk and gently set her down one hundred yards away from the road while Freddie went to work.

Freddie jumped into the air, instantly activating his asthma doser as well as his powers, and landed in front of the vehicle. It smashed into his legs and ground to a halt, its front end crumpled. I instantly used my abilities to grab all three guns and toss them out the vehicle's windows.

"Patrick," I yelled, "tie 'em up!"

Patrick always carried a small bundle of high-strength wire, developed by Bentley and Haywood, in order to bind criminals for eventual capture and arrest by human cops. Before I'd even drawn a full breath after giving the order, he'd finished the task, and all three hoodlums sat slumped against the vehicle in the street.

Sirens blared in the distance.

"Alright, gang," I said, "our work is done. Let's get out of here. On me." Everyone rushed to my position, and I lifted us all into the air and over the countryside just as the first police car arrived on the scene below.

$$\text{⚡}$$

Sneaking into the house after late-night ops was a lot more difficult now that Dad was working second shift, and without the aid of a teleporter. Dad was almost always awake into the wee hours of the morning, and of course he was watching television when we walked in the front door.

Without looking away from the TV he asked, "You guys stay safe tonight?" He knew that we regularly went into the greater world to find crime to stop, and honestly, I'm not sure he cared about the behavior as long as we were safe.

"Of course," Patrick said, arriving by Dad's side before finishing his sentence. I heard the faint sound of Dad roughing up Pat's hair. "Glad to hear it. Anything I need to know about?"

"No," I assured him from the kitchen, where I was gathering cookies and milk. "Just routine stuff."

I was fifteen years old, nearly sixteen, and probably had a more adult lifestyle than 99 percent of the kids my age on this planet. I routinely fought and defeated criminals, I had dealt with evil and death . . . routine for me was almost certainly a definition most humans would call a roller-coaster ride.

We'd stopped a kidnapping involving a planned $3 million ransom, but even that wasn't really a big deal in the custodian world. And I was far more concerned with actually making a difference than I was with bragging or impressing others with my stories.

"Glad to hear it," Dad said, suggesting he knew we'd probably at least come close to risking our lives, despite our success. He stood. "I need to talk to you boys about something," he said, striding toward the kitchen table.

Patrick made it to the television, changed the channel to Wheel of Fortune (his latest obsession), and made it back to the table before Dad had even reached the kitchen.

Dad sighed. "Alright, can you at least try to pay a little more attention to me than to the game show?" he asked.

"Sorry, Dad," Patrick said before zipping over to turn off the TV and returning to the table in the blink of an eye. Just sharing living space with Pat could sometimes be exhausting.

Dad pulled out a chair and sat down. For a few moments, he said nothing, almost as though searching for a perfect set of words.

"Phillip, you remember when the board asked you if your blood was drawn at the airport?"

"Yeah," I said. "Bentley said it probably had something to do with custodian DNA."

"It did," he said flatly. "Boys, the Department of Homeland Security has figured out our DNA is different. We've suspected for a while that this was coming, and now it has. We have an eyewitness account of a custodian's blood and hair samples being taken by DHS agents, followed by an apparent arrest." Dad paused, seeming to take this news harder than even I did. "Phillip, if there's ever a *next* time for you . . . I'm afraid it could become the *last* time."

It'd been five weeks since the incident with the plane, though everything about it remained fresh in my memory.

Each of us had heard whispers in school of the DHS's supposed custodian prison, and the rumored horrors that took place inside its walls. But if the government was keeping custodians prisoner, it meant they had figured out some way of barring or counteracting their use of powers.

"I don't understand," I said. "Why didn't this guy fight back or try to escape?"

"This particular custodian, guy named Davison, was a mental, like Henry," he explained.

"How did they even know he was unique?" Patrick asked before I had a chance to.

"He'd already been first-stepped, like your brother, and he was spotted at the scene of a very public incident. He and his partner stopped a hostage crisis at a theme park. They probably saved thousands of lives. His partner hadn't been first-stepped yet—though he has been now—so he was allowed to leave. He's the one who saw them prick Davison's finger before leading him away."

"So the prison thing is real then?" I asked. "I mean, kids say stuff at school, but I thought that's all it was."

"I can't answer that, Phillip. I don't know any more than you do. But they took him somewhere. And I don't want you to ever find out where through firsthand experience, do you understand me?"

I nodded my head.

"This stuff you do at night . . . I get the general sense it's all pretty low-profile stuff." He paused. "Is that a fair assumption for me to make?"

"Yeah."

"I don't want to have to tell you to stop being the person you feel you need to be, son. You either, Pat. But Phillip, if you're caught at the scene of any event likely to draw DHS's interest . . ." he trailed off, not wanting to finish the sentence.

Patrick finished it for him. "He's toast."

The dream was always the same. Had been for six months. I'm underwater, drowning, unable to use my powers, watching bad guys swim away with my little brother in tow. I always wake up right before I die from the excess water in my lungs.

I sat up with a start.

Sleeping, at least for long stretches of time, had become difficult for me lately. Insomnia kept me from getting to sleep quickly in the first place, and then dreams like this one combined with a general restlessness to make getting *back* to sleep even tougher.

I stumbled out into the kitchen, poured myself a glass of filtered water from the fridge, and sat down on the couch. I flicked my finger, sans remote, and the television leapt to life.

An old episode of some sitcom was on. I turned my wrist to change the channel several times, landing on one of the many twenty-four-hour news channels. At this point in America's culture, custodian stories were the kind of lightning rods news channels could count on to always bring in viewers. News, commentary, editorial, panel shows, interviews—the more custodian-related content they could create, the more viewers they could lure.

Tonight's program was a roundtable discussion show famous for casting its debate rosters with members of opposing viewpoints. Should custodians be forced to come forward and register? Two blathering idiots apiece on both sides of the topic were firing away in furious debate.

"These people are trying to help," one shouted.

"Not all of them," said another.

The DHS, and indeed Americans at large, would have been more primed to welcome custodian citizens with open arms were it not for the steady increase in custodian-related criminal activity.

After Finch disappeared, a half dozen would-be evil villains popped up in his place, and each had steadily grown a following of loyal, corrupt individuals with abilities. As often as a custodian was filmed rescuing someone from certain death, another was filmed committing some horrible crime or act of selfish gain.

"These custodians should be treated like regular human beings," one of the pundits shouted. "Some of them are good, and some of them obviously won't be. Why should we open our nation to gay marriage, racial equality, and general tolerance, only to treat these exceptional people as lesser beings subject to our discrimination?"

I liked that guy immediately, even if I had no idea who he was or what he stood for politically. He was making the point I would have made, and therefore he became an ally in the moment.

"Just look at the math," an opponent roared. "Two out of every three 'custodial events' is criminal in nature. That's factual. That's a statistic," he screeched. "You can't argue with the math here. These things are dangerous!"

I left the television playing, stood, and walked to the sliding patio doors leading to the backyard. I opened them, both screen and glass, and closed only the screen behind me.

I walked five or six paces until I'd left the patio and was standing in the grass. I lay down on my back, listening to the world around me as well as the news commentators echoing faintly through the screen. And I finally fell asleep.

# 6

# TAPPING THE BRAKES

School was going fine. I had an above-average mind, so it seemed, and basic schoolwork rarely seemed to challenge me—not that I was complaining. And this year, I was still able to get the best of grades while paying the least amount of attention. The only year grades had ever really been bad was that year mom died, and then only because I literally just stopped trying.

That attention went to daydreaming, of course, about my first date with Emmaline, which was still nothing more than a figment of my imagination. Other than the occasional chat at SuperSim practice or the polite greeting during school, I hadn't even really spoken to her much. Which gave my friends plenty of ammunition whenever they wanted to needle me.

"Maybe you should just ask her out and stop thinking about it so much," Bentley offered kindly.

"Or maybe," Henry offered, mouth full of chicken nuggets, "you should just get over your fears and be a man and tell her how you feel!"

"I'd take that advice," I admitted, "if I felt like it was coming from someone who had actually followed it himself at some point in life."

"Hey, I had a girlfriend once," Henry protested.

"Oh, yes, the infamous Sheila from Philadelphia," I mocked.

"She's real," he insisted as Bentley and Freddie laughed.

"What's so funny?" Patrick asked while sitting down to my left.

"Nothing," Henry said immediately. "We were just laughing at your brother for taking so long to talk to his girlfriend."

"Girlfriend!" Patrick had not yet heard about Emmaline and my crush on her, by my own design.

"Thanks a lot," I said sarcastically.

"What, he didn't know about Emmaline?" Henry laughed. "Well, he knows now."

"You have a thing for Emmaline?" Patrick asked me excitedly.

"No. I hate her. She's ugly and standoffish. Don't you have friends your own age?"

"Since when has this been going on?"

"Can we change the subject?" I pleaded. "Bentley, you got any word from Haywood yet?"

"No," he responded. "And you should ask her out."

"Dammit!" My friends knew exactly how to get under my skin, and it drove me crazy.

Emmaline was sitting with Luke and his pals, as usual. Luke Miller was her best friend. He'd also moved here from Goodspeed. They'd grown up together, and even though they weren't an item, I was still worried he was somehow competition for me.

Thankfully Penelope and Delilah showed up at just that moment, which would at least put Bentley on his best behavior for a few minutes. Penelope and Bentley had been close for years, and no one was really sure when they switched from friends to dating partners. It was gradual, I guess, but natural. They shared a physical frailty, but they bonded most over their differences.

With the girls present, the conversation shifted from giving me a hard time to actual constructive talk, which pleased me greatly. "The first SuperSim is only a few weeks away," Bentley reminded us. "And we still haven't settled on final rosters."

I waved my hand in dismissal. "We still have several practices left, though. We'll sort it out. I'm much more worried about how we continue our extracurricular activities, given the whole DNA thing."

"Phillip," Bentley sighed, "you know the easy answer to that problem."

"What? We stop? I don't accept that."

"So sayeth the court," Henry mocked. "You might end up going out alone if you insist on choosing stubbornness over patience here, buddy."

"I could probably handle it," I boasted, not really meaning it or wanting to prove it. "But that's not the point of these things," I said, steering the conversation the way I wanted. "It's as much about team building as it is stopping crime."

"There are plenty of ways to build comradery without risking our lives, you know."

"I know, Bentley," I agreed. "I just don't like being told what we can and cannot do."

"Well, like Henry said, you need to choose between how stubborn you want to be and how safe you want to be. Remembering, hopefully, that there are more lives than just your own at risk each time we go out."

He was right, as usual, and it angered me, as usual. I wanted to rant and boast about our abilities, which I knew to be more than capable. But the criminals were no longer the only concern. We now also had to worry about our own government. None of us wanted to find out if the rumored custodian prison was real, because none of us wanted it to be real—to say nothing of possible alternative explanations for the disappearance of custodians around the world.

"So what do we do instead?" I asked.

"Sleep," Henry blurted out.

Everyone else nodded or vocally signaled their own desire to catch up on sleep. Heck, even I wanted to catch up on sleep. I just knew that in my case, it would be impossible anyway. Having enough time to sleep had nothing to do with my issues, but I didn't really feel like getting into the whole thing with them anyway. "Yeah," I fibbed. "I think we can all use some extra sleep for a couple weeks."

Obviously, we immediately scheduled a late-night sleepover at Bentley's house for that evening, because even sleep-deprived kids can't resist living it up on an unexpectedly free evening.

Olivia, the Crittendon's nanny, was chaperoning us, as usual. She had her four-year-old, the adorable Abby, in tow. We all loved that kid anyway, but Abby typically joined us only out of necessity. Olivia's husband—Bentley's father's former right-hand man, Ted—had been killed in the Battle of Freepoint against Finch's forces. Every time we gathered at Bentley's guesthouse, we were silently reminded of the carnage we'd both helped cause and helped end.

Tonight's non-SuperSim agenda, created by Henry and Bentley, included pizza and movies. About half the kids from the Ables SuperSim teams had shown up. It was a great chance to bond and have fun, and just generally soak in the jovial atmosphere—something I hadn't experienced enough lately, I'm afraid.

Twenty or so of us kids wolfed down some Jack's Pizza and settled in for a showing of *The Champions*, the single most popular superhero film Hollywood had ever released. We'd all seen it a dozen times, and we collectively conducted our own audio re-creation along with the movie as it ran on the HD screen.

HD meant literally nothing to me—the highest resolution I was ever going to see was the Henry feed of my glasses, which was still well below HD standards—so I hung toward the back, sitting on a stool near the granite countertop bar next to the kitchen. A few minutes into the film, with most of the gang fully engaged and lobbing jokes and commentary at the screen, Bentley made his way back to where I was seated.

"Big group tonight," he used as his opener.

"Yeah, I was worried we'd run out of sleeping bags, or floor space," I said, playing along.

Bentley cleared his throat nervously. "You know nothing's ever going to be the same again, right?"

I sighed. "Yeah. I'm beginning to realize that," I admitted.

"There's more at stake than just you, me, and Henry."

"I know," I allowed.

"Good," Bentley said assuredly. "I know how stubborn and competitive you can be."

"Not in the face of risking the lives of my friends and my brother," I assured him.

"Look, Haywood will have something for us soon that will help us avoid detection," he offered as an olive branch. "Pretty soon most of this stuff won't even be an issue."

"You're right," I said, knowing he was correct and also knowing something else was going to change the game at some point down the road to make him incorrect.

It happened that night.

I woke earlier than everyone else, which didn't surprise me, and decided to go outside for some fresh air. I wasn't able to use Henry's vision, since that lazy bum was still snoring, so I tapped my cane through the Crittendon's garden until I found the bench I was familiar with and sat down.

"You're up kind of early," Bentley said from the nearby fountain.

I jumped at the surprise of his voice. "So are you," I countered.

Bentley was typically a bubbly guy for whom words posed no challenge, but this morning he seemed unusually quiet. Eventually he spoke again. "My dad's gone."

I wasn't sure what to make of this statement, since Bentley's dad was regularly "gone" for business reasons. So I left it alone for Bentley to fill in the blanks. After another long pause, he did.

"He left two days ago for another summit with the US government and never returned. None of them did."

I was still playing catch-up to this news, in part because Bentley was delivering it so nonchalantly.

"Itseems our latest peace envoy has been abducted entirely," he whispered.

"Are you . . . okay?" I wasn't sure what Bentley was feeling. I could only imagine what it would be like if my father were missing, and tried to convey the right amount of concern and worry. Bentley's relationship with his father had been complicated since I'd known him, and even now his true feelings were impossible to read.

"Yeah, surprisingly, I am," he offered. "I guess I'm not entirely surprised, given recent events."

A weak "Yeah" was all I could muster.

Another long pause as Bentley walked around the fountain. "There's only one way this thing ends, you know," he said in the most causal manner possible.

I knew he meant war. "Yeah," I admitted.

"I think maybe we should start training the Ables for more than just

SuperSim competitions and low-level criminals."

"I'm way ahead of you."

The next Ables practice was all business. No soccer, no lingering around—just straight to work. And it was the single most physically brutal practice we'd ever held.

"Look, these sessions are supposedly training for the SuperSim. And nobody has to think any differently. Everything we will do at these practices from now on," I said in my best wise-leader voice, "will still be of use to you during the Sims. But the recent disappearance of Bentley's dad and the other negotiators is a clear sign that things are going to get much worse for custodians in this country before they get any better." I channeled Mrs. Crouch a bit with my conclusion. "We're not doing you any favors if we act like the danger isn't suddenly more real. We're a family here. And today is the day we decide family means more than just sports practice. Understood?"

Heads nodded all around.

"Some of you are pretty young. Your exercises this evening will be graded by age and physical size. But make no mistake, we aim to do the best we can to start getting you ready to face real-world criminals as soon as possible."

"Or worse," Henry said, "actual soldiers."

Everyone shuddered at the thought of our own government potentially mounting an attack against custodians. The natural healer in me wanted to immediately assuage the group's fears by offering up something positive. But the reality was that Henry was correct. And if I was going to be any kind of help to these kids, I needed them to understand the true scope of the situation. So against my nature, I let the scary thought linger a moment.

"Anyone who wants to beg out of this and just be a member of the Ables on SuperSim nights, that is totally okay. We're not going to judge you." I paused. No one moved. "Now's the time to say something." Again, nothing. "Alright, then. Let's head over to the main field and split up for some drills."

As everyone began to head that way, I jogged up to Emmaline. "Hey," I said.

"Hey," she replied and smiled, standing up from tying her shoe.

"Listen, Bentley has something he wants to talk to you about, okay?" I pointed at Bentley, who was huddled fifteen yards away with Henry and Nero—a second-year Able who was a conductor, meaning he could manipulate electricity. We called him Fuse. Fuse was every bit as laid-back and casual as a stereotypical surfer, which created a charming mix considering his ability's rarity and great strength.

"Um, yeah, okay," Emmaline said, a bit confused. "Sure."

"Great, thanks. See you out there," I called as I turned to run toward the soccer field.

As I jogged I looked over at Bentley, knowing what he was asking of Emmaline and Fuse, and not 100 percent sure either would say yes. Then I turned and looked at the assembled Ables. I suddenly felt old. Was it really so recently that my own friends and I had been brash young twelve-year-old heroes, gathering in this very spot? I saw my own immaturity and optimism in these kids before me, and again I felt a weight at the responsibility of preparing and protecting so many lives.

It lingered in my thoughts all throughout practice. We put the kids through a number of drills, including evasion, tracking, tailing, physical combat, improvisation, and tactical thinking. Bentley had spent a night in the library prepping an ideal series of exercises and routines, and if he spent more than an hour researching something, then you knew he had gone deep.

Thirty minutes into the drills, Bentley and the others joined us. Henry gave me the news. *She's in, dude. They both are.* I smiled and quickly returned my focus to the field. "Alright, switch stations, everyone," I shouted.

# 7

# EMMALINE

As another practice broke up, I lingered a bit. I was feeling reflective. Worried.

The practices were just us going through the motions, pretending nothing was wrong in the world. And I wasn't sure how much longer I could do that. Were we spinning our wheels out here? Was there something else I should be doing to prepare these kids for a possible fight to defend custodial rights?

Bentley and Henry caught their usual ride home from Patrick. Those with powers of speed, flight, or teleportation often served as chauffeurs after practice to get the other kids home rapidly.

*Ooph!*

"Hey," Emmaline said. "I'm about to shuttle these mongrels home. You want a lift?" In hindsight, I wish I'd realized she was kind of reaching out to me in that moment. I was too caught up fretting the current state of custodial politics and my responsibility to these kids; I just didn't think to turn on my inner fifteen-year-old boy.

"I think I'm going to walk," I announced. "I've got some . . . stuff to think about."

"Fair enough," she replied.

*Ooph!*

And she was gone. She typically ferried home at least eight to ten Ables team members after each practice, saving each one a long walk or a parental car ride. And she never seemed put out by it. Maybe that was because travel between physical space was instantaneous for her. But I still saw her actions as generous.

I guess that anything a person does in kindness for another—that they didn't technically *have* to do—was generosity in my eyes. Or my mind, I guess. "*In my eyes.*" It was scary how quickly I'd adopted any and all normal speech patterns and idioms related to sight after finding Henry's assistance.

I regretted not taking her up on the lift home. But the walk by myself gave me time to think. And I did think.

As usual, I spent a bit of time thinking about the past. James's life would always be on my mind, as well as how and why it ended so early. Donnie too. And my mother. I felt I would never escape the memories of my dead loved ones, or the regret that always accompanied them.

What decisions would I make differently, and how would those better decisions have impacted my life? The lives of others? The world at large?

It seemed I was doomed to be fixated on things that might have been.

But I spent the time thinking about the future, as well. It certainly felt as if the near future held unlimited dangers for custodians. Heck, even the present seemed perilous.

I remember growing up feeling like the government was safe. They were on my team. My mother—ever overprotective of her blind son in New York City—used to tell me to seek out cops or firemen if I was ever in trouble or lost. "Or even someone at the library or the post office," she used to say.

And for all I know, those government agencies and the people working there actually were safe when I was a kid. For me, at least. Obviously abuse of power in government has been a fixture for most of humanity's existence.

But these days things seemed radically different than they had even two years ago. The government no longer seemed friendly or safe. This Ettinger woman that they'd put in charge of the new custodian division of DHS, she had a fervor about her—a passionate distaste for custodians. Why? What had I personally done to this lady aside from the uniqueness of my DNA?

Then I thought a bit about how likely my concerns for the future were to turn into just more regrets for me to mull over in the coming years. How many more bad decisions did I have in me? How much longer would people follow someone who keeps messing up?

I thought about how many years the future could go on before a disaster was a mathematical inevitability.

I also thought about alternate futures. Ones where my mother was still overcelebrating Christmas and squeezing my neck too hard during hugs. Where Donnie was still around. Every action created an alternate universe . . . or so the theory went. I readily entertained any and all of them that made me happy.

What if I hadn't pushed for the creation of a SuperSim team of disabled kids?

What if I hadn't tried to take on Finch in the cornfield?

What if? A lot of my internal dialogue these days seemed to start with the words "what if."

Maybe too much.

*Ooph!*

The noise was unmistakable. "Hmmm," I said, feigning confusion, "I wonder who it could be."

For a moment, as I heard nothing, I panicked thinking this was some official custodial teleporter before me with urgent news. And then . . .

"You already know my teleporting noise signature?" It was Emmaline, and she sounded only a tiny bit disappointed.

"Well," I said, trying to not miss a beat, "it was either you or my dead mother." I paused, instantly realizing I'd made a mistake. I tried to cover. "That was wrong. That just came out. That's obviously not . . . a joking . . ."

Emmaline, being gracious, tried to help. "What? I don't even . . . I didn't even hear . . . I mean . . ."

"I just meant that I don't know any other teleporters besides you." I wanted to die. "And I guess my mom . . . which is why I . . ." I sighed heavily.

"I get it." She grabbed my right elbow and hooked her hand around it. "I got done taking the kiddos home and thought I'd make sure you made it home safely as well."

"You think I can't handle myself?"

"You never know when a trip to anywhere might come in handy. A teleporter is a rare friend to have." Every single thing she said enraptured me.

"I think I'd like to have a friend like that."

"You already do."

The fact that I managed to avoid tripping or passing out as she said these words is a minor miracle.

"I guess maybe a typical girl wouldn't just come out and say something like that. I don't know what normal girls are like. But . . . I didn't want to risk the chance you hadn't been picking up on my signals. You know, being blind and all." I heard a smile in her voice as she said the last words.

"Ha!" I blurted out a laugh before I could stop myself. I tried to recover and change the subject. "Everyone else get home safely?"

"Yep. This is a shockingly small town, if I'm honest." There was a playful tone to her voice, like maybe she didn't take things so seriously all the time. I needed someone like that in my life. Well, someone like that who wasn't Patrick.

"Good."

"Are we really going to do this break-in?"

I sighed but felt instinctively that telling her the truth was the best route. "I've never seen him this worried. I don't think we have much choice if we want to get more information."

"Seems like every day someone new gets ghosted around here," she added.

"I know. My dad's off investigating it. Custodians have been disappearing a lot lately." I paused a moment, replaying some memories. "This kind of thing happened a few years ago, but the kidnapped custodians all showed back up either dead or working for . . . Finch. This time's different. Bentley's brothers disappeared weeks ago and haven't been heard from since." I didn't know how much she knew, but it was a small town and even top secret custodian information typically took only a few days to filter down through the community. I didn't see any reason to be extra careful with what I knew.

"Yeah," she agreed. "Oh—" she uttered in alarm as her balance gave out briefly. I brought my other arm in quickly and caught her by the elbow fabric of her jacket.

"You okay?"

"Yeah, sorry." She paused. I could tell she was hesitant, but only for a moment. "I'm gonna fall down a lot. It's just part of who I am. I thought about making up a story blaming it on caffeine and sugar just now, but that would all have been a lie. And I think I should be honest with my team leader, even if the truth is actually more embarrassing than a lie now that I say it all out loud . . ."

I paused a bit. Clearly I had been interested in her before meeting her. I couldn't deny that. But now that I did know her, now that I was able to spend time with her, she was just this pure and open thing—this honest bird, singing her melodies as much for her own enjoyment as for any listeners'. I wasn't infatuated; I was drawn . . . bonded.

"I wouldn't have believed the thing about the caffeine anyway," I said reassuringly.

She squeezed my elbow with the hand she had hooked inside my arm. "Alright, boss."

*Ooph!*

And she was gone. No goodbye. No goodnight. Just . . . poof.

I stopped for about forty-five seconds on the porch, just to catch my breath. Then I went inside and lost it all over again.

Dad hadn't returned yet from his latest business trip. He'd been due home this afternoon.

There hadn't been any voice mails, emails, or any other communication that indicated he might be home later than expected.

Patrick was awake. Scratch that—he was hopped-up on jawbreakers and cola, pacing around the house at five times the speed of normal human walking. "Where is he?" It echoed from all around me as he sped around the house while still speaking at a normal rate of speed.

"Patrick, you have to calm down." He looped around me twice more before I finally grabbed him by the front of his shirt, stopping his momentum and lifting him up into the air. "I am worried about Dad too. But if you can't calm down, I'm going to have to put you to sleep."

His body shrunk a bit in self-defense as I realized my poor phrasing.

"Give you a sedative, I meant—Jesus, Pat, like I would ever kill you! But I'm thirty seconds from knocking your ass out cold if you can't get it together. Your choice. Sleep for ten hours or help me figure out a plan."

He slowly walked to Dad's recliner in the living room and sat down. He reclined fully and sighed long and fictionally for effect. "I am ready."

I spent a few minutes lying to my brother, giving him reasons to believe Dad was fine and just didn't have a means to check in right now. Eventually he bought it. I reminded myself that soon enough he'd grow out of being so easily convinced of things by his older brother. He was goofy and hyperactive, but he wasn't stupid. He just had a bit too much trust in me.

Reassured—and tired out from the sedatives I'd slipped him—Patrick went to bed, and I finally had a few moments to myself. I reheated some leftover lasagna and sat down in front of the TV to eat. I started on the national news. The main story seemed to be about the impending elections. America was about to see its Congress change hands . . . or else it wasn't. Things were too close to call. It felt new and scary, yet still oddly familiar. Like having déjà vu inside a dream.

I smiled briefly at the idea of politics being important to people in a world where superheroes and supervillains were real—utterly *clueless* to how entitled and ignorant I was being. I was dismissing politics, but it had led to the current leadership of Homeland Security, and therefore the Custodial Relations Department.

"A brazen attack today on a farmer's market in the Midwest . . ." The newscaster interrupted my thoughts, directing my attention back to the broadcast momentarily. "A single custodian causing thousands of dollars' worth of damage."

The footage sounded exciting enough, but from an auditory standpoint it amounted to a series of bangs, crashes, and shouts.

Eventually I got tired.

I left the TV on, even after that channel had gone off the air and was only static. I liked white noise. It helped me avoid focusing.

I opened the sliding door, ambled out past the patio into the backyard, lay down on my back, and fell asleep to the ambient noise of the neighborhood streetlights.

I probably should have kept a pillow out there—or at least an alarm clock.

# 8

# A WALK

I woke up late, of course, because I'd fallen asleep in the yard and not my bed. Again.

Thankfully the sedatives I gave Patrick last night were strong and hadn't worn off yet. It was Saturday, and the family calendar didn't show any events, which meant that I would be dealing with Patrick all day. Whether he woke up as Panicky Patrick or Pleasant Patrick was yet to be seen.

I decided to do what I could to tilt the scales in the favor of Pleasant Patrick by cooking breakfast.

One of the skills I'd picked up in mother's absence was cooking. You'd be surprised how little importance eyesight actually has in determining a dish's readiness.

Is the steak cooked to the right temperature? That's judged by touch in any self-respecting steak house.

Have the mussels opened? Sight can help, for sure, but you can hear it as well if you're paying attention.

The doneness of pasta can be judged by biting into a piece.

Seasoning can make or break a dish, and you sure as hell can't judge seasoning with your eyeballs.

Other than general situational awareness, blindness didn't hinder my cooking aspirations one bit. It might even have accelerated and exacerbated them.

Patrick was a huge fan of carbs. So when it came to breakfast, the boy enjoyed pancakes, french toast, waffles, biscuits, and toast. If I could slip an egg or two in there, maybe a piece of bacon, I considered it a win.

It's not as though I expected Pat to wake up with no memory of last night, though the sedatives would probably keep him pretty groggy for much of the morning. I just needed time to talk to him where he wasn't freaking out. So . . . groggy kid wakes up . . . maybe something weird happened last night? Eh, who cares when there's clearly the smell of pancakes coming from the kitchen! That was my hope.

Mom always cooked as healthy as possible. She wanted us to be physically fit and ready to live as long a life as possible. Lots of veggies, organic stuff, homemade instead of boxed meals.

I was the opposite.

Custodians were, just by basic math, more likely to die young than humans—by a pretty shocking margin. So I was determined to eat based on desire and taste rather than health. I liked my ground beef high in fat content. I liked my fries greasy. I liked my garlic breadsticks dipped in warmish processed cheese.

And Patrick liked his pancakes with blueberries *and* chocolate chips. So that's what I was making.

I'd just flipped the first batch on the griddle when I heard him shuffle into the kitchen and sit down at the table. For a speedster, he moved pretty slowly in the morning. I didn't want to provoke him, but I was dying to know his state of mind.

"Morning," I said in as manly a way as I could muster. "Sleep good?"

He grunted. I heard him grab the remote and turn on the television.

The channel I'd left it on last night was currently showing animated mouse vs. cat cartoons, which brought a quick chortle out of my kid brother. Which caused him to leave the TV on that channel for the time being while he guzzled the orange juice I'd left on the table for him.

I cleaned up the dishes while he watched cartoons. I smiled at how motherly I'd become in my mom's absence. I turned the water off and dried my hands.

"Do you think he's coming back?" Patrick didn't sound panicked like last night, which was promising. But clearly he was still consumed with thoughts of our father's well-being.

I didn't miss a beat, if only to bolster my own optimism. "Definitely."

"Why do you think that?"

I didn't have a reason. I wasn't even sure I actually believed it. But I had to pretend. "He's too strong, Pat."

"You're way stronger than he is," he countered. "Dad's never lifted an entire train, Phillip."

"Raw strength is one thing, sure," I allowed. "But I'm talking about a deeper strength. The strength of experienced wisdom. Knowing when to act and when to hold back. Which situations to engage and which to leave alone. You should hear the way Bentley gets animated when he discusses the Tri-State Triangle or any of the other famous events Dad was a part of. No . . . if life is chess, our father is Kasparov."

"Who?"

"Oh, forget it!" I threw the hand towel at the wall in frustration and stormed out of the kitchen in temporary defeat.

I decided to go for a walk. I loathed exercise, but I knew it was good for the body as well as the mind. And my mind, at the very least, could do with a boost.

As I strolled down the street we lived on, I thought about Mom. I thought about how the last three years might have gone differently if Mom was still around. I thought about my best memories of her. And eventually I thought about the sad memories. When Finch had zapped her. When she'd died.

Before I realized it, I'd walked nearly a mile. I was now near the school. I turned north and headed into town, wiped my tears, and decided to turn my train of thought toward something more productive.

So I thought about how I could find my father. Or help him. Or both. I let my mind wander a bit while I considered the various possible scenarios that had led to him going missing. Had he been kidnapped? Was he just deep undercover somewhere?

From there I found myself thinking about my friends' fathers. Bentley's father was distant and stern, perhaps worse. Henry's dad was kind and warm, but he was not physically able to do a lot of the traditional father stuff. Henry's father was so distracted it made it hard to even guess how much he cared. I didn't know much about Penelope's dad. Emmaline's was seemingly important—one of only two members of our city's board who had not gone missing—which also made him a bit distant, though clearly more involved in her life than Jurrious was in Bentley's.

I had it pretty good, I realized. My father had mostly good qualities. He was encouraging and open. He was tough but fair. I made a note to tell him how much I appreciated him the next time I saw him.

A tractor trailer passed by, hitting a pothole which jostled the load in the back, which sent a piece of industrial equipment tumbling out the back doors. I didn't know any of that; I merely heard the noise it makes when a five-ton hydraulic press smacks pavement.

In a nanosecond I was in fight-or-flight mode. I hit the ground in the prone position and darted my head around listening for more information about the impending attack on my person. Someone or something was trying to kill me, that much was clear. This is what PTSD looks like, but one never realizes it when it first begins.

I began panting in fear, wondering what cover might be around that I could hide behind. My hands flew up to my head, clutching my ears in an attempt to quiet the rising white noise of my racing mind.

And then, just as quickly as it had started, it passed. The sounds of the truck driver shouting into his radio and the other nearby drivers and citizens rushing to help and reacting to the accident finally began to register true to my brain. And I realized what must have happened.

I rolled over onto my back and sighed, laughing in shock as I exhaled. I covered my eyes and breathed deeply.

"That's a weird looking workout." The voice was unmistakably Emmaline's. It was coming from the north, and she was about twenty yards away, give or take a few.

*Where am I?*

I worked backward, filtering through the sounds and smells I'd ignored over the last few minutes.

*I'm on grass.* I sniffed. *Lilac. Reynolds Park!*

Reynolds Park was one of five city parks in Freepoint maintained by the city for the enjoyment of its residents. Unlike Boyd Park or Harris Park, which were sports oriented, Reynolds Park was all about nature and relaxation. There were over fifty varieties of trees, a butterfly garden, a walking path, and a nice little fountain.

There were benches every fifty feet or so, and Emmaline was sitting on one such bench and had clearly just witnessed my entire panic attack.

I stood up and wiped the leaves off my sweater. "I don't suppose you had your eyes closed the last couple minutes?"

"Nope. Sorry."

"Great. Perfect." I walked toward the bench. "This is going to cost me some cool points, isn't it?"

"I don't know," she allowed. "You're talking to a girl that regularly faints from walking too fast, so maybe it's all relative?"

"Mind if I sit?"

"Please."

I sat and then lifted my right leg up and crossed it over my left knee and leaned back into the bench as I sighed.

"So . . ." she said. "Panic attacks, eh?"

I took a deep breath. There was no point lying to her. "Yep. Awesome, right?"

"Hey, don't beat yourself up. That noise was super loud. It would have scared anyone."

"Scared, yes. But not everyone would hit the ground like they were in the trenches of World War I." I decided I'd been self-deprecating enough for one morning and changed the subject. "So, what brings you out to lovely Reynolds Park this fine morning?"

"I like it here," she said enthusiastically. "It's so peaceful, and it smells so pretty. I like to come here to read."

"And what are you reading?"

I heard her hold up the book before realizing her mistake. "Oh, sorry. Um, it's *Catch-22*. You ever read it?"

"Can't say that I have. I've heard of it. Is it good?"

"It's freaking hilarious, man. This guy, he's stuck overseas in this badly mismanaged military. Circular logic comedy. It's all about situations where you're damned if you do and damned if you don't, if you know what I mean."

I wasn't sure I did. "I think I do."

"I love it. I've read it six times already." There was something refreshingly honest about Emmaline. She just said what she was thinking. She didn't filter her thoughts, probably because she wasn't likely to have ill thoughts about anyone. And she appeared to look for the positive wherever she could find it. God knows I needed someone like that in my

life. "You can borrow my copy if you want." Another brief pause before she realized her mistake. "Oh, crap! Sorry, I keep forgetting you're blind. Well, not forgetting, but . . . you know what I mean."

It was fun hearing her act flustered. "I'd like to read it. I'll have my dad order it from the braille place."

"It's probably in my top five."

"I'm guessing you probably haven't read many comic books," I said sheepishly.

I could hear her smiling. "Tell you what, Phillip, you recommend your favorite comics and I'll recommend my favorite books, and we can both go on new reading adventures."

"Deal," I held out my hand.

"Deal," she shook it.

"Do you wanna . . . you know . . . go out on a date with me?" I blurted out suddenly.

"Well, duh." She pulled her hand back from the shake and smacked me in the head playfully. "Been waiting on you for a few weeks now, kid. I'd have worn a shirt asking you to ask me out if I'd thought you would have gotten the message."

"Oh, I see," I replied. "That's blind humor right there. I'd know it anywhere."

She clicked her tongue. "I'm new to it, but I think I've already got a pretty good feel for the genre."

I stood up, stretched a bit, and said my goodbyes. "I'll let you get back to the circular logic book. Let's grab some dinner together on the twenty-first, what do you say?"

"Sounds like a plan," she confirmed.

I floated back home, buoyed not by telekinesis but by unadulterated teenage hormones.

# 9

# TRUANCY

"Why do you three seem to show up only when I'm extremely busy?" Haywood was walking quickly between his classroom and his office, mostly because his next class started soon.

"Kind of just seems like you're always busy," Henry said.

"Or at least acting busy," I joked. Then I tripped.

"Ha ha!" Haywood laughed before catching himself. "Oh, that's not funny. You're blind! What was I thinking?" He lifted me back onto my feet.

I wasn't offended. Haywood was notoriously honest and off-the-cuff. He said things as they came into his mind. But he was pure of heart. And he was helping us here, so I wasn't about to give him grief.

"Students who care about their education are already in class," he yelled out to those in our way. He meant it, but he was also frustrated with the crowd.

"What about teachers who care about—" Henry was interrupted immediately.

"What about teachers who are on their free period, which they should be using to grade papers but instead are using to help a few ungrateful vigilantes continue doing illegal superhero work?"

Henry cleared his throat. "Fair point."

Haywood opened the door to his office and stood aside to let us file in. "Are you three even attending any classes anymore?"

We were, but he wasn't out of line to ask. Enough custodians had gone missing—including teachers—that lots of area parents were keeping their kids home instead of sending them to school. Some kids with less-than-attentive parents used the kidnapping crisis to their advantage by simply skipping school and lying to anyone that cared to ask.

He sat down behind the desk with a sigh. "Afraid I have some bad news for you gents."

"Oh?" I said.

"I'm not going to be able to finish the masks for you."

I had never known the man to shy away from a challenge or fail to finish a project. My mind raced with possible scary reasons for this revelation. Perhaps the DHS had begun to pressure custodians enough that he was no longer okay with helping kids get out onto the battlefield. Maybe someone caught wind of him helping us and he'd gotten a reprimand. Maybe he didn't like us anymore? My anxiety often functioned in this way, creating a dozen potential problems in an instant and before I've even gotten all the information at hand.

As usual, the reason turned out to be nothing as bad as I had feared. "Unfortunately, I'm not going to be able to do much of anything around here anymore—including teaching. And no, I haven't been fired."

Henry and Bentley looked at each other quizzically.

"I guess you could say I've been drafted."

*Drafted?*

"Seems we've lost enough custodians in the field that even some of us civilian types are being called into service. I, uh, I'm leaving tomorrow morning."

"But your powers aren't . . ." Bentley trailed off before finding his thought again. "Surely they're not going to make you fight out there?" A hitch in his voice reminded me of his special bond with Haywood, beyond just their similar abilities.

Haywood laughed. "Oh, no. No, no. I'll be helping with strategy for the most part. Putting the old noggin to use for the greater good." He thought he sounded proud, but I could tell he was only pretending. Taking Haywood out of the classroom was like stealing a songbird's voice. It robbed him of his joy and his purpose.

Or maybe I was just projecting, hearing my own sadness in my teacher's words. "I don't know what to say."

"Me neither," Henry agreed. "You're basically the coolest teacher I've ever had."

"Relax, kids, I'm not dying! I'm just not going to be here in Freepoint for a while. And thus, unable to finish these." He pulled a file folder out of his drawer and plopped it on the table. "These are all my notes, designs, and calculations so far. I want you guys to have them."

He slid the folder toward Bentley, who opened it and leafed through its contents.

Haywood continued. "I haven't even gotten to prototype stage, I'm sorry to say. But there's some solid science there. I felt pretty confident I was going to figure it out pretty soon. I'm sure you can as well."

Bentley didn't agree. "Right," he said, chuckling sarcastically.

"I'm serious."

"I'm . . ." Bentley stammered, "I'm not half the mind you are. How could I ever complete this invention?"

"Do you know what your biggest weakness is, Bentley?" Haywood leaned forward, pointing his finger to underscore his point. "Your self-image. Your brain, son, is massive. I'm in awe of it. You're doing things at your age that I wasn't doing even in college. The only thing that can keep you from completing this invention"—he paused for effect—"is you."

Now it was Bentley's turn to sigh. He closed the folder. "You better be back. Next semester, next year—whenever this all blows over. You know what I mean?"

"Absolutely, buddy. You have my word."

"Why are we even still coming here?" It was all I could think about since Haywood said goodbye this morning.

"The cafeteria?" Henry mumbled, mouth full of chips.

"The school." I took a sip of my water and continued. "I mean look around." I gestured around the cafeteria, which was less than half as full as it should have been. "No one's coming anymore but us and the kids whose parents are still in town. Everyone else is out there doing something more important than school right now."

"You don't know that," Bentley objected. "I bet most of the kids who aren't here are playing video games and sleeping until noon."

He had a point. "Okay, sure. Yeah. But we would do something constructive with that time. We could try to stop crime or maybe save some lives." The frustration in my voice grew proportionate to its volume. "Instead of slouching around half-empty classrooms and makeshift study halls because half of our teachers aren't even showing up anymore!" I tossed my half-eaten roll onto my tray.

"Emmaline's not coming anymore, apparently," Bentley said, noting her absence from the table.

"She's actually just sick, she said."

Henry smiled and lifted his eyebrows playfully. "You guys messaging each other regularly now?"

"What? No, I . . ." I cleared my throat. "I mean, no. She just . . . she messaged me to say she wouldn't be here today, but mostly because she also won't be at practice later tonight." That was the truth, but that didn't mean it was going to get my friends off my back.

"You know what I think you're doing?" Henry asked, like the setup to a joke. "I think you're sitting in a tree, mister. I think you are sitting up in a tree right now, and I think you're not alone up there."

The others all giggled, including me. But I still objected. "I am not in the tree! I'm not in a tree!"

Patrick chimed in, elbowing Henry. "I wonder what they're doing up there?"

"I bet it involves lips," Freddie joined in.

"There's no tree. I'm not in it. There's no sitting or kissing, and the first one of you that starts singing or spelling is getting a slap in the face."

"Guys," Bentley said, "he's right. We shouldn't tease him so much. At least not until he actually makes a move or something."

"Seriously, Phillip, I don't know what you're waiting for." Penelope had been so shy when I'd first met her three years ago. She'd come out of her shell quite a bit since then. "She clearly likes you."

"Right," I agreed sarcastically. "Clearly. I suppose she told you this?"

"No, actually. I can just kind of tell. I think everyone but the two of you can see it plain as day that you like each other."

"Maybe vision would help me see it better," I snapped back in a bit of bitter blind humor.

"Oh, shut up," Henry countered. "I give you vision all the time, even around Emmaline. You can't use that excuse on this one!"

Nothing aggravated me more in life than Henry being right.

"Fine. You're right. Can we get back to what I was saying already? About school, and the pointlessness of continuing to come here five days a week?"

"Well, what's to stop us from not coming?" Bentley asked, always willing to talk through things logically. Well . . . for the most part.

"My parents," Henry said right away. Henry's folks weren't in custodial public service. Mr. Gardner had been injured on the job and was on disability. His wife basically took care of him and ran the rest of the household as well. They were likely to notice if Henry started sleeping until noon and playing video games instead of going to school.

"Mine too," Penelope added.

"Okay, that's fair." My own father hadn't been gone that long but it had already become normal to me, to the point that I hadn't considered my friends' parents were still hanging around *parenting*. "We should consider that for sure."

"Would the school do anything?" Patrick wondered. "They still take role, right?"

"Well, sure," I agreed. "But with half the school already missing days, there's way too many kids to keep track of. It's not like there's a truancy officer out there running us down and dragging us back in here."

"What's truancy?"

"Skipping school."

"It's a word you learn when you don't skip too much school," Bentley jabbed.

Patrick was surprised. "They have officers for that, like police officers that track down kids who ditched school?"

"Well yeah, in some places. But my point is that we don't have them here. No one's going around trying to find all the kids who aren't here right now. So no one's going to come looking for us either."

"So we'd have to find a way to keep Henry's and Penelope's parents from knowing they're skipping school," Freddie summed up, "but otherwise we should be good, right? Like, can't they both just keep leaving the house in the morning but instead of going to school they go . . . wherever else?"

"I think so, yeah." I couldn't think of any reason it wouldn't work.

"And so what do we do with all this free time?" Henry asked. I felt pretty sure he thought I wouldn't have an answer ready. But I did.

"Look around this town, Henry. This is not a handful of weird kidnappings anymore. There's a crisis happening, and we're in the middle of it. There's no more board in Freepoint—the members are almost all gone! My dad's gone. Someone has to get to the bottom of this. Someone has to figure out where everyone's gone missing to and why. I feel pretty confident we could fill all the hours in the day pursuing those kinds of answers, right?"

Henry was defensive. "Alright, alright. You sold me. I didn't mean to get you so riled up. I just asked is all."

"We'll hopefully find some leads two nights from now," referencing our planned mischief. "Hopefully Emmaline is over her illness by then."

Just then the bell sounded to end the lunch period. Most of our fellow students throughout the cafeteria stood up and began shuffling back down the hallways toward their next classes.

Everyone at our table remained seated, looking around at one another.

I can't make true eye contact, obviously, but through Henry's peripheral video feed showing me what my camera was pointed at, I could totally "look directly at" people. It was my version of eye contact.

I looked at Henry, then Patrick. Then Penelope, who looked away but smiled a tiny bit. Then Bentley, who met my gaze. Then back across the table at Freddie, then Henry again—you could never fully trust that scoundrel without checking him twice.

I looked back at Bentley, and we nodded at each other.

I slid my hand into the center of the table, palm down. One by one, my teammates stacked their hands on top until we were all represented.

"Let's get out of here," I whispered.

We stood collectively and then marched down the hallway and right out the school's main entrance.

It was so cool! I'm telling you, if it had been a movie, we would have been walking in slow motion with some kind of cool song playing loudly in the background.

# 10

# NUMBERS

"I'm so excited," Henry giggled. Indeed, he was practically rocking back and forth in his wheelchair. "We haven't been breaking and entering in ages!"

"It's hardly breaking and entering, Henry," I corrected. "We've got the key."

We were standing outside Jurrious Crittendon's home office, joined by Bentley, Penelope, Freddie, Emmaline, and Patrick.

"The way I figure it," he countered, "using sneaky methods to enter any place we're not technically supposed to be counts as breaking and entering."

Penelope was confused. "Are you trying to get a longer rap sheet?"

"Street cred," Henry cooed. "It's all about street cred. The ladies love a man with a reputation." It goes without saying that Henry didn't have any better clue about what the ladies loved than the rest of us did.

Bentley pulled the key from his shirt pocket, inserted it into the lock, and turned it. "Try not to break anything." The dense wooden door swung open with a faint creak, and we all filed in silently.

The office was spacious and ominous all at once. It was the most intimidating room I'd ever been in. The bookshelves taunted me with their ancient knowledge while the handcrafted oak desk made me feel two feet tall.

I sighed, overwhelmed. "What are we even looking for, Bent?"

"I don't know," he admitted. "I just know that Dad kept most of the important custodian business in here, away from the family. And now that he's gone . . . now that the board is gone . . . I'm just looking for clues."

"Should we try the computer?" I offered.

"Oh no," he laughed. "I've tried everything to break into that thing. It's hardwired to some central custodial server somewhere. It's basically unbreakable without my dad here. No, just look for anything that might be a clue. Papers, notes, anything that looks askew or out of place . . . maybe something he was working on or thinking about before he was taken will shed some light on who took him."

Everyone started looking around near where they were standing. Within a few minutes, all pretense was dropped and everyone was rifling through whatever book or shelf or drawer they could find. We tore that place upside down.

And yet, thirty minutes later, no one had found any kind of clue.

"It's the most boring office I've ever seen," Emmaline stated bluntly.

"Your dad was important," Henry told Bentley.

Bentley assumed he was done. "Thank you."

"No," Henry continued. "He was important. This office is not important. This office is . . . what a secretary to an important person's office might look like."

"I haven't found anything that looked even remotely useful," Patrick offered, "and I've been moving pretty quickly." Pat had shown a recent flair for puns related to his superpower. But because Dad and I were desperate for anything tying Patrick to education or learning, I looked the other way for the most part. I hated puns in general, though, probably because my father enjoyed them so much.

"Hmm," Bentley breathed.

I turned my head. "What?"

"What?" he returned.

"You said 'Hmm.'"

"Out loud?"

"Yes."

"You did," Penelope concurred.

"Well," he said slowly before drawing a long breath. "I always suspected my father had a secret office."

"A secret office . . . in addition to this one?" Freddie wasn't having it. And I'll admit it sounded odd. The office in which we stood had been pretty well protected on its own. And the computer was locked down tight. Just because we hadn't found any hidden messages or clues didn't mean there had to be another office.

Everyone weighed in at that point, and a murmur rose up from the room. "I've heard the rumor too!" "We're wasting our time." "Curfew is in thirty minutes!" "Does anyone have any gum?"

"There is an odd bit of architecture here, though." It was Emmaline. "These windows here don't match up with this photograph from the outside of the house." She gently removed a framed photograph from the wall. "You see this outcrop here?" She placed the frame on the desk, turned on the lamp, and pointed. "There's no way to get here from either this room or the hallway outside. That has to be it."

"Wait a minute," Bentley objected immediately. "I'm not even sure there is a secret office. And I don't know where this photograph came from. I've never seen it before tonight!"

"Let's just talk for a moment," I offered, hoping to please everyone at once.

"Screw that," Emmaline said.

Bentley tried to explain. "I brought James here once. He and I also thought there might be a secret room here, but . . . we couldn't be sure. And with James . . . if I couldn't give him any kind of picture as though I'd been there myself . . . it was just too risky. We even fought about it once . . . I probably pushed too hard."

"You fought with James?" Lots of information today was new to my ears.

"Phillip, that's not the poin—" His words were interrupted by a familiar sound.

*Ooph!*

Emmaline had jumped from this room into the space she assumed another office existed, and she'd done so while we stood here arguing.

"Oh," Penelope gasped.

"Christ!" Henry exhaled. "She's an impulsive one, isn't she?" He laughed aloud. "She might be dead or encased in brick right now, but I still respect that move! Holy crap!"

She was, indeed, impulsive. To the point of danger. And yet I did find myself smiling about it rather than freaking out. And I was prone to freaking out of late; PTSD is real, and it was haunting me. My therapist had even suggested that the events a few years ago with Finch had permanently altered my emotional DNA. That sounded like scientific hooey, but I liked my therapist and I felt better whenever I left those sessions, so I just ignored the parts that sounded like hooey—or tried to.

A few seconds passed and nothing happened. I'm sure it felt like more time than actually passed, but we were all on the edge of melting down when she returned.

*Ooph!*

"Okay," Emmaline breathed. "Definitely a secret office in there. Not enough room for all of us. Who wants to come?"

We all waited a beat, soaking in the new information, and then . . .

"Don't you *ever* do that again!" Bentley railed at her like I'd never seen. "If you'd died encased in that wall, do you have any idea how bad that would be? My father would disown me! I'd never be able to sleep in this house again knowing your corpse is rotting in the walls! God!" He gasped in frustration.

Emmaline turned to me, seemingly surprised at the outburst. "What's with him?"

Ultimately, after everyone calmed down, we left Patrick and Freddie in the main office and the rest of us went to inspect the secret office. Unlike the main office we'd just been exploring, which was extravagant in its furnishings and imposing in its stateliness, the secret office was downright Spartan. It was practically empty—a metal folding chair, a laptop on a table, and a discount office lamp.

There didn't even appear to be a proper door into this room.

For a few moments, we all glanced around and took in our new surroundings. Emmaline had turned the lamp on when she'd first come into the room.

"What's the point of a secret office if it ultimately feels like a prison cell?" Bentley was thinking out loud again, but I had no counterargument. If this was all it was, there didn't seem to be any reason for the room to be so hidden. "There's nothing here!"

"I don't know," I said. "It's sparse for sure. But this feels . . . important."

"Maybe he hasn't finished building it out yet?" Henry suggested.

Bentley just shook his head in confusion.

"Maybe it wasn't an office where he *kept* secret things," Emmaline wondered, "but an office where he *did* secret things."

"What kinds of things could that be, though?" Henry blurted out.

Emmaline was ready. "Phone calls, meetings, emails, online searches . . . any number of things. But whatever it was," she said and pointed at the table, "the answer is on that laptop."

She was right, and we all knew it.

We all sighed, almost collectively. I put my hand on Bentley's shoulder in support. He pulled the chair back, the rubber feet micro-rumbling across the concrete floor. He sat down and carefully opened the laptop.

But we all knew something we hadn't said out loud: we wouldn't get anywhere without the right password.

I, for one, believed Bentley had it in him to figure out the right password, whether by intuitively guessing his father's mind games or via some scientific fingerprint-dusting-type method. Henry's thoughts betrayed Bentley's concern, as I heard his brain mutter "*Oh God, oh God, oh God,*" over and over.

We were all wrong.

Bentley opened the laptop, and the operating system booted up without any password or eye scan required. I guess Mr. Crittendon figured the room was so secure and hidden that the computer didn't need security.

Bentley started doing his hacker thing immediately.

His power truly was incredible, but because it was so rarely presented to us in a visual way it was often overlooked. The flashier powers tended to get noticed more. That guy over there can fly! The guy next to him can freeze things with his fingers!

My friend, Bentley, could learn like no other. Math, science, street smarts—it didn't matter. He was a sponge made up of smaller sponges, and all he longed for was more information and knowledge.

His fingers danced over the keys like he was playing a concerto. He barked out progress updates as he typed without his hands missing a beat. "This computer was exclusively used for video calls." His hands tapped some more. "And two voice-only calls. All over an encrypted private network."

His fingertips stampeded across the keyboard as his code sought the machine's purest truth. "There's an auto-erase program designed to scrape the laptop of data after every call." He typed some more.

"So we don't know anything?" Henry was frustrated, mostly because he was impatient. He was probably also a little hungry.

Bentley typed like he hadn't even heard him. "Every call has been routed through dummy connections . . . but they've all got one port of connection in common. One underlying IP address."

"So he comes in here," I said out loud, while really just working through the logic myself, "to have conversations he doesn't want anyone to record or know about?" I let it linger a beat. "That doesn't seem so bad," I concluded.

Bentley didn't appear to even be listening to me. He was on his own track. "I've got it. Someone got a pen to write this down?"

*Ooph!*

*Ooph!*

"Got it," Emmaline said, pretending like none of us knew she'd just gone to fetch it from the larger office next door.

"Emmaline, are you sure you didn't write it down wrong?" Bentley had tried the IP address several times, using multiple computers and various web browsers. He'd even inverted some of the numbers in case of a typo.

But nothing. He'd even checked the wireless router's connection twice, just to make sure. The IP address appeared to be a fake.

"Or maybe it's not an IP address at all," I thought out loud.

"Didn't he pull it from the code of the videoconferencing app?" Freddie was correct, but that still didn't deter my mind from this new idea.

"He did. But what if it was planted?"

Everyone looked up at me, and we all appeared to agree collectively that we needed to explore other explanations for the numbers.

"What about longitude and latitude?" It was Emmaline, and her words sparked a flurry of ideas.

"Someone read it back again," I yelled.

After some scuffling, I heard Henry's voice ring out. "It's 108.55 P-40.wo."

"That doesn't sound like longitude and latitude," Emmaline concluded.

"Sounds more like made-up names for missiles and airplanes than anything else," Patrick offered.

"Maybe a part number or model number?" Bentley threw out. "Some kind of username maybe?"

Henry's impatience fueled his theories. "Is it possible we're overthinking this? Maybe it's nothing. We're searching for meaning in a few characters of computer code from an old-as-hell laptop that was in a cave of a closet of a secret room? It's just some numbers and letters and decimal points! It doesn't mean anything!"

Something churned within me. The word "decimal" had triggered a thought. I tried to concentrate. "Everyone shut up," I blurted out. "Hang on, hang on," I said, rummaging to refind and hold onto that lightning bolt. "Dewey Decimal System!" I finally shouted triumphantly, much to the chagrin of everyone around me.

"That has to be the nerdiest thing anyone ever shouted in joy," Henry teased.

I was unfazed. "Everyone, come on, hurry!"

Mere seconds later we were all picking through Jurrious's bookshelves. Unfortunately, the elder Crittendon was *not* a fan of the Dewey Decimal System, and his shelves were organized by other criteria—or perhaps organized by no criteria whatsoever. It wasn't alphabetical by title or author, and it didn't appear to be topical either. We would have to check every book, one at a time, looking for the right number on the spine.

Fortunately, we were custodian kids with superpowers, and we wanted to make the search go by as quickly as possible. So Emmaline I used my ability to rapidly move the books into a row of vertical stacks along the floor. Once we were done with that, I just wound up Patrick and set him loose down the line of stacks. He whipped down and back so fast he was a blur, and within about twelve seconds he'd found the book we were looking for.

He read the title aloud, "*Picking Sides: The Psychology of the South Side/North Side Chicago Divide*, by Andrew Wickum, PhD." He handed the book to Bentley with a shrug.

Bentley checked the number on the book's spine to confirm it as a match and then began flipping through it.

"Was I the only one expecting a book that contained maybe a more obvious clue?" Henry was speaking, but I was thinking similar thoughts. The book's title was anticlimactic and didn't give us any outright answers.

But it was a clue. It was more than we had an hour ago.

"I guess I've got some reading to do," Bentley announced, closing the book and sighing.

⚡

It felt good to finally have some progress, to better understand the mystery of the threat we faced.

I'd been through enough as a young custodian to know that some battles were long. And long battles often had small victories or losses along the way. And today's discovery had been a victory.

We knew where we had to go—Chicago—and we knew, to an extent, what we were looking for.

Even Patrick seemed upbeat at the thought that following this lead about Jurrious might also bring more intel about our own father. He zipped around the kitchen cleaning up after another dinner catered by Jack's Pizza, humming the theme song to his favorite sketch comedy show, *Chuckleheads*. It was a terrible and unfunny show, but the theme song was catchy.

Maybe I was an awful big brother, but my approach was to just leave him alone and let him be whenever he was in a good mood. This went for the current situation, but it applied even before Dad went missing. Why mess with a good thing?

He had friends who were his own age—many whom he met online—and he had a full evening planned, which for him involved eating a few thousand calories and playing multiplayer video games with them.

I sat in Dad's chair listening to the television. One of those fundraising commercials featuring homeless dogs came on. I simply couldn't stand them. Even just hearing them, they were oppressive in their guilt shaming. I loved animals, but I hated being shamed—like it was personally my fault thousands of dogs and cats were going hungry or getting sick. I had to change the channel whenever one of those things came on. As it happens, the channel I flipped to was a national news network, and it was covering a juicy breaking story.

". . . the latest custodian act—that we know of. Again, for those of you just joining us, the DHS has foiled another attempted act of violence by a so-called custodian. Tonight in Midtown Manhattan, this man attempted to rob a jewelry store but was chased off by agents before he could do anything more than break a window."

I was listening. I knew Patrick was listening.

A familiar noise breezed into my ears as Pat sped from the kitchen to the television in a nanosecond.

"Uh, Phil . . ." my brother stammered.

I just grunted, because I knew some kind of bad news was coming and I knew I probably wasn't ready for it.

"What's that teacher's name that helps you guys with secret inventions?"

"Haywood?"

"Yeah," he said slowly. "Haywood. So . . . he just tried to steal some diamonds in New York City."

"That doesn't make any sense, Patrick. Haywood's not a criminal. I just saw him a few days ago. And his powers are mental—he's like Bentley. Haywood robbing a bank would be like Bentley robbing a bank."

"I'm sure you're right, but I'm telling you, it was him."

"You weren't even sure what his name was. How can you be sure it was him?"

The phone rang at just that moment. Henry had seen the news as well. "It was him," Henry confirmed. "What the hell is going on, Phillip?"

My breath became short as a shiver ran through my body. Dizzy, I steadied myself with a hand on the couch. "I think . . ." I felt overcome with a sudden fear I couldn't identify. I didn't know the source. Haywood on the news doing a crime was going to affect me, sure, but something else was happening. All this anxiety and PTSD stuff was new enough for me that I still struggled to recognize the signs as they were happening.

*What's the youngest anyone's ever had a heart attack?* I wondered. *Oh wait*, I remembered, *I know what this is. Aw crap.*

And my head smacked the carpeted living room floor.

# 11

# REFLECTIONS

I sat up quickly, the way you do when you're desperately hoping that memory in your brain was a dream.

I was wrong.

All around me were familiar faces, and I knew instantly that I must have passed out. Patrick called people he knew to come and help.

But it was an odd mix. Bentley and Henry were here. I knew Henry was because I could see. Emmaline was here, and I was instantly embarrassed; I wasn't even immediately sure what clothes I was wearing. Mr. Farris—the father of Pat's friend Neal—was here, because I presume Patrick simply doesn't know very many adults. But also our neighbor Mrs. Fanny was here. She sometimes checked on us in the past when our parents would go on extended missions, and I think she went to the church we used to go to.

Basically, without having the time to process it all, I could tell upon sitting up that my poor little brother had probably had his own panic attack after seeing me pass out. Poor kid probably just tried to find any and every person he could to come help.

While it was not my first panic attack or even the first time I'd lost consciousness, it was the first time Patrick had been present. I briefly wondered if he was doomed to a life of emotionally scarring events, poor kid. He was only fourteen and had already seen too much pain and violence. Then again, I was barely a year older than him, so the same could be said of me as well.

"Oh, thank goodness," Mrs. Fanny exclaimed.

Patrick was less courteous. "You are never allowed to do that to me again, you hear me? If you ever do that to me again, I will freaking kill you!"

Emmaline swooped in, put her arm around Patrick, and skillfully guided him off to the kitchen to let him vent.

"Mrs. Fanny, you can go home," Mr. Farris said. "I'll take the boy to the hospital." She must have agreed with his thinking, because she shuffled away.

"Please don't take me to the hospital," I pleaded. "I'm fine. I just passed out. I had a panic attack. It's . . . happened before."

"What?" I heard Patrick scream from the kitchen, still lashing out emotionally after the trauma he'd been through. Bentley got up and used one of his canes to amble into the kitchen to help Emmaline keep my brother from having an attack of his own.

"Son," the man replied, "I have a responsibility here as the adult to make sure you're okay."

"It was just a panic attack, sir, I promise. I have anxiety medicine in the bathroom I can show you."

Henry turned his head at that news, but he said nothing.

"You hit your head pretty hard on the floor here," Mr. Farris objected. "You could have a concussion. I can't in good conscience just leave."

I wasn't winning this debate. I figured it was time to be blunt. I motioned for him to lean closer with my finger, then, in a hushed voice,

I said, "My father's been missing for two days, my favorite teacher was on the news tonight for a jewel heist he is incapable of performing, my mother's been dead for three years. I don't think this family can handle any unnecessary trips to the hospital these days, much less afford them financially. And my brother is currently freaking the hell out not eighteen feet from here, and I'm not sure an ambulance trip is going to improve that situation, so would you kindly get lost and let me and my friends calm my little brother down? I promise I will have somcone wake me up every two hours tonight to watch for a concussion, okay?"

I'll admit I was probably a bit too harsh.

But it worked. He silently stood, put on his jacket, and left the house. We were finally adult-free again.

"If Haywood really was there tonight in New York, I mean, how do we even begin to explain that?" Bentley was just thinking out loud here, but we were all wondering the same thing.

He and Henry and I sat at my family's kitchen table drinking hot chocolate. We were old enough to have tasted coffee, but we'd hated it, so our late-night conversational hot beverage of choice was hot chocolate—though, in his defense, Bentley had inquired about tea.

"Maybe the disappearances are part of something deeper," I wondered. "Haywood definitely didn't go to New York of his own free will to steal diamonds and get rich. That's obvious." No one disputed it. "But he was there. He was there," I repeated, still not quite putting my finger on things.

"Maybe," Henry said cautiously, "he was forced to be there?"

"How?" Haywood was strong-willed, like me. I wasn't buying it just yet.

"Maybe they blackmailed him? Or threatened someone he loves? Forced him to do a crime on their behalf?"

"Isn't he single?" Bentley asked.

"Just because he's single doesn't mean he doesn't love anybody," Henry shot back.

"Well, duh," Bentley agreed in his own snarky manner. "That's not what I meant. But the kind of leverage it must take to get a guy as noble as Haywood to commit a crime like this would be astounding. I didn't know Haywood to be all that close to anyone. No wife, no kids, no siblings that I'm aware of."

"Maybe it wasn't a friend or family member. Maybe he . . . owed money to someone?" Henry seemed to just be searching for answers, but Bentley's patience was thin. It was quite late, after all. But Bentley pounced on him.

"Right, Henry. Haywood, schoolteacher to superhero kids, owed money to the mob, probably for sports gambling debts—you know how much he loved the ponies!" Every word dripped with angry sarcasm. "But this isn't your ordinary mob, this is a mob that loves diamonds! They love diamonds so much they use superheroes that owe them money to rob jewelry stores for them!"

"*Enough*," I bellowed. It was my house, after all, and I was tired of this fight. "You're both going to regret this argument tomorrow. We're all exhausted, and if you wake up my brother by screaming at each other I'll kill you both with my brain right here and now!"

A stunned silence followed, wherein several deep breaths were drawn and exhaled. Eventually the two of them stood and headed for the door, as though collectively understanding what I needed.

I stood to follow them to the door just as Emmaline snuck out of my brother's room. She tiptoed toward me and whispered, "He's finally asleep." She'd spent two hours in there comforting and consoling him, talking him down from his own anxiety and letting him vent. Before tonight I thought she was cute and I might enjoy dating her. After tonight, she was a saint. She'd demonstrated more positive qualities by babysitting my brother tonight than most humans had shown me in their entire lifetimes. Future me will look back on this evening as the time I fell in love with her.

Henry and Bentley waved a silent goodbye from the doorway and shut the door behind them.

"I should go and help them get home quickly," Emmaline said. "Just . . . you're a great guy, and it meant a lot to me to see how much you care about your brother. Night."

*Ooph!*

I awoke in the backyard again. The fall air was creeping in lately and I'd clearly spent some part of the night shivering, as I was now covered in the blanket from the back of the living room couch.

After collecting myself and stretching out the kinks, I slid open the patio door and entered the house to find the television on and the smell of breakfast lingering in the air.

"Patrick?"

No response.

I ambled over to the kitchen counter and started feeling around for the source of the smell, because I was utterly starving. My fingers found a piece of paper first—a transcribed note!

One of Bentley's best inventions of all time, at least from my biased standpoint, was his note-translator. It was a small rectangle, the size of a foot-long skinny candy bar, and it could turn any handwritten or printed note into a braille version in thirty seconds. Which is why Patrick never bothered to actually learn braille, since he had no reason to.

I read through his message with my fingertips. "Off to see Neal and play some video games. Will tell Mr. Farris all is well. Made some eggs; they're in the microwave if you want some. Be back for dinner." The note was signed "Pat" and the postscript read, "Since when do you sleep outside?"

I tossed the note on the counter and went after those eggs.

Later I made my monthly trip to the cemetery.

"Are you out there somewhere still? Do you ever hear the things I say?" I was sure that wherever Donnie had gone, he couldn't hear me. And yet, I refused to believe he was truly gone. Away? Sure. But dead? No way. I would likely never see him again, but he was out there. I was sure of it.

I placed my usual flower arrangement at the base of the statue and then slowly wandered over to my mother's grave. There were many graves and memorials in this cemetery that now held personal value to me. Dozens of former classmates. A few friends. A couple relatives. Every time I came here, I felt like I could spend days here and still not have time to convey my respects to everyone who deserved them.

The Freepoint Cemetery was nearly a football field in size, with several overgrown acres of Mr. Charles's former cornfield to grow into.

When I moved here just under four years ago, the cemetery had 232 graves. Today it had 995.

Times were changing, whether or not we wanted to admit it.

These recent disappearances and the strong rhetoric from Ettinger and the Department of Homeland Security weren't just hot air or empty threats. Our very existence was under direct threat.

Standing among those graves brought things into clearer focus for me. Custodians were under attack. We could run, hide, or fight back. Give you one guess which one I leaned toward.

I thought about the graves that weren't here and might not ever be. For people like Haywood, who had apparently crossed over to the dark side, even though that made no sense—if he had died in that jewel heist, would he have gotten a gravestone here in Freepoint?

I thought about my own grave. My own stone. What would it say? Would my own desires for my tombstone even remotely line up with what my peers would write? Let's face it, no one gets to write their own epitaph. Had I lived a decent enough life that my friends and family would have nice things to etch into my permanent grave marker?

There's no good reason for a fifteen-year-old to think this much about death. But I'd long ago accepted that my life was not normal.

I made certain to leave time to visit James's gravesite. It was one of the newer ones here. His mother put fresh marigolds on his headstone every week—they were her favorite flower. I couldn't imagine her pain.

I was unable to find any words this day; I just cried a bit and nodded. I still wasn't ready.

On the way to grab some lunch, I ran into Henry and Barb leaving Jack's Pizza. Barb was a new student this year, and one I knew very little about. I was actually surprised that she was out with Henry, as I didn't realize he knew anything more about her than I did.

"Oh, hey, buddy!" I exclaimed.

He seemed happy to see me. "Phillip! Finally I can introduce you to Barb! Barb, Phillip!"

We shook hands.

"I thought I might grab a slice," I offered. "Any left?"

"Oh yeah," Barb responded. "Lots."

"We're going to hit up the yard sale over in Bentley's neighborhood," Henry informed me. "Catch up tomorrow?"

"Sure, sure," I agreed, not remotely meaning it nor thinking Henry was buying it for a second. The conversation had the feel of one being played out for the benefit of Barb alone. But I was happy to do my part to help out. He and I had felt some distance lately, maybe only because we'd both started dating recently, or attempting to date.

Honestly, the distance probably had less to do with dating woes and more to do with my own issues. I'd been somewhat distant from everyone lately, not just Henry.

They headed off on their quest and I went inside for a slice of pizza, but really to get out of the house a bit while still being in an environment that felt safe to me.

After coming here for three years, I was more than a regular; I was family. I didn't even need to place an order. Just walk in, join the line, edge my way down to the cash register, pay, and eat. Slice of pepperoni and a fountain drink, $2.95. Once a week or more for three years.

This was almost a home away from home.

I skipped the video games today and chose a booth in the back corner where I could enjoy some privacy.

Sometimes I just needed to be alone with my thoughts.

# 12

# TIES

One block away from Emmaline's house, my anxiety kicked in and I started sweating.

*Maybe she's just humoring you? Maybe someone is paying her to prank you with a long con where she pretends to be friendly for months before breaking your heart? Maybe she's blind like you are!*

I think love's greatest trick is that even when it is present and developing, it can convince both parties that they are hallucinating . . . that they are only one-sidedly experiencing the euphoria.

Looking back it's pretty clear she was as interested in me as I was in her, but neither of us really knew it at the time. We were both wanting to explore it and willing to nudge things but still also hoping the other one would be the initiator.

Which is how we ended up on the most awkward first date in the history of dating.

For starters, I had banished Henry from being anywhere near the proceedings. I decided I'd rather be audience free than have sight.

So, of course, I tripped on the sidewalk leading up to Emmaline's front door. *Great*, I thought. *I've scraped my face on the sidewalk, and now my clothes are messed up. Nice first impression, Phillip.* But it was too late to go home and change and freshen up, so I carried on, not realizing I'd done much more than scrape my cheek.

By the time Emmaline's father opened the front door, I looked like an extra from some zombie prom movie. Naturally he shrieked at my appearance, leading Emmaline's mother and both her brothers to rush to the door to see what the fuss was about. One of the brothers immediately began recording video on his phone, while the other called a friend and started telling him the story.

*Oh, nothing to see here, folks. Just a bloody teenager hoping to take your daughter out for pizza.* I was mortified.

It turns out I wasn't mortified enough.

I knew I was bloodied from the fall, but in reality I was utterly gushing blood. Emmaline's parents called 911 immediately, and I ended up in a hospital bed with eleven stitches in my face and a family's worth of strangers gathered around me—most of them giggling at my clumsiness.

This is how I met Emmaline's family. This was my introduction. If I'd been a turtle, I'd have never again emerged from my shell.

Side note: If anything was going to bring my father out of a possible extended undercover assignment, it was me being hospitalized. And yet he didn't show.

Fine. Fair enough. I hadn't thought he was undercover, actually. I'd been entertaining much scarier thoughts. Like the idea that he'd been kidnapped or imprisoned. Or killed in secret.

Regardless, he didn't show.

The hospital decided to keep me overnight. I couldn't tell if it was because no parent or guardian had shown up to claim me or for purely medical reasons.

I didn't care.

I was happy to have a night to myself—free from the rest of the gang, free from superhero work, free from Patrick, who was spending the night at his best friend's house.

I expected I might not ever be able to face Emmaline again after tonight. I was so embarrassed. I knew on some level that she wouldn't hold my klutziness against me, but I still felt like I'd blown it.

I was going to have a nice little scar, the nurse said, from the edge of my right eye down my jawline across my cheek. She said it would make me look tough. I'm pretty sure she thought I was younger. Or maybe she's just not great with teenagers—or blind kids. I didn't want to look like a badass. I couldn't even see. My physical appearance mattered quite little to me.

I cared about the appearance of my personality, my reputation as a person. I was always aiming for hero but felt like I ended up making a goof of myself more often than not.

I struggled to sleep. Anxiety was one thing, but sleeping in beds that were not my own was another level of discomfort. Whenever we used to go on family vacations it would take days before I adjusted to the new bed and could sleep through the night.

My mind played out contingency plans for bad news I might get about my father. *Maybe he's never coming back. Maybe he's been killed.*

I thought about what that would do to Patrick. Could he and I survive the death of another parent? I wasn't sure we could.

A few moments later I was chuckling morosely at myself for worrying about my dad turning up dead tomorrow.

But this was my reality. My father was, if nothing else, risking his life out there right now. He actually could be killed. And if it happened,

I'd be expected to just pick up and carry on somehow. And I was only fifteen. It kind of made me angry sometimes how much weight I had to bear.

I turned over to my other side and rearranged myself to try and get comfortable.

I heard light footsteps as the night nurse made her rounds. A few minutes later she popped her head into my room, where I was pretending to be asleep. I wasn't hooked up to any monitors or IVs or anything, so I was pretty sure they were just babysitting me for the night. She lingered only a second, then she shut the door and moved on down the hall.

I thought about Homeland Security's new fervor for custodians. Was our way of life really about to change? Or even end? Why would they be so angry when we just want to help?

I knew some of these answers, of course. I knew, for instance, that power and control drove pretty much everything—at least in America. Whenever the actions of people in positions of power appeared to be strange or even morally wrong, you can bet there were motivations behind them that drew from power and control. Money? Sure . . . because it buys power and control.

It was most frustrating, I suppose, to see so much of the public turning against us. So many had seen personal firsthand proof of our intent and ability to help stop crimes and save lives.

But not all evidence weighed the same.

A few bad apples doing shady things and suddenly everyone had forgotten about all the good things we'd done over the years.

And Haywood. What in the heck had happened there? The man we knew would never commit a robbery. Even under duress. He was incapable. And yet there was video proof that he had tried—or something that looked like him. Henry had a conspiracy theory that someone was creating doubles of custodians to commit these crimes with. I'd filed the notion alongside other harebrained things Henry believed, like his theory that the government put listening devices in restaurant saltshakers or his insistence that some animals could speak English but just chose not to. When a friend says ridiculous stuff like that all the time, he tends to get a label.

It wasn't doubles. I don't know how I knew, but I just knew. Someone was forcing good heroes to do bad deeds. And I had to figure out who and how, in that order.

⚡

Two hours later I still hadn't fallen asleep. I'd tried every sleep position known to man, some of them two or three times, but slumber was still a distant speck on the horizon.

I decided to get out of bed and go for a walk. I wouldn't leave the hospital, but I had to try and burn off some of this mental energy.

I found my clothes folded neatly on the windowsill and changed out of my paper gown.

I crept into the hall quietly and tried to get a sense of the ambient noise out there. Little noises most people take for granted or ignore could be incredibly helpful to a blind person like me. Electronic beeps and the whirring of machinery. The spin of a computer's hard drive. A distant cough.

I could get a decent lay of the land this way. For instance, I now knew that the hallway was much longer to my left than to my right, where a wall or pair of double doors twenty feet away cut off the sounds and bounced them back. I decided to go left.

I tapped my cane lightly, not wanting to make much noise but also needing it to avoid a collision.

Most of the rooms' doors were closed, and I had no interest in disturbing anyone. I wasn't even trying to explore really. Just mixing it up. Lying in bed for hours hadn't brought me sleep, so I was going to try walking and see what that brought.

And what it brought was an unexpected encounter with a terrible memory.

Fifty feet down the hallway, I came to a perpendicular hallway that formed a T. Something tugged at me mentally, and I turned left down this new hallway without really knowing why. But ten steps later I knew. There before me was the room. That room. The room where Mom had died.

I couldn't see it, obviously. And I'm not sure what combination of my other senses helped me know where I was—some team up of smell and muscle memory. I don't know. But I knew it was the room.

My body stood there, catatonic, while my mind clicked right back to that night.

I was there in that moment all over again. The doctors shouting and the stampede of panicked staff members. The wailing of alarms and the incessant beeping. I heard my younger self's cries echo through the hallway. It was a powerful reminder of how sensory memories can be. I hadn't remembered or recalled Mom's death that vividly ever before. But being in this spot where it happened opened up the floodgates.

Like an audio echo dancing around a canyon, the memory repeated and eventually faded.

Only then did I realize there was someone nearby. I could hear labored breathing, coming from a height and distance suggesting someone was seated on a bench just down the hallway.

"Hello?"

"I thought that was you." It was the voice of an older woman, maybe in her late fifties or early sixties.

"Excuse me?"

"You used to be friends with my boy," she replied.

I cocked my head and she apparently understood that I was still confused, because she continued.

"Donnie. Donnie Brooks. I was Donnie's foster mother."

I was floored. "Mrs. Brooks!"

"It's Delmar now. Been divorced about two years. Things never quite got back to being right in our home." She stopped, as though realizing something. "Well, you know what I'm talking about. You been through loss."

I had half a mind to consider her a figment of my imagination. But I carried on talking, assuming her to be real. "What are you doing here?"

She let out a long sigh. "I got the cancer. Lung cancer. Too many years of smoking. Don't you never take up smoking, son! Don't you dare!"

"I would never," I assured her. I took the initiative and sat down on the bench next to her.

She was struck by a sudden coughing fit. I wondered how no one in the rooms around us was awoken by it. Just when it died down, it picked back up again for another fifteen seconds of hacking. It was uncomfortable, because I knew it meant she was pretty bad off.

"They came to our house, you know. Them government types. Came by and said Donnie'd done a good thing. He'd saved some folks. Even gave him a statue, they did."

"It's a lovely statue. I visit it often."

"Gave him a gravestone too," she added with sadness.

I nodded. "I visit that as well."

"You know," Mrs. Delmar blurted out, "I ain't never gotten a good explanation as to what happened to him. No one ever been able to help me understand." Her voice cracked, and I could tell she was choking up.

"Did my boy die? All I heard was 'black hole' and 'disappeared.' I ain't been able to accept that as dead, son. I just can't do it." She wiped her face with a tissue or handkerchief. "I just know he's out there. And he's coming back here someday. We'll see that boy again," she said, with not much confidence. Almost as a question. She was asking me to agree.

"Donnie isn't dead," I assured her. "I've never thought he was. He's definitely out there somewhere . . . being kind to everyone he meets." I heard her cry a little. And yet, I felt the truth was better than a lie. I'll never know if I was right about that, but I continued anyway. "But I don't think he's coming back." I didn't. "Space is basically infinite, Ms. Brooks—I mean Delmar. Donnie sacrificed himself to save all of us, and the black hole ability sent him somewhere off into space. Even if he wanted to come back here, I'm not sure he could."

She cried a little while longer, and I sat there holding her hand while she did. Then she squeezed my hand, stood up, and thanked me for being honest before shuffling into the room nearest the bench to go to bed.

As for me, I was finally ready to escape this awful world and head off to dreamland for a bit.

Mrs. Delmar died a few weeks later. They gave her a grave right next to Donnie's.

# 13

# PIZZA

"Well, Chicago is the destination for certain," Bentley said. "The book says that by title alone. I've skimmed through the thing and am still working on a couple theories, but I do not yet understand how this book is supposed to help us."

It was a crisp fall Saturday, and we were warming up at Jack's.

"What's it about?" Henry asked.

"It's about . . ." Bentley blustered, "it's about Chicago! It's about the differences between North Side and South Side Chicago."

"Maybe the title is more literal than you're giving it credit for," I offered. "Like, maybe there is or was or used to be a physical line between North Chicago and South Chicago . . . and whatever we're trying to find is currently at *that* spot?"

"A physical line?" Bentley scoffed at first, before thinking it through and realizing I might be onto something. "A physical line!"

So where was the official line between the two Chicagos, and why did people choose one side over the other? And what the *hell* kind of important custodian item would ever get stored out there in the first place?

Bentley went to work on some new research avenues, typing away furiously on his tiny little laptop.

"Just a suggestion," I added.

"I'm confused," Patrick confessed. "Are we going after this lead because we think it was left for us on purpose or because we think we were never meant to find it?"

"What?"

"Did his dad leave that for us to find or did we find something no one was ever supposed to find?"

"I'm not sure it matters," I replied. "Whether he meant for us to find it or not, it's clearly an important piece of information. Something worth hiding in a secret office. Something he was investigating just before he disappeared perhaps. It's worth us chasing it down no matter what Mr. Crittendon's intentions were."

Bentley instinctively shivered and looked up from his computer. "Can you not do that please?" he asked playfully. "I hear Mr. Crittendon, and I hear my dad talking down to me. I don't think he's called me Bentley since I was in grade school."

If I had a nickel for every time Bentley said something intriguing about his father that I did *not* follow up with more questions out of respect for my friend, I'd be rich. Filthy rich. Crittendon rich. "Sorry, buddy. My bad." I valued his feelings more than my own curious itches being scratched.

Bentley returned to his internet research.

Just then Freddie walked in with a pair of our younger Ables members: Owen, who I'd taken to just calling Lead Foot, and a kid named Porter that everyone called Leper. It was a crude nickname only loosely related to his powers; he could regenerate limbs the way a lizard regrows a tail, only he could do it really quickly.

As I said, it was a crude nickname, one I hoped to change over time. For now, I began by calling him by his given name. "Hey, Freddie, Owen . . . hey, Porter." I held up my closed fist as they walked by the table on their way to the front counter, and all three bumped it with their own fists as they passed. If there was one thing I was willing to give myself credit for, it's that I was probably a cool coach and mentor.

"Where's Emmaline at?" Henry was always talking with his mouth full.

"She's sick, she said." If I sounded disappointed, it's because I was. Our rescheduled first date had again needed to be postponed because of this illness, and it was beginning to feel like fate was conspiring to keep us apart.

"Maybe she's just keeping her distance after you bled all over her front porch." My little brother was a dick sometimes.

"Funny," I said sarcastically.

"She seems to get sick a lot," Henry noted.

"Yeah," I agreed. "I think it's probably related to her disability. I know the dizziness can lead to throwing up. And maybe by 'sick' she just means that."

Freddie sat down with a piping hot pepperoni slice right then. "Oh, bad timing. Maybe talk about puke somewhere where people aren't eating, dude."

"Gross," Greta declared. Penelope and Greta were at the end of the table on my left, working on some calculations they had yet to share with the group.

"Oh, you're not even eating yet. Calm down," I said to Freddie, taking Greta's side. "And don't be gross."

I looked up and down the table, again taking for granted Henry's ability to use just his subconscious peripheral vision to send me my glasses' camera feed. I was so proud of this group. We were all so different, but working together. We hadn't broken down into bickering and blaming, at least not too much. We were just all friends working collectively.

And it was a school day! I laughed a bit at how quickly we'd gone from deciding to stop attending school to forgetting what it was like to ever attend school at all.

"Are you ladies ready to share what you're working on?" I asked.

"No," Greta barked.

"Zip it," Penelope said at the same time.

"Lovely. Great. Awesome."

"Okay, okay, okay," Bentley said excitedly. "There are a few variations that people like to argue about, but apparently there is some kind of ceremonial line between North and South Chicago."

"Okay, great," I said.

"Awesome," Freddie said, not even having any idea what we were talking about.

"But they're all several miles long," Bentley added, sighing.

"Maybe the title was super literal but there's some further clue inside the book itself?" I offered, just honestly trying to be helpful.

"Like I have time to read a whole book right now," Bentley shot back before realizing he'd gone a bit over the top on the anger. "I'm sorry, Phillip. I'm just a little edgy. I'll see if I can find an e-copy of the book and run it through some phrase filtering software." And with that he disappeared back into his invisible research shell where he pretended nothing around him really existed.

"How does this pizza taste so freaking good?" It was Owen, but it could have been any one of us that was eating today. Jack's wasn't just a good hangout spot with video games; the pizza tasted outstanding. I used to live in New York City and never had a slice there that tasted as good. I'd long ago learned why that was, but I decided to let someone else teach young Owen in the ways of the Jack's Pizza.

"It's all about the ingredients," Patrick said, as though he'd invented this spiel instead of learning it from me. "Lots of pizza places claim to use the best ingredients. Most of them are just using clever marketing or employing the power of words like 'organic' and 'natural' that sound like they have hard scientific meaning but, in the food world, are merely narrowly defined labels that don't correspond to science at all."

I had to admit, Patrick was better at telling this story than I was. He had more passion. More enthusiasm. He was a better orator than I was. He was animated and gestured wildly as he spoke.

"Jack doesn't care about those labels. And Jack doesn't care about price. In fact, one of the ways you know Jack's is using the best ingredients is because it costs so much per slice to eat here!"

"Preach it," Henry chimed in.

Freddie added his own "Amen!"

Pat didn't miss a beat. "Jack imports most of his pizza ingredients—including the olive oil, herbs, and cheeses—from Italy. Because Italy invented pizza. And even though it's *super* expensive to put that stuff on a freaking boat and chug it all the way across the Atlantic, it makes the pizza taste better. And that's all Jack cares about, baby!"

Owen had finished his slice by the time the story was over. "I had no idea what I was getting into by asking that question."

I put an arm on his shoulder in a moment of mock bonding. "Lead Foot, Jack's isn't pizza—it's a way of life."

Later that night, as I lay in the backyard, those words echoed around my brain.

A way of life. A way of life.

A thesis for a person.

I'd been joking about Jack's pizza and its carefully sourced ingredients being a way of life, of course. Everyone knew it. But the joke had possibly exposed a hole in my own life: I had no compelling philosophy. I had nothing driving my actions.

Sure, I was a "custodian," whatever that ultimately meant. I knew that I had special abilities—namely telekinesis—and that I hoped to use those abilities to help my fellow man.

I guess. I mean . . . I think I did. I felt pretty sure that I did.

But didn't everyone want to do good? Didn't many dream of being heroes? Wasn't it only the truly evil and vile that daydreamed about doing wicked things or had wicked goals?

I had goals, and was certain that they were not wicked, but still I wondered . . . what was my North Star? My inspiration?

I'd been to church off and on my whole life. The whole thing about God's son sacrificing himself for our mistakes . . . that seemed so lovely and romantic. I adored its poetry. For years I wanted it to make sense to me. I longed to feel it in my gut as the answer. So many around me had.

But I never connected to it personally. I never felt drawn to its mission or lifestyle. Millions did, and I often wished I could be one of them, but I was not.

I was only fifteen, but that still felt like an age where people begin to figure out their drives and inner callings. Was mine really so rote as to just be another hero in a line of heroes? Another son following in his father's footsteps?

What mattered to me?

Patrick did. And my friends. My dad. But aside from people, what thoughts mattered to me? What truths and theories? What ideas mattered to me?

For instance, I met a man once on a school field trip to the Metropolitan Museum of Art. He stood on the steps outside "preaching" his version of some kind of gospel. It was about the moon landings being fake. And he was as passionate and loud as any preacher I'd ever encountered.

But I wasn't sure I'd come across any issue or mission statement that fired me up even 10 percent as much as moon-landing guy. My therapist thought moon-landing guy's passion may have been somewhat drug or alcohol boosted, and that seemed like a fair argument. But I still wanted that passion. I wanted to be fired up about why my life was worth living.

I thought perhaps it could be family. But then I remembered how messed up my grandpa turned out to be, and I realized my life philosophy wasn't going to be family based.

For a brief moment, I considered if my purpose was to live in a way that allowed my mother to be remembered by others. But she'd taken care of that with her own lifestyle. And even though she'd died young, she'd touched myriad lives with her kindness and generosity.

Kindness and generosity. Did I even possess those qualities, let alone in volumes enough to make them part of my mission statement? I wasn't sure that I did.

I had an uncanny ability to be honest with myself in areas where I felt instinctively weak. I often danced around the line between brutal honesty and harsh self-doubt. If I made a silly grammatical error, I might go hard and call myself a moron.

It seemed possible that a person's life philosophy would be informed by their parents or those who raised them. So I thought about the pearls of wisdom I'd had passed down to me.

Mom always focused on emotions. Happiness was her pursuit, though more for us than for herself.

Dad used to tell me, back when I was in elementary school, "Do good to others, because maybe they'll do good back to you. But even if they don't, you'll sleep well at night."

What would be my nuggets of wisdom I'd pass on to my own future kids?

What did I want them to say about me at my funeral? Did I want them to praise my actions or my intentions?

As usual, I fell asleep before I figured any of it out.

# 14

# SEARCHING

There are, as it turns out, at least a half dozen divider lines between North and South Chicago. There's no consensus among scholars or residents as to which is *the* line, and each has a fervent base of fans and supporters. This has led to three separate lawsuits, multiple community rallies, and several protests—including one where a famous local running back got arrested for protesting while he was also on Injured Reserve, which netted him an NFL fine of $10,000.

With no way to discern between the various supposed "official" divider lines through the city, we had no choice but to make a more broad decision in planning our search.

We decided to begin on the East Side. "We are here, and we are about to go west along the modified North/South line Bentley created," I said, pointing to a map. "We're not actually following any of the lines they say could be the true line because we're following an amalgamation of all six lines. It sounds messed up when I say it out loud, but Bentley says this increases our odds of finding something useful."

We were at Arvey Field in Grant Park. This was a loose staging area for us to begin working our way west across the city, and our intention was to investigate along the line as far as we could before the morning commute.

Of course, we didn't even know what we were looking for, so our efforts were hard to define.

"Are we looking for some kind of underground hidden chamber or . . . what?" For once, Patrick spoke for everyone present.

"For the last time," Bentley screeched, "I do not know! I am taking some hidden information and trying to interpret it on the fly. I have no *freaking* clue what I'm doing. And you are not obligated to follow along with me as we go forward."

In his defense, it was about the tenth time someone had asked Bentley a question since we'd gotten here, and that would test anyone's patience.

No one knew what we were looking for or how we would know if we had found it. We were taking a wild leap of faith here. We were in uncharted territory where anything was fair game. I just wanted to find the missing custodians. And we had but one legit major clue. I was willing to be wrong half a dozen times if we eventually got it right and found our way toward some answers. But it was late, cold, and we were still a group of high schoolers. There were bound to be conflicts.

"We'd make better time if Emmaline were here," Greta griped.

"She's still sick," I said. "Besides, who says the point here is speed? We're trying to find a needle in a haystack. Scratch that . . . we're looking for a needle in a football stadium full of hay. Now we have a clue that something important is near this area, and that's literally all the information we have to go on. If we move too quickly, we run the risk of running right by the very thing we're looking for without even seeing it."

"Should we go under this overpass?" Patrick asked. He was moving in the wrong direction, headed east toward the Field Museum and Shedd Aquarium. We'd intended to head west, and Bentley thought landmarks like those were too obvious to be our target anyway.

"Well, only if you want to be by yourself," I shot back. "You're going the wrong way."

"I'm sorry," he said, sounding genuine, as he zipped back over to my position. "I didn't realize we were going to be doing so much walking. I thought you were going to, you know, tele-connect us all over the place."

"Tele-connect" was Patrick's favorite way to turn my powers into a verb. It drove me crazy, which is part of why he enjoyed it so much.

"I'm not your personal chauffeur," I said. "Besides, why don't we look around here before we worry about moving anywhere?"

Bentley ambled up to Penelope and Greta. "Time to make the reveal?" he asked. They smiled and nodded their heads excitedly.

Turns out that Greta was a bit of a coder, and her father had been an audio engineer with the navy. With a pinch of assistance from Bentley, they'd invented a kind of sonar device that worked in water, underground, and above ground through open air. They called it Gretalope, which was just a combination of their names and sounded awful. I made them promise to consider changing the name to something more palatable.

Tonight it was helping us look for hidden rooms and chambers, both above and below ground. We believed we were after a room of some kind. If a hollow area existed near us, the Gretalope would help us find it.

But truth be told, we were guessing. We had a lead that suggested we should come here to this nebulous line between the top and bottom of Chicago, but beyond that we were playing the lottery. Whatever was out here could be right in our faces and we might not realize it.

We didn't get very far this particular evening because of a drunk driver.

If you've never driven in Chicago, you should give thanks.

Folks from Boston like to talk about bad traffic. Those in Atlanta do the same. And I've sampled both, and they are equally terrible.

But nothing is like Chicago traffic. It's *all the cars*, and *all at once*. It's bumper-to-bumper traffic while everyone's going ninety miles an hour.

It is, on a good day, a very dangerous place to drive. The sheer volume of cars and constant rate of speed can be deadly.

Tonight, a drunk driver on the nearby Lake Shore Drive merged when he should not have merged, and did so just as he was approaching the overpass near our position. The large truck behind him slammed into the drunk's car and pushed it partially up onto the trailer of the flatbed semi directly in front. And fifty yards later, twenty individual vehicles were crashing and crunching into each other on one of the busiest streets in the city.

Two cars leapt off the elevated overpass toward where we stood in the field and looked to smash into the ground below. We raced into action, and I was able to suspend both vehicles just above ground to avoid a couple of deadly crashes.

I set both vehicles down gently. The passengers inside gaped at me in wonder. It's one thing to see a custodial act on the evening news or see a reporter blather about it over grainy handheld footage. I imagine it's another thing entirely to see one in the flesh. And not just as a spectator on the sidelines, but as a near-victim—as one of those who was saved by the deed. They'd just had a front row seat for an act that probably didn't make sense to their brains.

*We didn't wear masks*, I thought to myself in both realization of fact and disgust at my own lack of careful planning. If this family in the minivan here on my right wanted to pull out their cameras and start taking pictures or video of us right now, there'd be little I could do to stop them short of using my powers even more.

I had bigger problems, as it turned out.

The crash had snarled traffic on the roadway above and brought out the emergency vehicles as well as the news choppers.

News choppers were antithetical to the Ables accomplishing their mission tonight. And just like that we'd gone from a reconnaissance mission to one of survival.

Hiding under the overpass was easy at first. There were so many lanes on Lake Shore Drive that massive shadows were cast down there. Lots of darkness. But we couldn't stay there long. Surely witnesses up on the loop would tell the first responders and the news reporters about the two vehicles that flew off the road. And when those vehicles were discovered unharmed, the occupants would probably just point their fingers over in our direction and give our position away.

We started creeping farther east. We needed to stick to the shadows.

I noticed a thick line of trees running like a grove along the front of the Field Museum. We didn't have to be all that quiet, as the commotion above was enormous. But we stayed as quiet as possible as we ran from the shelter and shadowy comfort of the overpass to the tree line.

From there we moved slowly again, working through the trees toward the far end of the grove near Shedd Aquarium.

But once the DHS drones were deployed, we had to give up creeping and just run. I shouldn't have been so surprised at the department's quick reaction time to the crash. They probably monitored police bands for any events likely to draw out custodians.

DHS drones were equipped with cameras, massive dayglow lighting rigs, and tear gas, and that was basically it. If they couldn't blind you into submission, they'd gas you. That didn't work on all custodians, but it was enough to slow most down a bit at least.

"Let's go—move it!" I barked.

They came at us fast from the area of the crash, likely deployed from a mobile DHS command unit at the scene.

"Penelope, a little help?" I blurted as I ran.

Soon enough a fog began to develop between the drones and us. It wouldn't stop them, but it might buy some time. Maybe a few seconds.

"We didn't even get a full look at everything back at the landing zone," Henry complained. "Now we're already on the run?" He used the word "run" loosely, as his motorized wheelchair did all the work and was faster than all of us except for Patrick.

"What about the Gretalope?" Greta cried while running. "Are we just going to let it get destroyed or stolen or whatever? We're just leaving that behind?" In the commotion we'd forgotten about the device she and Penelope had worked so hard on. I felt bad for her, but there was no turning back to get the box now.

Bentley, for once, was living in the moment. Maybe even ahead of the moment a few beats. He'd already found an entrance into the sewer line and popped open the cover. "Down here," he urged as we all approached.

The word "sewer" has a pretty negative connotation in the English language. Typically most folks associate it with human waste. And for good reason.

But taken literally, the word sewer just means "a conduit for carrying wastewater."

After a playful clarified definition like that, the concept of using sewer pipes to break into a famous aquarium almost sounds romantic, doesn't it?

Look. The fact of the matter was that Shedd Aquarium, like any major aquarium, sent away hundreds of gallons of wastewater per day. It sounded like a gross plan, but it would work.

A few minutes later we were inside, drying off with towels we'd found in the divers' locker room as we strolled through the darkened facility's exhibit hallways.

For a brief few moments, the panic of the incident just a short while ago melted into the back of our minds. The subdued lighting and utter lack of other patrons made this feel like a private VIP tour of the aquarium—like backstage access.

It was dreamlike.

We moved slowly, independently but as a group, taking in the impressive collection of underwater specimens. The habitats glowed with internal lighting, sending shimmering wave shadows to dance across the building's walls and ceilings.

We pointed at our favorite fish. We called out to each other to share newly discovered animals or exhibits. In the performance hall, Freddie— the only one among us who'd actually been here before and seen the show—regaled us with a detailed account of all the tricks the dolphins would perform.

We laughed and forgot our troubles, the way that regular kids did when they came to this place.

That is, until I realized we were not alone.

I knew what was there even before I turned my head. The drone motor noise was unmistakable. How foolish I'd been to let my guard down so quickly.

"A drone," Greta cried out as she spotted it too.

Freddie tapped his aspirator, grabbing the drone in his giant fist as he grew to about half his full size. He easily crushed the machine to bits and pieces. He panted and then looked at me and said in his deeper, giant-Freddie voice, "Still too late, though, right?"

I nodded. It was definitely too late. The drone had certainly already done its damage by merely sending images of us to its owner.

"How long was it there?" Patrick panicked.

"I don't know," I said honestly. "It doesn't matter, really." I looked up to face him. "They know where we are."

# 15

# UNDERWATER

We were fairly well surrounded at this point. DHS had agents all throughout Grant Park, and they were slowly advancing on the aquarium.

*I am such an idiot.*

*Not the time to be kicking yourself, man,* Henry told me silently. *You can kick all their asses!* He paused. *Right?*

"How many of them are there?" I asked out loud. My anxiety kicked in, and my chest started pounding. I tried the breathing exercises I'd been taught. They seemed to work, for a bit.

Henry looked out the nearest window again. There were dozens of police vehicles, a few DHS SWAT trucks and ambulances, even a fire truck and some kind of armored SUV thing. He glanced up into the sky and revealed two circling helicopters as well.

"How many what? People? Vehicles? Chances for us to die?" As usual, Henry peppered his mission intel with his own personal feelings of doom and gloom. If you looked up "glass half empty" in the dictionary, you would find a picture of my pessimistic friend Henry.

"I'd give good money if you'd just tell me something useful or actionable," I shouted, losing my temper yet again because of the overwhelming stress.

But Henry was as tired of me as I was of him. "You are seeing the same exact thing I am, Phillip. Why don't *you* come up with some actionable intelligence! Maybe you can throw some sharks at them or something!"

For half a second, I thought about it.

"I'd like to formally register a complaint against using any of the aquarium's specimens as projectiles." Penelope was our resident animal conservationist. She was passionate about wildlife, and while she was typically shy, she never hesitated to speak her mind about issues related to animals.

"Relax, Penelope," I assured her. "We will not be using any of the animals as weapons." I looked around, trying to find something useful among all the aquatic enclosures. There was a flagpole. A few stanchions and ropes to guide lines of customers. It certainly would have been easier to fight our way out of this if we had more than fish lying around.

"Custodians," a voice bellowed from outside. "Come out with your hands up and do not attempt to use your abilities. You have sixty seconds to comply."

"Well, crap," Bentley sighed. "That didn't take long."

"Are we sure they mean us?" Henry joked.

"Maybe you could shut your yap if you can't be constructive," I said.

"Maybe you've turned into a real jerk lately."

I started to respond in kind but was cut off.

"Or maybe," Penelope chimed in snidely, "we've wasted a fourth of the time they gave us by arguing about it?"

"She's right," I said. "Let's focus on solutions."

Henry was apoplectic. "What? Solutions? You can take them all out on your own, man! Just . . . go take them out!"

"Henry, we are in a city of ten million people, and we are in its heart! What do you think happens for custodians if I make tonight's news by killing a hundred DHS soldiers? I can't hide my identity with the masks Haywood never finished. I can't stop them without doing some serious damage. You're asking me to plaster my face all over the news. You're asking me to become the FBI's most wanted!"

"If the alternative is that *all* of us get locked up, maybe . . . yeah! Maybe you should!"

"Custodians inside the aquarium," the voice from outside echoed, "you are down to thirty seconds."

"Really wish we had Emmaline tonight," I said aloud, mostly to myself.

"Maybe if you weren't in love with her," Henry started.

"Can we go back to where you and I aren't angry with each other? Because I don't even know what happened to make us angry."

"Big surprise," Henry spewed.

The outside voice returned for another unhelpful update. "Fifteen seconds."

"Great," Freddie breathed. "Now we're all gonna die because you two got into a pissing match."

Henry was looking out the window again. "They are advancing, and quite rapidly. With machine guns."

Glass broke suddenly all around us as tear gas canisters breached the aquarium's windows and started spewing out clouds of gas. Despite all our insane planning, we were somehow not equipped to deal with tear gas or any other gas.

As the general murmur of panic began to grow among my team, the distinct sound of breaking glass came from above.

We all looked up while also instinctively shielding our faces from the falling debris. Then—*thump*—a man landed in our midst. I instantly recognized him.

"Dad?" I went into shock.

"Dad!" Patrick's squeal brought me out of shock. I'd forgotten we even brought him along on this mission.

I went into battle mode and attempted to catch him up to speed with as little information as possible. "We were looking for the meridian. The DHS is about to raid us. What do we do?"

He didn't speak. He didn't move. He didn't even look at me.

"Dad?" I thought he might be in shock from breaking through the skylight or the hard landing. Or possibly he was mad that I'd gotten myself into trouble again.

Finally, he turned his gaze in my direction. I smiled. Most kids have experienced a moment of true fear only to have a parent show up and make them feel better instantly. That's what happened to me. I didn't know *how* he was going to do it, but I knew my dad was definitely going to save the day.

He drew his left arm up and around the opposite shoulder, as though stretching his tricep or trying to scratch a hard-to-reach spot on his back. And then he paused. And then he smiled. I will never forget that smile; it was slow and hollow.

Instantly his arm released from its position, as though it had been held in place while gaining momentum like a car on *The Flintstones*. Then it swept down to the floor in no time. Before I even knew what was happening, we were all two hundred feet in the air, flying over the edge of Lake Michigan, the wind—and probably the confidence—knocked out of us good and hard. He'd blasted us all back through the skylight with his telekinetic power.

My father had just sent us all soaring to our deaths without batting an eye.

I came to and opened my eyes to find myself below the surface of Lake

Michigan. My blue jeans and all my gear were getting heavy quickly and sinking me. And my vision was gone. Henry!

Henry would be sinking even faster than I was, due to his wheelchair. And if I wasn't getting any vision from him, it meant he was probably unconscious . . . or worse.

My ears were overwhelmed with new sounds like rushing currents and sonar noises from the harbor. I'd never learned to swim, and my body began to flail in panic almost as soon as it realized it was underwater.

I began to suck in water as my lungs hyperventilated. Bentley's leg braces would probably drag him down as well. A half dozen other potential catastrophes entered my mind.

Patrick! Well, Patrick knew how to swim, I knew that for sure. Maybe he'd be able to get to the surface and find help for the rest of us. It seemed like a long shot the moment I thought of it, but I didn't have any other threads of hope to cling to.

Suddenly, a familiar sound . . . though somewhat dampened.

*Oophul!*

I was still underwater, but we jumped before I could even process.

*Oophul!*

*Oophul!*

*Oophul!*

Eventually we were all dumped out in Charles Field back in Freepoint, sucking wind and wet as hell, each of us with a dozen quality questions.

"You can teleport underwater?" I was the first to blurt something out.

"Well, duh," Henry chided. I was just glad to know he was okay and to have my sight back again.

"I didn't know," I countered. "That's amazing," I said to Emmaline directly. "And thank you, obviously. How did you even know we were in trouble?"

Emmaline just tilted her head to the right, where Patrick stood next to her. It took a moment for him to realize what was happening, but then he sheepishly accepted responsibility for the good deed. "I'm so small that I don't pass out easily, even when most folks would. And I can run on the surface of a body of water, so . . ."

I knew my kid brother was wicked fast, but I didn't know he was *that* fast. He'd run from Chicago to Freepoint in seconds, just to save our lives. And it had worked. I made a mental note to give Patrick a break now and then and to start treating him as more of an equal than a subordinate.

Without warning I spit up a few mouthfuls of swallowed lake water and wheezed as I tried to regain my awareness. "Please tell me this doesn't count as our date," I joked between breaths.

She smiled at me and then suddenly turned her head and zapped over to where Penelope was. They exchanged a few hushed words, then Emmaline disappeared.

A few seconds later she reappeared, holding Gretalope. Greta shrieked with joy as both girls hugged Emmaline, who then keeled over and threw up, no doubt overexerted from the incredible underwater rescue.

⚡

"What was he even doing there?" I asked.

The news was running footage of my father at Shedd Aquarium ad nauseam. Every network had a slightly different angle, but they all showed the same thing: Dad rising up from the aquarium and using his telekinesis to fling some cops about for a while before flying up into the clouds above Lake Michigan.

The news channel pundits were ready to act shocked and scared. "Here is a so-called hero. For those who care, we have finally identified him—a custodian named John Sallinger. And he's just . . . look at him go. He's just breaking into places and flying off whenever he wants. The cops are powerless. These are the folks we're being asked to accept into our society as regular citizens? Hell no, I say!"

"I don't know," Emmaline replied to my question honestly. She had, once again, been a great help in calming Patrick down tonight. And she'd stuck around for moral support, as had Bentley and Penelope.

"You're sure it was him?" Bentley just wanted to give me options. I would have done the same for him. But the truth was the truth.

"Yeah," I admitted reluctantly. "It was him."

"You know Henry's got that theory about doubles."

"I have heard and dismissed that theory, yes. I guess I can't say anything for certain anymore, given the rapid exponential rise in scientific discovery and my own reputation for stepping in it."

Ettinger was nothing if not punctual. A mere nine hours after the events in Chicago at Shedd Aquarium, she was on TV with a statement and a press conference.

"These so-called custodians cannot be trusted. We *need* more oversight. Clearly most of them are good-hearted and well-intentioned, but the bad seeds among them—like this one here in Chicago who attacked the aquarium—they do exist, and they sully the name of custodians, I believe."

A softball interview ensued, where she was asked a series of questions designed to help her make us look bad.

"Why are you so concerned about custodian behavior?"

"I'm only concerned about the behavior of unregistered custodians. The ones we have on file, the ones we know about and understand their powers and know where they are, we have no problem with them. It's the rest of them I'm worried about."

"How so?"

"Why won't you let us take your picture? What do you have to hide? The custodians want us to believe they have our best interests at heart and only want to help, but when we ask for first and last names they shrink back into the shadows. And that kind of makes me nervous, I won't lie."

# 16

# A HEIST

The doorbell rang. I assumed it was the Jack's delivery guy with our pizza, so I let Patrick worry about answering it.

We'd been ordering dinner from Jack's three or four times a week, easily. I'm sure the FDA would have had a fit about our imbalanced diet these last several weeks. I know Dad would have, and he was generally pretty lenient when it came to diet.

But calories and sodium content weren't major concerns for me right now. As long as both of us ate, that was good enough. We were under a tremendous amount of stress. The last thing we needed was me trying to force green beans into the meal discussion.

I heard the murmur of conversation at the front door, then Patrick yelled, "It's Bentley, for you," and then scampered back down the hall to his bedroom.

I turned around and peeked my head over the back of the couch. "Hey, buddy. Come on in."

Bentley ambled over slowly and joined me on the couch. "I've got good news and bad news," he declared.

"Alright, hit me."

"The good news is I figured out how to finish Haywood's plans for the masks."

"That's amazing!" I exclaimed.

The events in Chicago had nearly been our end. Our faces were seen, by citizens as well as a DHS drone. This almost certainly meant that we were all stepped up another level from our previous status, maybe even up at level two or three after the aquarium, we couldn't be sure.

Clearly my father had been the focus of the news coverage and the public statements from the DHS personnel. For some reason they had, so far, chosen not to out us as custodians. But they could—and they might. Especially if we gave them a good reason, like doing more custodial work without somehow being able to hide our identities.

Getting Haywood's masks working would be huge.

"So what's the bad news?" I asked.

"We need boron."

"Sure. Of course we do," I said, pretending to know what he meant. "I figured. It's always boron, isn't it?"

Bentley ignored my joking. "Boron is perfect. It used to be used a lot in fiberglass construction. It's what we need to use here because of how well it bonds with other elements. I'm not sure why Haywood overlooked it, but his plans never even mention it . . . like it didn't occur to him."

"Bent, I love you, but I don't have the patience these days to pretend I care about the science behind all this."

"Right," he agreed. "So the problem is that boron is super rare."

"I see." And I thought I did. "It's one of those rare earth elements, right?"

"Actually, no," he said.

Even when I tried to care about the science stuff I got it wrong.

"Rare earth elements aren't even all that rare, in terms of abundance, and it's kind of a misnomer in that regard because—"

"Bentley!"

"Right. So . . . we have to steal it. From NASA. That's the bad news." He paused and then, as if sounding it out himself again, he repeated, "Steal it from NASA."

About sixty full seconds went by where neither of us said anything. Both of us were kind of just processing.

"I feel like that's not going to be easy," I said slowly.

Bentley just kind of made one of those sighing sounds that suggests he kind of agrees but also doesn't completely agree.

I continued my train of thought. "I feel like, in fact, stealing from NASA is going to be quite difficult. Maybe even impossible. Are you telling me there's not an easier way for us to get some boron, Bentley?"

He choked on his shock at my ignorance. "It's produced only by supernovas and cosmic nuclear events! The only reason it's even ever found on Earth is because of meteorites!" He scoffed some more, making sounds that fell between gasps and coughs.

"I'm just saying . . . NASA? No one else has any we can steal it from?"

"There's some in Turkey, Russia—it's not impossible to find. But I still think this is the best play." He was so matter-of-fact, it drove me crazy. Like that was common knowledge or something.

I shook my head in disbelief at what I was about to agree to. "Okay, if you say so. Let's go steal some boron from NASA. Maybe I can keep a journal and make it into a science fair project if we ever end up going back to school."

"Alright," he stood up. "Call Emmaline."

"What? You want to go right now? Immediately?"

"Sure. The place we need to break into is closed right now." I could hear his arms and the rustling of his shirt as he spun, looking around the room. "I don't see anything around here that you seem to be too deep into."

I sighed and grabbed the phone.

$$\lightning$$

We needed Emmaline for her teleportation. But we didn't want to bring everyone on this super illegal adventure. So the only other Able we needed was Henry, so that I'd be able to see.

But I wasn't able to get him on the "mind channel." Sometimes Henry would leave his ability to hear thoughts turned on in a kind of passive sleep mode, and if I thought "loudly" enough it would oftentimes reach him and he'd think back at me. Tonight it seemed he'd closed his brain off to the world entirely.

I tried a more old-fashioned approach; I sent him a text message. "Hey, buddy. You around? I need your eyes."

A few moments went by, and there was no response.

"What's going on with you guys?" Bentley asked.

"I wish I knew," I said honestly.

"Maybe it was the smiley," Emmaline suggested unhelpfully. "Some people hate those things. My mother can't stand 'em."

I ignored her and tried another text message to Henry. "We've received a supersecret mission from Bentley."

This time I received a reply. "At the movies with Barb."

And that was it.

I rubbed my forehead in frustration and then typed out another message. "Don't you even want to know what's going on?"

About twenty seconds went by before I received a notification on my phone telling me Henry had blocked my number. "What in the hell?" I didn't understand the hostility. "He blocked my number!"

"What?" Bentley asked, just as shocked as I was.

"Rude," Emmaline added.

"Well," Bentley said, thinking out loud, "I guess we go without him."

"Go without him! How am I supposed to see?"

"We can't afford to wait. We need those masks. Who knows how long it's going to take him to get over whatever he's mad about! Besides, your telekinesis doesn't require eyesight. And we hopefully won't even need to use your powers on this assignment anyway." He closed by repeating his earlier statement. "We go without him."

"Oh, this is going to go smoothly for sure," I snipped sarcastically.

"DHS aren't the only ones with fancy drones." I could hear the smile of pride in his voice as Bentley lifted the antenna on his touch screen tablet.

He took something from his interior jacket pocket, clicked it a few times, and then set it on the grass next to the three of us. I heard the whir of the tiny drone's motor, and there was a tiny burst of cold air as it rushed by my face during lift-off.

"I can't believe you freaking made that thing." Emmaline was still coming to grips with the raw output of brilliance from Bentley's mind. I was more than used to it by now.

"It's just basic physics," he said dismissively. He wasn't trying to be a jerk; he just honestly didn't believe that he deserved a compliment for making something that, to him, seemed straightforward and rudimentary.

"Where are we?" It was a strange mission for me. I had gotten used to the "vision" I received via Henry's powers. I'd gone soft. It was extremely weird to not be able to see any of the details around me.

"We're about a half mile from a NASA storage facility in Texas." Bentley went back to concentrating on flying the drone, guiding it by watching the camera feed on the tablet.

"Oh," I said, before thinking of another question. "Are we like . . . hidden? Or are we exposed right now out in the open?"

"We're in the trees along a ridge. Would you stop asking so many questions?"

I quieted down and let him work, even though I did, in fact, think of a few more questions I wanted to ask.

By now the drone was inside the building, having flown through an exhaust duct. "Alright," Bentley said, sounding pleased. "We are now in the main vault. Let's find ourselves some boron."

I guessed what the vault might look like. I'm sure my idea of a NASA element vault was probably way more snazzy and high tech than it actually was in real life.

"Alright. Boron. There we go." I heard him set down the tablet and dig around in his bag. "Okay, Emmaline, this is for you."

"What is it?" she asked.

"Homing device, with a slight modification or two. Just hold it between your thumb and forefinger."

She gasped. "Oh my! I . . . I can feel it!"

I was about to scream for lack of detail, but thankfully Bentley began to explain. "So there's a bit of electric shock in there, along with the homing signal. I took the idea of Penelope and Greta's all-purpose sonar device and combined it with a version of that button your mom used to use, Phillip, to jump straight to where you were. Basically trying to give Emmaline here—or any teleporter, I suppose—the ability to almost sense the drone's location so that snap-teleporting to that spot should be a cinch."

"Yeah," Emmaline agreed. "I can tell it's working. I'm ready to try it out and get inside there."

"We'll be back in a minute, Phillip," Bentley said.

"Wait, what! You're leaving me here alone?"

"You're a big boy," he said. "You'll be alright."

*Ooph!*

And just like that, they were gone.

"Hello?" I knew no one was there to answer.

Inside the vault, Bentley and Emmaline found a cabinet full of boron samples, each labeled with weight as well as original discovery location. There was some initial discussion, I'm told, about which sample they wanted to take. Or if they wanted to take more than one. Or if it mattered.

But once they lifted one of the samples off the shelf that had been holding it, all hell broke loose outside the facility. The shelves were weight monitored.

Suddenly drones raced out from inside the walls and I heard the voices of soldiers below the ridge I was hiding on.

*Great. I'm all alone, about to be spotted by drone and discovered by NASA cops, and I'm blind. Why'd Henry have to go and get all angry tonight of all nights?*

A great many details about this mission had gone unplanned. Perhaps Bentley was just overly excited to be on the verge of completing Haywood's invention. Maybe Henry's sudden anger had distracted us. But we had left a great many things to chance that we shouldn't have.

We hadn't known the specimens were kept on weight-sensitive shelving. We didn't expect drones. We for sure hadn't thought there'd be soldiers on guard here.

And, perhaps worst of all, we'd forgotten to bring our damn radios.

# 17

# A SLOPPY FIGHT

*Dammit!*

I'd just reached up to activate my team radio to call and tell Emmaline and Bentley about the incoming forces, only to discover we'd left the radios at home.

I had no way to reach them, and they had no way to know I was in any kind of trouble.

*What do I do? Do I just start blasting the air all around me? I don't have any way to aim.*

I cocked my head to-and-fro, listening for any sign the drones or soldiers were drawing near. For now, I heard none. If this facility was this well protected, I had to assume it was probably also in an area that was quite remote. Maybe it would take the drones a while to find me.

We'd done so little preparation and had left so hastily. I cursed myself silently for being such a bad leader. What if something happened to Emmaline? I would never forgive myself.

And then a thing happened that I absolutely should have seen coming. It makes so much sense that here, alone in an arid desert with enemy forces bearing down on me and my friends out of reach, I would have a panic attack.

As I understand it, panic attacks can vary a bit from person to person. Some cry uncontrollably. Others hyperventilate. The idea of a panic attack alone is terrifying. That lump of brain mush we all carry around is responsible for so much more than just thinking; that brain, all by itself, can cause physical suffering. Unreal.

I hit the deck and got ready for the vomiting. I was pretty new to anxiety, but it seemed my attacks contained puking more often than not. I gagged a bit and choked before coughing up a bit of phlegm.

My breathing grew shallow, and I knew I was going to be too dizzy to stand for several minutes. And that's about the time the first drone found me.

This was a DHS drone, exactly like what had chased us in Chicago. I could tell by the pitch of the rotors. Much like personal recreation drones, these were quadcopters. I thought it was a pretty telling detail about Homeland Security's reach that a NASA storage facility was now being protected by DHS drones.

The drone had been sweeping the landscape when it spotted me, stopped, then rapidly descended to hover over my head. I could feel the heat of the powerful search light's lamp. I was bracing for the tear gas when I remembered something Bentley had said earlier in the evening about my powers not requiring sight.

The drone was close enough that there was little doubt as to its position. I merely pointed both palms at that spot and grabbed at it with my abilities. A half second later I brought it sweeping down to earth and shattered it on the ground.

But the drone's operator could now notify the other drones and the foot soldiers, so it was about to get insane.

I'd stood up instinctively when taking out the drone, but now my knees buckled as a wave of dizziness hit me. It struck me as odd that unexpected distractions could temporarily bring me out of an attack or convince my brain to forget about the attack for a few seconds. It also made some sense. One of the techniques I'd been taught to deal with a panic attack is to have someone ask me a bunch of easy questions rapid-fire—stuff like my name, where I live, my school's name—because it was just a simple brain hack where a momentary distraction can ease the effects of panic and anxiety.

"Over there," I heard a voice call out from behind me. The soldiers were heading this way.

I had one trump card here to play, and that was flight. I could hit the air anytime I wanted, and could probably get up there fast enough that bullets would struggle to hit me. And I could reach altitudes even the drones couldn't.

So I could save my own skin here. Easily.

But then Bentley and Emmaline would return to this spot and be surrounded by bad guys right away.

I couldn't do that to them. Granted, for all I knew they'd been captured inside the facility and weren't ever coming back here. But I sensed that was wrong, that they were fine. And in fact they were. They would later tell me they were utterly oblivious to the alarms and the guards and drones until they returned to the ridge with the boron.

"This way!" I heard another soldier yell. They were closing the distance. Conflict was imminent, though I had no idea how many of them there would be, or how many waves.

I decided to give it my best blind shot.

Knowing my hearing was impeccable, I opted for a crude take on human echolocation. It would be highly imperfect, but it might help a little bit.

And so I screamed. I screamed my ass off. It was loud and shrill and sharp. I snapped my head to the side, slowly sweeping my ear across the landscape. Sure enough, a patch about twelve feet wide returned the scream's faint echo to my ear while everywhere else the scream just kept going into the night air.

So I still didn't have much to go on, but I did know how wide the group of approaching soldiers was. And that would be enough to do some damage. Some quick math gave me the rough "shape" of the telekinetic blast wave I wanted to send out, designed to be twelve feet wide by the time it reached the men.

I didn't really want to hurt anybody, but I also didn't have a lot of options. I reared back and blasted them with an invisible forceful wall. I heard startled cries and grunts, and it seemed clear I'd knocked most or all of them down. How much time that would buy me remained to be seen.

And then another drone showed up.

"Oh, come on!"

I stood up to unload on the new drone, but my stomach wasn't ready to be done being upset just yet, and before I could do any heroing I was felled by another vomiting spell. I rolled over onto my back and blasted the drone out of the sky while turning my head to the side so I could continue spitting and coughing.

In the moment, the stress of a panic attack can overwhelm the mind. Sometimes it can be so uncomfortable that evil things like comas or death start to look like relief. I didn't know how much more fight I had in me to counter this physical attack by the guards and drones if I couldn't shake this physical attack from my own mind.

As the spinning increased, I began to think of reasons why death wouldn't be all that bad. I wouldn't have to worry about babysitting Patrick anymore. Or chores. Or responsibility of any kind. I might get to see Mom again. Maybe even Donnie, though I hoped not, because I didn't want to believe he was gone.

Morbid stuff.

I'd nearly been captured. It began to feel like capture was even a little bit inevitable. And, of course, it was.

*Ooph!*

"Oh thank the high heavens!" I screamed.

In reality, Emmaline and Bentley had been gone for only two minutes and forty-eight seconds. From their perspective, very little time had passed at all.

So unsuspecting were they that anything nefarious was going on out here that Bentley immediately let go of Emmaline and bent down to start packing his bag, without even processing what I had said or the urgency in my voice.

Emmaline did hear me and looked up to the horizon to see a half dozen armed soldiers almost on top of our position.

She was closer to me than to Bentley, and her first instinct wasn't to flee but to fight.

Like a rag doll, she lifted my skinny frame up to standing height and grabbed my right wrist. She pointed our connected right arms to the right deliberately and shouted in my ear, "Sallinger!"

Somehow I knew what she wanted, and I let loose a telekinetic blast with all my might.

It must have been too much power and I certainly hurt someone badly, as her reaction was instantaneous. "Oh God. Dial it back to 50 percent." She jerked my arm to the left ten degrees. "Hit it!"

Bentley had finally allowed the commotion to reach his ears and be translated by his brain as something amiss. "What's going on?" he asked, but right then Emmaline spun the both of us eighty degrees to the right in a tight circle, and our outstretched right arms smacked Bentley in the side of the head.

He hit the ground pretty hard, and I would have taken the time to check on him had I not been carelessly whipped around in another half circle the other direction and commanded "Fire!"

"Okay, look," I began to object, "I'm not a gun—"

"*Fire!*" she screamed, and it carried the weight of a scream a wise person would heed if they valued their life.

I let loose another blast—forgetting in my haste to dial it back to 50 percent like she'd said to earlier, so again I probably broke some legs or spines of soldiers who were very likely just nice people following orders who didn't actively hate me.

"Jesus," Emmaline breathed, clearly in awe of the raw power I had displayed . . . and maybe a little disgusted by it as well. I couldn't tell. I didn't want to know, to be honest.

One more spin and she put a hand on Bentley. And even though I could hear incoming footsteps from charging soldiers that were clearly only a few feet away, Emmaline saw a window and used it to teleport us all back to my living room, where this entire escapade had begun.

Emmaline and I both slumped backward into the couch with a crash. Bentley leaned hard into the love seat and then sat down.

We were all breathing heavy. Both of them were probably still processing things, since they'd shown up to a fight they didn't expect and then made several instinctive gut decisions.

"We must have tripped an alarm when we lifted the boron from the shelf," Bentley said.

"*How*," I bellowed, "did you manage to *not* know that place had weight-sensitive shelving?" I was in disbelief. I'd made my own planning errors tonight and before now, and I owned them, but Bentley was the planning wizard. If it could be read, hacked, printed, or discovered about a place we were going to, he knew it already. That was his thing. And he'd totally dropped the ball tonight.

"I don't know," he said softly. "I was in too big a hurry. I was . . . distracted."

A few more deep breaths and I was ready to be done being angry or placing blame. Exhaustion has a way of hastening us toward the truth.

"Oh, I don't care. I don't blame you. We didn't bring the radios either. And we didn't set up any contingency exits or key words. It was just sloppy all around. I'm sorry I yelled. I was just freaked out about having almost died."

"I'm sorry you almost died," he gasped back.

"Tell me this," I said. "Tell me we at least got the freaking boron."

Emmaline unzipped her backpack, a smile in her voice as she answered. "Oh yes. Twice as much as we need . . . just in case we have trial and error."

"Alright, Emm," it was the first time I'd ever shortened her name to one nickname syllable, but I didn't think anything of it at the time—and I certainly didn't make the connection that "Emm" is what my father used to call my mother, whose name was Emily. "You go home and get some rest. Bentley, you get to work on those masks. And I've got a telepath I need to clear the air with."

# 18

# THE TRUTH HURTS

Emmaline and I were on our way to our makeup makeup first date. The conversation was lively, and I'd thus far managed to not trip and bleed to death. So things were already progressing further than ever before.

We had nearly reached Jack's when she spotted Henry wheeling away in the other direction. It's possible he saw us coming and wanted to avoid any conflict. Or maybe it was just a completely coincidental encounter. But I had been through enough of an ordeal on one adventure without him to let this fight go on any longer.

Thankfully, Emmaline had been on the same adventure, and she shared my enthusiasm for healing this particular friendship rift. She told me that she would be fine on her own and that I should go after Henry.

I left her at the restaurant and scampered after my friend. Knowing only his position when I started after him and having a general feel for the layout of the town, there was no guarantee I'd even be able to find him. I put on my glasses in the hopes that he'd let me use his vision once he heard me calling his name.

Two blocks later I stopped jogging and called out, "Henry? I'm blind, buddy. I . . . I can't chase you through the whole town. But we gotta work this out. I love you too much for us to be this angry. Please. If you're there . . . if you can hear me . . . please talk to me."

A few seconds passed, and then suddenly I could see again. Henry had reactivated his vision sharing. I looked up and spotted him about twelve feet to my right, near the ATM at Freepoint Bank.

"Hey."

"Hey."

It started to rain. It had been threatening for two days but had been holding off for some reason. Perhaps even the weather wanted to weigh in on this fight between us.

I thought about our first encounter three years ago, as two scared kids in the hallway outside the special education classroom. Even then there had been a spark of connection that seemed genuine and unforced.

We'd been through so much in such a short amount of time.

"Let's go over to City Hall and get out of the rain at least," Henry suggested, nodding his head southeast toward the building where we'd argued together for our right to participate in the SuperSim alongside able-bodied kids.

I just nodded and started walking. I knew we weren't done fighting, so I wasn't going to add to it by also fighting about the location we chose.

We traveled the distance—about two hundred feet—in relative silence. Neither of us said a word as the fat raindrops pounded the brick sidewalks below our feet.

City Hall, as it turned out, was hilariously empty. Despite the fact that it was just after lunchtime on a weekday, there were few signs of activity. A handful of cars in the parking lot. A few lights turned on up on the second floor, where the offices were.

But on the main floor in the rotunda . . . crickets. The lights were on, but I didn't hear or see anyone around. Not even a security guard. The information desk sat unmanned as well.

I chalked it up to the general confusion of all custodian life these days. So many had gone missing. Others had just quit caring or trying and had gone into hiding.

I figured what we had seen at the school—masses of students and teachers just abandoning pretense and ceasing attendance—was probably happening at buildings and businesses all throughout custodian cities.

For a few beats, it seemed we were silently debating which of the two of us should go first in these proceedings. I honestly didn't care.

"Well, what did I do?" I finally asked.

As a result of the emptiness of the building, my words bounced off the walls and the curved rotunda ceiling. So my question came off as much more foreboding than I had intended. The echoes added to the overall volume in ways I didn't predict.

Henry sighed heavily. For a moment, I wondered if this meeting was a mistake, if maybe I was forcing him to lay it out there before he was ready. But then he spoke, and it was too late to turn back regardless.

"That night we rescued that kidnapped rich girl from the speeding car south of Chicago . . . you remember that?" He said this with the measured confidence of someone who had written it down and rehearsed it a few times.

"Yeah," I said. And I did remember it—though I was about to learn exactly how poorly I remembered it.

"I made a joke about Penelope's fog blinding us heroes as much as it also blinded the bad guys we were chasing. It was just a joke. And I know my jokes can be too much sometimes or go overboard. But it was just a joke." His voice cracked the tiniest bit. I was shocked that his response to the memory was so emotional.

In my mind, this rescue event had ended with us getting the girl, tying up the bad guys, and saving the day. And, in fact, that is exactly how the events had played out. But my memory left out a simple detail that had stood out to Henry. And after standing out, it had begun to fester.

"You told me," he said angrily, "'Just shut up and do your job.'" He sucked in a batch of air and spat back out again in bitterness, "Just do your job."

I looked down as the words echoed around me like a pinball. I remembered the moment now. I had spoken in haste and frustration. In a moment of crisis, he had cracked a joke and I hadn't been in a place to tolerate it.

"As though my job—my very reason for existence—is to provide you with sight." Tears ran down his face. "As though I don't have any purpose or power or ability . . . nothing I can add to this team except to help make you a better you. Henry show me this. Henry show me that. I'm *tired*, Phillip. I'm tired of showing you everything! I'm not a pair of binoculars. I'm not a tool to be utilized! I'm a goddamn *person*!"

It was at this point I became glad no one was around in this building, as things had gotten loud and personal in a hurry.

"Maybe if you hadn't stopped trying to advance your abilities, then I *would* see you as more than a pair of eyes," I said with no small amount of venom. There had been an element of discovery and experimentation in our early days together as the Ables, and lately that had faded away.

"What!"

"You haven't offered to fog anyone up in months, and you haven't tried to explore your powers since you learned to fog in the first place. You've got all this potential, but you just mope around because you're in a wheelchair."

I knew as soon as it came out of my mouth that I wanted that sentence back. It was too late, of course. And it landed like a dagger.

"Imagine," he countered, "if someone showed up who could make me walk again, but they had to be around me all the time and never stop giving me that ability. And after a while, I took walking for granted. And then one night that guy wanted to go on a date with his lady friend and not have me tagging along, but I was so offended about losing my legs for a few hours that I wouldn't even let him have his own stinking *life*!"

We both took a break for a moment and sucked in some deep breaths while we thought about the discussion so far. It felt like we were both angry because we felt the other one no longer had the same vision of the future, but neither of us truly had reason to think that.

Eventually, I realized how wrong I had been these last few months. And I also came to grips with exactly how little energy I had left for hate. I was here to heal, after all, not to continue hurting or facilitating hurt.

"You're right," I admitted. He looked at me, surprised. But I was done fighting. "I took you for granted," I continued. "I really did. I didn't realize I was doing it. But—having just spent time on a mission *without* you by my side— I'm ready to admit that I took you for granted, along with the empowerment you give me along with the eyesight." I sniffed a bit, mostly to avoid having to find a tissue. "I don't have any excuses. I was wrong."

Henry was shaking his head, either in disbelief or in mutual surrender.

"Nah," he started. "I was the one in the wrong. I think I just get jealous sometimes of the attention you get from people at school or whatever. I don't know. I mean . . . I know I don't have anything better to offer but being your eyes. And I should be thankful for the chance to be part of what you're doing."

"Oh, forget that nonsense," I argued. "I'm telling you, you have so much more strength yet to discover. It was so easy for you to learn how to send me images . . . and then to perfect it as an almost subliminal act? Don't sell your abilities short. You're probably more powerful than any of the rest of us, if you think about it."

"I don't mind being your eyes," he said weepily.

"And I don't need to abuse that privilege like I have or take it for granted," I sobbed back. "I value you, man. I absolutely cannot do this hero shit without you, man. I need you."

I leaned down, and we hugged.

By the time we released the embrace, we were both giggling.

Oddly, I had never doubted this outcome's eventuality. Even at my angriest, I knew our rift was temporary. Henry and I were true friends for life—as was Bentley. Our bond had come at a formative age and a time of identity crisis for each of us. Wherever one of us went, the other two were virtually guaranteed to follow.

By the time Henry and I finished our talk and resolved all our differences, Emmaline had left Jack's Pizza. I knew only because Porter was in there playing Tekken and he'd seen her get a phone call and leave suddenly about twenty minutes prior to my arrival.

Another date foiled. I knew she would understand. She herself had strongly encouraged me to ditch the date and patch things up with my friend.

Just as well. I was empty right now. I'd shed all my emotions in that exchange with Henry, and I had nothing left to give, positive or negative.

I decided a nap was in order and pulled out my cane and began tapping my way home.

# 19

# PERSONAL DAY

I woke up the next day in a fantastic mood. I'd managed to sleep a full eight hours and didn't even feel bad that I had to take a sedative to achieve that.

Having healed things up with Henry was just the boost I needed to be optimistic again.

Tomorrow we were headed back to Chicago to keep searching. Our latest theory was that the thing we were hunting for was the much-rumored custodian prison—where folks like Bentley's brother and father might be.

But today was a free day. Nothing on the agenda. Patrick and I had long ago abandoned the use of the family event calendar.

It had been a couple months since Dad had disappeared. My one encounter with him during this time didn't make any logical sense, but most of all it did nothing to suggest he was going to be coming home to us again anytime soon.

Our favorite teacher was gone. Half the authority figures in town were missing or off looking for others who were missing.

I and the other teens in Freepoint had done a pretty good job not messing things up in the absence of appropriate adult supervision. And while I didn't expect any praise for that, I did see it as an accomplishment. Something deserving of praise.

Or a reward even.

"Hurry up and finish your breakfast," I said to Patrick.

"Why?" he mumbled, mouth full of cereal.

"We have an important errand to run."

"Oh yeah?" He was intrigued, but I was playing it straight enough that he was ultimately unsure about things.

"Shouldn't take too long." I left the room and walked down the hall.

He called after me. "Where are we going?"

⚡

"Okay," Patrick said, running down the list of clues he'd managed to get out of me so far on the walk to our destination. "I'm not going to hate it. I might like it. It won't cost a lot of money, but it will have a price that won't be cheap."

I smiled. It had been a long time since he and I had bonded in a fun way, and knowing ahead of time that he was going to greatly enjoy this errand made it a little sweeter a thing to savor.

"Am I forgetting anything?"

"I don't think so."

"How much farther?"

I gauged our remaining distance. "A little bit."

"You do know you're blind, right? I mean, we passed the shops downtown a few blocks ago, and I wasn't sure you knew that."

"You think that I could lose my way around Freepoint? Seriously? I know you know me better than that," I teased.

"So are we not going to a store for this errand that has a great price?"

"We are *not* going to a store, actually."

His steps slowed briefly, betraying that I'd just blown his mind a little bit. His entire line of guessing up until now had been based on the notion that we were headed to a store to make a purchase of some kind.

"I swear to God if this is about some kind of chore or you're taking me to a dentist or something I'm going to be three states away before you can even breathe."

"It's not a chore," I laughed. "Well . . . not how you mean."

"And it's not a dentist?"

"And it's not a dentist, Jesus. It's a good thing—I promise. Just let me have a little fun with the mystery. Why don't we change the subject?"

I stuffed my hands in my pockets and tried to think of a new subject. I wondered what Dad would ask. Eventually I just started talking. "So do you have any girlfriends or anything?"

"What?" He laughed in a way that suggested I was silly for even thinking he had a girlfriend. "How can you live alone with me for the last however long and think I have a secret girlfriend? Or that I could have one without talking your ear off about her constantly?"

"I am blind, as you point out."

"Where would I even meet a girl? We don't go to school anymore."

For the first time since making that decision, I wondered if maybe quitting school hadn't been so wise after all. At least for all of us. Maybe Patrick was missing out on some key elements of what youth was supposed to be about.

"There are a couple girls in Ables squads that are your age," I noted.

"Eh, they're both super weird."

I laughed at that. "Brother, every single member of the Ables is weird."

"I mean extra weird. That girl Beatrice, she's got some kind of electricity power. Her body hums all the time, and it's creepy. I'm always afraid she's going to shock me."

I had noticed the girl's hum but had thought only I could hear it. "I think that's a little harsh. You don't know that."

As if he hadn't even heard me, Pat just continued. "And Maddie, she's just too much. That girl never shuts up. She just goes and goes and goes."

I made a note that Patrick could just as easily be describing himself with those words, and how ironic it was he was turned off by such qualities. "Well, maybe she's just nervous."

He was over this topic. "Can we just talk about something else? I don't want to talk about girls with you like you're Dad or something."

"I'm sorry. I wasn't trying to be Dad." I had, in fact, been trying to be Dad. Or act like him. Patrick saw through it and didn't appreciate it.

We walked in silence for half a block or so.

"I made up with Henry."

"Oh," he said quietly. "You guys were fighting?"

"Do you pay attention to anything?"

He laughed. "I'm sorry, I didn't know you were fighting. I mean . . . he made some snarky comments that night in Chicago, but I didn't know there was anything more to it."

"I had to do a mission without him where I was blind the whole time. He blocked my phone number!"

"Big deal," Patrick shrugged. "You just said you two made up. I can't get all worked up about the fighting now that I know that."

The little jerk.

"What were you guys talking about back when we were in Bentley's dad's office . . . about teleporters and walls? Why was everyone so freaked out that Emmaline just jumped without knowing there was a secret room there?"

"Well, let's start with the fact that if the wall is solid and dense, there's a good chance she would just get . . . instantaneously imploded. Matter can't occupy the same space as other matter. It's been theorized a teleporter in that situation might even liquefy on the spot."

"Gross, dude."

"You asked. Anyway, let's assume that she somehow manages to displace the concrete in the wall where her body ends up and she's suspended there inside the wall—which again, is a generous hypothetical. Escape from that situation just doesn't fit with how the ability works. Teleporters travel with anything touching their hands. That's why we do that touching thing every time we leap somewhere."

"I know that," he said, wishing I would hurry up.

"Well, imagine if Emmaline had jumped, but instead of an open room there'd been a solid concrete wall. She wouldn't have been able to jump back out without taking the wall itself with her, because it would be touching her hand."

"Whoa," he breathed. "So . . . could you not just chip away at the wall and cut her out?"

"Maybe. But without knowing her exact jumping location, we'd be guessing—running the risk of hurting her or chipping away at her body instead of the wall. And there's no guarantee we could get there before she ran out of air."

He pondered that for a moment. "Is that what happened to James?"

I instinctively turned my head away from Pat. "I'm not ready to talk about that." I knew that I should be ready. I should be talking about it.

It was the main question at every therapy session. I knew I needed to move on to the next stage of my grief about James, but I was still stubbornly hanging onto denial, as though that stage had done anything good for me.

"Well," he said, "speaking of Emmaline, you get that date with her yet?"

"No." I breathed in frustration. "The universe keeps conspiring against it."

"It's been a while, though, right? You can't just . . . be in the same place together at the same time and have a date?"

"Stuff keeps cropping up. We've got it rescheduled for a few nights from now. She hasn't been sick in a while. It's gonna happen."

"You know those people who have to witness it when you sign important documents?"

"Notary publics?"

"Yeah, them. You should bring one of them on that date. Otherwise I don't think anyone's going to believe it actually happened."

⚡

"We're getting a dog?" Pat exclaimed.

I'd learned a few weeks ago that one of the dogs on Greta's farm had given birth to a litter of puppies. The mother was a German shepherd, and the father was a golden retriever.

We'd passed all the shops downtown because we were headed to the farm, which was on the other side of Freepoint.

After turning up the gravel driveway and being greeted by Greta, I sent Patrick around the back to the garage and then I—and a dozen neighbors—heard his jubilation.

He sped immediately back to my position using his abilities, got right up in my face, and begged me to confirm. "We're really getting a dog?"

I smiled. That was all the confirmation he waited for before dashing back around the house and then zipping right back in front of me, this time with a puppy in his arms. "This one? Can it be this one? I like this one!" It was like those old cartoons when the mouse or the duck drinks too much coffee and gets hopped-up on caffeine. "I don't know why, but I like this one. I looked at all of them and this one seemed to be silently calling out to me, so I picked this one." I heard his voice change direction as he turned to Greta. "Can I have this one? This one isn't spoken for, is it? Please say it isn't!"

"You can have that one," Greta laughed.

Instantly he was off again, running ten times normal speed all over the farm, making figure eights and other patterns as he screamed for joy. "I can't believe it! Oh my God! We're getting a dog! You, you're the dog, you, little guy! We're getting you! We're taking you home!" This carried on for some time.

"You said he would react like this, but I just didn't believe you," Greta declared.

"You're sure he's not taking a puppy someone already spoke for?"

"Oh, no. He's fine. They all need good homes."

"We'll try and provide exactly that."

"What should we call him?" Patrick asked.

"He is so adorable," Emmaline said, scratching his ears.

I'd called over a few people to last-minute game-plan for tomorrow's trip back to Chicago. But if I'm being honest, I just wanted to show off the new dog.

And he was adorable. His fur was light golden brown with a white patch on his chest. He looked mostly like a German shepherd but with slightly fluffier fur.

"How about Wendell?" I suggested, though I wasn't sure how I had landed on that idea. I wasn't even sure where I'd heard the name before.

"Ew," Patrick replied. "He's not an old man in a nursing home, he's a puppy!"

"What about naming him after someone?" Bentley asked. "Like . . . Donnie?"

I thought about it a second. "Might end up being a little weird."

"Yeah, maybe," he agreed.

"What about something silly? Maybe something action-sounding like Tarnation or Whirlybird?" Only Henry could suggest names like these.

Everyone groaned.

"Proudfoot! Inspector Dog! Hyperbole!"

"Patrick you're just saying words now," I scolded. "You don't even know what hyperbole means."

"It's like you guys have never named a pet before," Henry joked. But then, when we didn't laugh, he froze. "Wait, have you never had a pet before?"

"No," I said, suddenly embarrassed about it.

"You're blind!" Henry shouted.

I just stared at him a moment, waiting for him to elaborate.

"You never had a Seeing Eye dog?"

"No, Henry, we didn't have enough money. Seeing Eye dogs are expensive. They need so much training, it's ridiculous." I could tell I'd killed the mood momentarily, so I tried to get it back on track. "But now we have this guy, and I did a lot of research. And German shepherds and goldens are supposed to be some of the most trainable dogs around, great for guide dog stuff, or even to help with my anxiety attacks and stuff." I gave the dog's head a quick rub. "We may have to train him ourselves, but he can probably help in a lot of ways."

"If he's a guide dog, you should totally call him Sherpa," Emmaline said bluntly, as though she wasn't making a suggestion but stating a fact.

"Sherpa," Patrick repeated. "Hey, I think I might like that. I definitely at least don't hate it."

"Alright, fine, we can consider Sherpa. But please for the love of all that is holy will you get him off the table. We eat there."

# 20

# THE LAST TRAIN

"Two and a half miles west of the Shedd Aquarium area and about five blocks south is a large Union Pacific rail yard. This is our target for a number of sound reasons," Bentley said in his mission-voice. Most folks considered me the "leader" of the Ables, even Bentley. But no one disputed that he was the brains of the operation and the head mission planner, and as such he had the right to give the briefings. And he clearly relished the task.

Everyone knew the plan. We had gone over it yesterday evening and two days prior to that, when we created the plan. And then again an hour ago when everyone had first arrived at my house to get geared up.

But after the chaos of our unplanned side quest to Texas, Bentley and I weren't taking any chances when it came to preparation. We were willing to go overboard prepping for this mission for the sake of not doing too little of it.

Bentley had pulled up a digital satellite photo of the area in question. "The rail yard represents a point of access, and there are dozens of train lines in and out of that area, making it easy to move people or equipment.

Storage containers are stacked row upon row. And the sheer volume of trains coming through this place in a single day is staggering."

The new puppy whined from inside the garage, and Patrick gave me an urgent look. But I shot him down with a shake of my head. This wasn't puppy time.

"Most importantly, there are two tunnels here . . . and here." Bentley used a laser pointer to show us the areas in question. "Now, I've been studying the activity in this rail yard for several days, including still photographs, satellite video, and I even hacked the rail yard server. By my math, these tunnels are the most likely places for us to find something."

"Why?" Henry asked.

"Because they never get used," Bent replied flatly. "No train ever leaves or arrives by either of these tunnels. You can follow both tracks back to the switch and neither are ever used."

We all let that compelling piece of information sink in. Why would those tracks and tunnels even exist if they were useless?

"Now this trip we have the good fortune of having Emmaline with us, so we will have a teleporter." A quiet—but genuine—quick round of applause went up.

Bentley was all business. "But we will have to split into two teams so we can cover both tunnels at the same time. Emmaline, you'll have to be ready to jump from one spot to the other if anything goes south."

"Got it," she said with confidence.

"It'll be Phillip, Henry, and Emmaline at tunnel A, and the rest of us at tunnel B." That meant Patrick, Bentley, Penelope, Freddie, and Greta. We typically didn't split up into even numbered teams because, frankly, Henry and I alone were capable of plenty in most cases. I'm guessing Emmaline was added to my team because Bentley knew I liked her. And I wasn't going to complain.

"And now for the fun part—gadget time!"

Everyone cheered in delight. Gadget time was rare; it basically occurred only prior to missions when Bentley had recently finished a new invention or upgraded an old one. So it was like tech Christmas.

I heard some oohs and aahs as Bentley laid down a mask in front of each person around the table. "I finally finished Haywood's plans. Feast your eyes on these bad boys."

They looked like ultrawide headbands, with a carbon matte look. There was one lens instead of two, but the rest of the device was stretchy so that it would fit snug around a person's head. I slipped mine on and flicked the switch on the side.

"These babies have everything," Bentley beamed. "To start, wearing these will make us unidentifiable to eye witnesses and cameras. In fact, with cameras it gets even more fun, as the scrambler Haywood developed is a tricky bastard. On video they won't even see our bodies . . . maybe they'll see a shoe or a hat. But the scrambler blinds the camera in a wide enough burst that surveillance video will be worthless as long as these are on."

"It blinds cameras but not people?" Greta inquired.

"That's right. The scrambling technology is on a different spectrum, one the human eye can't even process."

"Cool," she responded.

"In addition to that identity-hiding stuff, I've crammed some more useful gear in here." I was constantly amazed at the invention mountains Bentley could so easily climb and the casual way he could dismiss those feats. "Comms are in here, so we all have radios built in. You can view real light, infrared, thermal, and fourteen-color true-light night vision."

"Whoa," Patrick cooed.

"Spectrometer, accelerometer, range finder, five times optical zoom, and even a rudimentary heads-up display."

I noticed a small snap in the lower back part of the mask, no bigger than a centimeter wide. Then I realized where I'd seen it before, or I should say where I'd felt it before: Texas. It was the electro-homing beacon thing he'd used that let Emmaline jump directly to the location of his drone, which was the location of the boron. "Hey, is this . . . ?" I trailed off as I looked up at Bentley. He winked, and that was all.

"Does it play video games?" I joked.

"I thought about loading some basic ones on there, but figured it was . . . oh, you were joking."

I just laughed. "Amazing work, buddy." I patted him on the shoulder. "Okay, everyone—let's get to it. Keep your eyes out for each other. Everyone ready?"

Emmaline put her two arms out, palms up. We clasped hands around the table in ripple until we were all connected.

"Hit it," I told her.

*Ooph!*

I'd had a bad feeling from the start. Something seemed off. But when my father showed up, that's when I knew we'd been set up. Him appearing twice in the same vicinity right after we'd arrived? That was not a coincidence. It couldn't be.

And still, I thought I could take him. So I didn't panic. I cracked my neck. "Round two," I said.

I mentally ripped up a huge swath of train track off the ground near where he stood and wrapped it around him like rope in a lightning-fast twist of my fists. I could feel his own telekinetic powers fighting back against the tracks, trying to control them himself. Then . . . he seemed to give up.

I thought maybe I'd crushed him. I'd gone too far and smashed my father.

"Phillip!" I heard Freddie cry out from behind me. But it was too late. A shipping container fell on my position from above. Dad hadn't been crushed, he'd just diverted some of his powers to another task: throwing something at me.

No sooner did I realize I'd been trapped like a spider under a glass than a dozen loud thwacks resonated all around the outside of the container; he was sealing me in. He was using train tracks or some other material nearby to stitch the shipping container into place, with me under it.

*Ooph!*

"Hey." It was Emmaline. "What do we do?"

"Get everybody out of here, Emm. I'll hold him off as long as I can."

A cry of pain rang out. It was Patrick's voice.

"Emm, go. I'll be okay."

*Ooph!*

I'd learn later that Patrick, seeing his older brother trapped and bullied, did what any idiot little brother would do—he attacked the enemy himself impulsively. Dad had plucked the speedster off the ground with a tiny pinch of his fingers, tossing him out of the way like a nuisance.

I hit the radio. "Henry, find me something sharp." He began wheeling his head around in earnest, looking for something that fit the bill.

I knew what my situation looked like from the outside because of Henry's view. The shipping container had been placed over me in the vertical position. Which meant I had a good twenty yards or so of empty space above my head.

"Henry?"

"Still looking," he replied. I could see what he could see, so I joined the search. It's not like I had anywhere I could go right at the moment anyway. He swept his gaze past a construction area, and there were two large digging machines there. One had massive wheels. "Dude, giant hubcap." His head moved back to the left to center on the wheel of the great metal claw, giving me an optimal view.

I concentrated and pried the hubcap off the enormous wheel. The hubcap itself was twice as big as any dining room table I'd ever seen. I tossed it gently into the air about twenty-five feet off the ground and gave my right hand a sharp and violent twist to the right, spinning the hubcap in place like a saw blade.

It took no time for it to get up to a deadly level of acceleration, and I let it loose, firing it directly at my temporary metal prison. As expected, the makeshift hubcap projectile tore off the top of the shipping container like it was made of paper.

I flew easily out of the newly created opening and landed back on the ground next to where I'd been trapped.

For good measure, I'd lined things up so that after it set me free, the hubcap would be headed toward my father.

Unfortunately, he saw it at the last moment and jumped into the air to avoid the blow.

But right behind him had been a group of decoupled train cars stacked with metal barrels, and the hubcap hit with extreme force. Barrels blasted everywhere like shrapnel from a homemade bomb, and one smacked Dad in the leg, sending him flying off to the side.

"Get everyone out of here!" I shrieked at Emmaline, hopefully for the last time.

I turned back to face my father again to see that he'd lifted a nearby seventeen-car train into the air, wielding it like a giant iron whip with just his right hand as his left released a boxcar in my directly like a clunky spear.

Behind me I heard a series of air pops as Emmaline jumped to-and-fro collecting all the other Ables for an escape jump.

I took to the air and avoided the projectile as it crashed into the dirt where I'd just been standing.

And then, I lost my vision.

Emmaline, who was only following orders, had grabbed literally everyone except me for the trip home—including Henry, the provider of my sight. I hadn't really meant for Henry to be taken, but now they were too far away for the radios to work.

I was thirty feet in the air and dead in the water.

Then came the beating of a lifetime.

The locomotive was the tip of Dad's makeshift whip, and it smacked me from the left side. That alone should have killed me. Or at least it could have. Most of my clothes had been sprayed with Bentley's impact-dispersion stuff, but that wasn't designed to shield me from train engines.

I was reminded again that this man serving as my adversary right now was not my father. It may have been his body, but it was not his mind.

I stood slowly, my body aching head to toe. I remembered the position of a nearby caboose, so I lifted my hand up and prepared to pick it up and toss it in my dad's direction. But nothing happened. It was like I'd blown a fuse or something and my powers had gone out.

"Time to come home, Phillip," a female voice whispered from behind me.

And that's when everything faded to nothingness.

# 21

# INTERNMENT

The room was soundproof.

The walls, the floors, the ceiling tiles . . . even the door.

We used the same tech on our night-op gear. I could smell it, but I could also feel it with my fingertips as I ran them along the edges of the chair. Everything in the room had been "painted" with a special sealant designed to keep sound out. Or in.

Everything, that is, except the actual locking mechanism on the door, which was metal. It was a Tompkins 325 R model electronic dead bolt, if my ears were correct. And they had, on occasion, been wrong. On occasion.

The point is that I heard the lock moving, giving me a little bit of a heads up that I was about to have company. And after hours of being in here alone, you could say I was more than a little ready for some company.

I'd been in here for at least six hours, minimum. I'd been awake for six hours, but who knows how long I was in this cell unconscious.

In that time, I'd managed to ascertain that I was in a locked, windowless room comprised of standard concrete and drywall. There was a lightweight plastic table and chairs as well as a wall-mounted cot and a toilet in the corner. I had never been in a prison cell, but I'd heard enough about them to know that's what this room was.

Oh, and I was roughly three hundred feet underground. One skill I'd started honing during our battles in the Rocky Mountains a couple of years prior was the ability to sense my own position relative to sea level. Bentley had helped me focus the talent, and it had come in handy more than once since.

Everything about this situation—most notably that I had been knocked unconscious prior to waking up here unexplained—suggested I was a prisoner. And yet there were no chains. No restraints. Nothing but a locked door and some fairly flimsy wall construction keeping me here. So it seemed. Well, and the three hundred feet of dirt and rock.

They'd even left Bentley's custom-made mask with me, and it hung around my neck like a scarf. They might have inspected it or something and found it to be harmless. But whatever the reason, other than the cell, they hadn't done much else to make this feel like a regular prison.

The door finally opened, and I heard three sets of footsteps as a woman in heels entered and stood to the side while two people in work boots wheeled in some kind of cart. One of the wheels on the cart squeaked as it turned, and I found it incredibly annoying. Maybe that was the point.

I heard some scuffling, a few more light bumping and banging noises. Then the people in the work boots left and the door closed behind them.

I scratched my left hand, mindlessly relieving an itch.

The woman took great care to slide a plastic chair across from me away from the table in as slow and noisy a manner as possible. Then she sat down and slowly shuffled her way back up to the table, where she loudly dropped a large stack of papers from way higher than she probably needed to. I guess she thought she was intimidating me.

"Mr. Sallinger," she began, "my name is Marian Ettinger. I'm the head of Homeland Security's Custodial Relations division."

I said nothing. I'd heard of her—everyone in America had. She was on television more than most elected politicians or professional athletes.

"It's nice to meet you," she tried again. "I've heard a lot about you." Her voice projected absolute confidence. She was in complete control and wanted me to know it. She waited quietly for a few moments, demonstrating patience.

I decided to stage a subtle demonstration of my own. So I leaned back and crossed my hands, interlocking them behind my head, letting her know that I was aware of my lack of restraints and also that I was a contrarian teenage son of a bitch.

"I guess you must be wondering where you are," she offered. She had a pleasant, singsongy quality to her speech pattern. It wasn't just that she wanted me to know she was confident, she was also celebrating her confidence; patting herself on the back like this was the payoff of some decades-long con game. "Eh?"

I finally spoke. "Some kind of illegal off-books underground holding cell for custodians who haven't broken any laws?" I was good at playing poker, but I was also a typical kid who thought he knew everything. Of course I was going to pop off and say something snippy. It had never been anything but a question of when.

And I clearly hit close to home, as my interrogator choked briefly before responding. "There's that bite I've been warned about." I heard her lean forward. She lowered her voice a bit before saying, "I've been waiting for a real challenge. I'm glad you've arrived. We don't get enough firecrackers down here. I'm lucky to meet you, son."

As usual, I had overestimated my understanding of the situation. "You're lucky I haven't broken your neck with my brain." I'd known for some time that my eventual cause of death was almost mathematically certain to be "leaped before he looked."

There was a long pause as my captor calculated her next move. Finally she spoke. "What do you think you know about your current situation?" She behaved as though she had all the time in the world and none of her affairs were urgent.

Stupidly, I took the bait—it's just not very easy being a hormonal teenage boy with superpowers. "I know I'm not restrained right now. I know the walls are standard concrete and drywall paneling that I could blow through easily. And I know I don't owe you a thing and I haven't done anything wrong." I was ready to rumble.

By now I was on my feet, pacing back and forth like the caged animal I believed that I was. "And I know that no one read me my Miranda rights, no one gave me my phone call, and no one has offered to let me speak to a lawyer."

"I think," she interjected, "before you get too worked up and do something stupid, I should explain the situation to you fully. Let's make a deal," she offered. "You give me one minute to explain the situation, and if you don't like what you hear . . . you can do whatever you want with your powers to try and get out of here. What do you say?"

I sat down and then nodded, still believing the lack of cuffs and flimsy walls meant that I had the upper hand. If I was going to ditch this evil woman in a pile of dust and debris, I could just as easily do it a minute from now.

"You have been given an upgrade," Ettinger began.

Instinctively my right hand slapped over my left hand, without understanding why. Then I felt something I hadn't noticed before.

"Yep," she continued. "It's under the skin, FYI. And before you go ripping it out mentally, you should know something about that upgrade."

My fingers traced the recently-stitched-up wound on the back of my left hand as I felt my heart rate begin to race. I tried to focus on my breathing exercises as she spoke, trying to head off a possible panic attack.

"It's high tech, developed by your buddy . . . the Haywood fellow. We took his formula and perfected it. This thing is triggered only by your custodial abilities being activated—that means you trying to use your powers—and the trigger sets off a release of chemicals to your body's pain receptors. And honestly . . . you are simply not prepared to experience pain at this level."

She stood up and slid the chair back under the table.

"This is the AV portion of the program," she said cheerily, as though she were offering me a doughnut. "Only for you it'll just be A—audio only. You are actually my first blind custodian. My first . . . Able." I could hear the tiny whoosh of her fingers making air quotes as she said the word "able," but her vocal tone would have conveyed enough sarcasm on its own to know she was mocking me and the rest of my friends. And she was probably also trying to intimidate me by showing exactly how much detailed information she already knew about me.

"The video I'm about to play for you features a custodian named David Barnes. It was filmed about two weeks ago, just after we'd perfected the chip. It was filmed in this very cell, as fate would have it."

I could tell by her footsteps and the location of her voice that she was circling the room as she got to the meat of the speech. "Mr. Barnes decided to test us. He didn't believe our pain chips were real. Thought they were some kind of psychological experiment or placebo. So he, being a fireballer, attempted to melt down his cell door." She stopped, clapped her heels together dramatically, and then ended with a line so quiet it was almost anticlimactic. "Here's how that worked out for him."

I heard the natural room sound of the prison cell coming through the TV speakers—an amplified and echoed version of the baseline ambient noise I'd already come to identify with this room. Then came a male voice: "I don't believe you." I'd never met David Barnes, or even heard of him, so I hesitate to judge, but he sounded nervous and falsely confident. Like a person trying to talk themselves into adopting a position or truth that, deep down inside, they didn't really accept.

"I don't believe you!" he yelled this time. Much louder, but no more persuasively. "I'm willing to prove it if I have to," he continued to yell. There was no indication from the audio of the videotape whether or not anyone else was even in the room to hear his shouts.

"I don't believe you." If I'm being honest, it really did sound like he was maybe starting to convince himself that the pain chips weren't real. Maybe there was something to his whole "talk yourself into it" style of pep talk.

Sadly, the chip in David's hand's realness depended not on his level of confidence. And so he tried to melt the door anyway, and when he did the unfeeling chip did what it was programmed to do and lit David's pain receptors up like a 9-1-1 call center after an earthquake.

For maybe a nanosecond—the tiniest fraction of a second that you can imagine—what I heard was a war cry. The intention behind the cry began as boastful and positive. But it morphed so quickly that it's like the war cry part never even existed. It almost instantaneously shifted into something entirely more frightening.

I faintly recall an event from my childhood. It was a picnic . . . maybe a church event or a family reunion of some kind. Everything was great, and everyone was having a great time. One of those idyllic childhood days. Some were talking, others were playing tabletop games or tossing Frisbees, some were playing flag football. Then came the screeching tires and that sickening crash of metal and glass . . . followed by a great commotion as everyone rushed to see what the commotion was all about and to offer their general assistance.

And I remember that my cousin, Stephanie, had been chasing an errant tennis ball across the street when the car hit her. I remember the rapid ripple effect of the news traveling from those on the scene back through the rest of us in the crowd behind—until it reached my aunt Susan, my mother's sister and Stephanie's mother.

For a few beats, she refused to accept the news as fact. But her heart knew, and soon her objections gave way to her rawest, purest emotions.

I will never forget the sound she made. I couldn't if I tried; hell, I spent years in therapy trying. I think part of my PTSD relates back to it. The cry was guttural, at least two octaves lower than any sound a mother should ever make. Like a gravely wounded bear or other apex beast flat-out stupefied to finally meet some kind of an end. Deep, low, and long. Churning like waves through the air, bubbling like acid on the wind.

The kind of noise that makes you twitch for relief and shudder until it arrives.

And that's the noise David Barnes made. Not just anguish, but also horrified regret. Only somehow worse. Listening to it was one of the worst experiences I'd ever had—and I'd endured a *lot* of bad experiences. Shoot, one of my last memories before waking up in this place was getting smacked in the face by a train! Wielded by my father! Oh, I knew bad experiences, even ones that were too painful to put into words. But nothing like this.

The demonstration had worked. I wasn't about to try using my telekinesis in this place. But what exactly was this place? Who else was here? I knew my friends and the rest of the Ables wouldn't rest until they found me . . . but could they find me? Would they?

The manual labor reentered the room in their work boots, grunted at their boss, and wheeled the cart back out into the hallway.

Her heels slapped slowly across the floor as she moved to the exit. Once there, she spun in place and stopped on a dime, facing me. "Did I mention that our DHS scientists—best in the business, these men and women, most of them poached from the CDC and a private analytics

firm—our scientists have finally spotted the common marker in custodian DNA. We know how to pick you out by genetic data now."

I already knew this, of course, though I tried my best to hide that
fact from her.

She continued. "And there's a lot of genetic information out there
we can get our hands on. Which means now we have a list. A recruitment
list, if you will."

I lowered my head, because I was overcome with sadness. I just
hoped she interpreted my action as something else entirely, such as
general apathy or maybe even some manner of an emotional shutdown.

Whatever she noticed, she didn't betray. She just kept talking. "Two
other facilities just like this one went online this week, and three more
are in the construction phase. And that should give us a place for about
85 percent of custodians."

She shifted her weight slightly.

"Imagine living in a world," she continued in her patented shrill-
voiced format, "where 85 percent of its custodians are a figment of the
public's memory. Fading away quickly, as though they never existed at
all. That's the world we're building. And that world requires you to move
here and settle in permanently." I heard her lips smack slightly as they
formed an enormous and phony smile. "Welcome home, Phillip."

She shut the door behind her, and a guard typed a password into a
keypad, which closed the locking mechanism on the Tompkins 325 R
model electronic dead bolt.

# 22

# NIGHTMARES

My dreams were getting intense.

I'd always had pretty interesting dreams, and I seemed to be able to remember them more than most of my friends or family members could. But they were growing freakier by the night—more vivid and intense and scary.

Maybe it was the mental stress from being in this prison. Perhaps they were putting something in the food they were serving or pumping chemicals into the air ducts. I couldn't be sure. All I knew was my dreams had suddenly become violent and vivid.

Tonight I found myself soaring over New York City like Superman, periodically diving and swooping like a roller coaster. I danced and swirled about like a ribbon dancer in the sky. It was exhilarating, but for only a moment.

Because that's when the fighter jets showed up and started firing machine guns and missiles at me.

A thrilling dogfight ensued as I tumbled and soared, swirling away from them by inches at every turn.

A couple of missiles only barely missed me and smacked into the tops of famous skyscrapers like the Chrysler and Empire State Buildings, their brick-and-mortar tops exploding like confetti as I zipped by just missing the debris.

I raced away from my pursuers, out of the city and into the suburbs, hoping to give my enemies fewer landmarks to use as weapons.

I'm not sure what happened next. Dreams can be fuzzy sometimes on the transitions.

But after a bit of blurry fuzziness, I was in some kind of a warehouse. Some guys were loading a boat on the pier just outside. I must have been on guard duty, because I kept looking left and right, as though I expected trouble.

Suddenly everyone started running and shouting in some kind of foreign language. I must have understood it, because I immediately leaped into the air and dove into the harbor below. A submarine was approaching; I don't know how I knew that. But I brought both arms back behind me and slammed them together in front of me, sending a giant shock wave pulsing out all around me.

The wave met the submarine and started to turn its direction before just pulverizing it to pieces. I had a fleeting wonderment regarding how many underwater animals might have been killed by my shock wave maneuver.

Then more fuzziness.

Next I found myself working my way through a palace. It was ornate and gilded. Famous artwork lined the halls, and I walked over Persian rugs that covered the floor.

*Where in the heck am I?* I wondered.

It was a labyrinth of hallways. Silent sentries appeared here and there, standing guard for the king or queen of this palace, though I floated right by them without incident or them even seeming to notice me. I was moving too quickly to be able to linger on any one moment . . . and I'm sure that was ultimately by design.

I climbed several sets of marble stairs and circled a rotunda before finally arriving at a large oak double door. Two servants appeared from nowhere and opened both doors, beckoning me to walk through.

I did.

The chamber was dark, lit only by moonlight coming through the open window. I walked up to the foot of the bed, only to discover a small child in it—a prince, no older than three years.

He sat up, pointed at me, and giggled. I waved, and he waved back.

I reached out my hand, palm up, and the child grabbed my thumb momentarily and pulled on it before ripping his hand away completely. A sharp pain caused me to check my right hand, and sure enough, he'd drawn a bit of blood as his sharp fingernail scratched my skin.

The kid paused, saw my wound and my pained reaction to discovering it, and he cowered slightly, fearing rebuke.

A great commotion off to the right. I turned. It was the boy's father—the king—and his armed guards.

Before I even realized what I was doing, I grabbed the king by the throat, lifted him off the ground, and wiped my arm to the left, sending him flying out the high-rise window to his death below.

I turned back to the child.

His eyes widened and then he chuckled with pure joy and fascination at the voodoo going on around him. Probably seemed like a magic trick to him.

Then blackness.

Next I was running through a cave, with several men in army uniforms in front of me. We were all fleeing. Behind me I heard a growl that would have emptied my bladder had this not been a dream. Some kind of massive animal was chasing us, and I tried to run even faster.

Sudden daylight bathed me in warmth. I wheeled around, foolishly thinking the pursuing creature would be afraid to come out into the light. Instead, he walked out into it confidently, as though he was bragging. And well he should have been.

Before me stood a bear/wolf hybrid the size of a movie-based T. rex.

I lifted off the ground, hovering in attack mode.

The bear misinterpreted my actions as friendly and reverted to his human form. "You're custodians too?" he said excitedly. "Oh thank God," he exhaled.

"Indeed," I agreed with a smile. I gestured to my riflemen, who tranquilized the wolf bear instantly.

Another flash of a dream.

This time I was on horseback. I was chasing someone through a dense wood.

Another person on horseback? It sounded like it. I couldn't be sure until I got closer.

Soon enough I rounded a bend and saw my target on the road before me. I lashed the horse to increase speed. Suddenly, I threw telekinetic waves at the other rider with a sweep of my hand, knocking him off the animal and down the cliff next to the road.

"Why, Phillip?" I heard him, or someone, cry out.

I woke with a start, drenched in sweat and breathing rapidly.

If there was a silver lining to being incarcerated without being charged with a crime, it was that I was finally exercising. Everyone I knew wanted me to exercise—my father, my therapist, my physician. And now I was.

Push-ups, sit-ups, running in place . . . I was doing it all. My old gym teacher from back in Manhattan would be mind-blown to see me do even a single exercise.

Granted, it was only because I was so bored I couldn't think of anything else to do. I mean, they wouldn't even give me blank paper and crayons!

But still, I was ultimately going to take credit for these push-ups and sit-ups, and I'd been doing them a couple weeks now and was starting to sense a difference.

I think plenty of fifteen-year-old kids are exercise averse. Maybe even most of them. But I had the added knowledge that, at least as far as using my powers was concerned, my physical muscles meant nothing. I couldn't use my arms to lift a fifty-pound bag of dog food, but I could use my mind to pick up something a million times heavier. My physical muscles were borderline useless to me.

Exercise had always seemed like folly. Wasted effort and time with no real gain. Like running in place—which, coincidentally, was also a form of exercise!

But it passed the time. It helped me focus on an objective. And the exercise, in turn, made it easier to sleep.

Another of my favorite waking-hours activities here in this custodian prison was chess.

I'd requested a game, and the gatekeeper, Ms. Ettinger, had deemed a chessboard okay for me to have in my cell. I'm sure her decision was made based on her own criteria: Would a chess set allow him to escape? No? Then he can have it.

For me, it was as much about sharpening my strategic mind as it was passing the time through the use of a board game.

My sense of touch allowed me to track the different pieces on the board. I obviously played against myself. I was able to keep myself honest and make moves based on each player's best interest, but it was still predictable and anticlimactic chess.

I quickly realized the game held no draw if I was the only opponent.

I opened my eyes to find myself in what simply had to be Antarctica. There were a few penguins nearby, though they shuffled away as soon as I appeared. It seemed excessively cold, and the wind burned my face with cold as it blew by.

Without warning, the ice beneath me began to quake and break into a fault line. I leapt to the side as the rift grew bigger. And then a giant squid burst from the water and jumped into the air like a show dolphin. While it was in the air, the squid's tentacles fired tiny bits of ink in my direction.

Assuming it was poison ink, I drew forth a wall in front of me, constructed out of nearby snow and ice, and the wall took the brunt of the squid attack.

And everything went black yet again.

When I again regained my sight, I was on a golf course. I'd made seven birdies and one eagle thus far in the round and was on the verge of besting the local course record.

I strolled to the tee and smacked a seven iron with a perfect draw. It spun in the air as it traveled, hitting the ground with a built-in distance reduction of at least twelve feet, purely because of the backspin.

I'd never been a better golfer than I was in this dream, and that alone made me want to stay in the dream forever.

But then I blacked out again.

One of the ideas I had to try to manufacture my escape was related to food. Well, bugs really. But also food.

Every day they gave me two trays of mostly tasty food. All I did was take the sweetest tasting dish from each meal and put a bit of it in the northeast corner of the cell, on the floor.

It had been weeks since anyone had physically entered my cell. They just slid food in and took away the old food trays. That was it.

But what if I could cause an infestation? What if I could create a pest-based crisis so urgent they would be forced to remove me from my cell, even if only for a moment?

Sure enough, after a few days, the ants started showing up. Which should be a lesson to all you fancy builders out there: no matter how tight you make your seams and cuts, no house is built tightly enough to keep out ants.

Sadly, instead of the ants leading to an evacuation of the cells for a bug bombing, the prison guards just slid a few ant traps into each cell and left it up to us whether we wanted to share our living space with ants or not.

I chose to put the traps out.

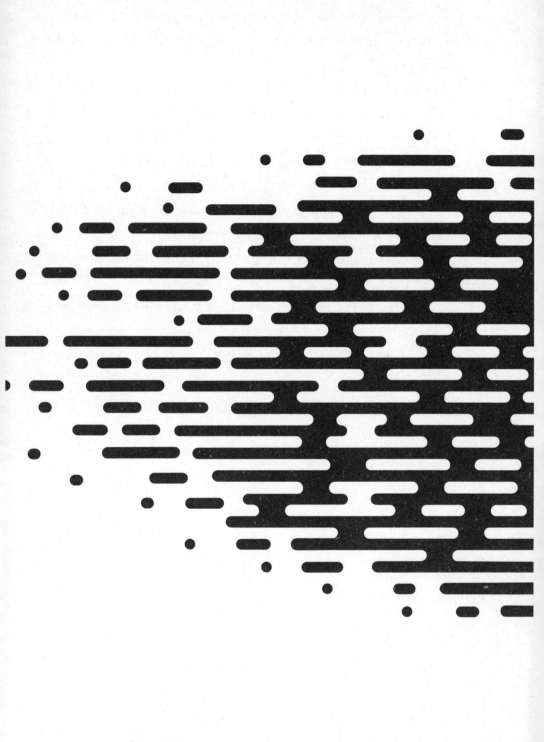

# 23

# RELEASE

I'd been scratching my left hand so much since coming here that the original incision still hadn't healed from where they put the implant in. I wasn't doing it consciously or secretly.

My therapist had told me more than once that I exhibited behaviors that suggested a strict upbringing: picking at wounds, biting my nails, things like that. I figured this hand-wound-scratching stuff could be chalked up to that.

Or maybe I just hoped it could.

My childhood certainly hadn't exactly felt strict while I was living in it in real time. But in hindsight, I could see the label applying.

My folks had definitely guarded me when I was younger, shielding me from activities they thought might be too dangerous and keeping me from seeing entertainment options that were considered too crude or R-rated. Which was certainly part of why I was drawn to those activities and programs as a teen.

I wondered briefly what my therapist would have to say about my current situation. What "proactive steps" would he see in this environment that I should be taking?

Some of it was obvious. I knew for a fact he would tell me to exercise in this cell. Exercise has a wonderful effect on the stressed-out brain, in that it alleviates anxiety and releases endorphins.

Best I could tell, I'd been here three weeks. Other than the initial visit from Ettinger, I hadn't had a single visitor.

Twice a day the slot opened and someone slid in a tray of food, but that was it for human contact. And the soundproofing in the building meant I had no idea how many other inmates were here with me.

The food was pretty great. I would love nothing more than to further trash the reputation of this illegal custodian prison, but they did feed us well. I figured it was some kind of psychological warfare or experiment.

But I was stubborn. I grew more restless every day.

I doubted my captors were familiar with my full mental health history. I don't think they knew I was prone to panic attacks. They certainly hadn't even pretended to give me any kind of medical screening or checkup, which even the dirtiest, seediest standard American prison would do, if only to cover their own ass to prevent a lawsuit.

The dreams were getting to be too much for me to handle, and I'd begun actively avoiding sleep. And when you take a sleep-deprived teenager and combine with anxiety and paranoia . . . you get something quite unpredictable.

I was rubbing my left hand's wound again, tracing the small rectangle that represented the microchip they'd implanted in my skin. I forced myself to stop and deliberately moved my finger over to the right hand's knuckles, sliding along the peaks and valleys from the smallest finger's knuckle to the thumb's. Which is where I felt something that, at least initially, seemed new.

A small scratch between the two knuckles on my thumb.

I wasn't sure at first what I was feeling, so I kept running over it until a deep memory connected and popped back up to the surface.

*The prince from my nightmare! He'd scratched me in that exact spot!*
*Wait.*
*Wait!*
*That was* real*? That really happened? It wasn't a dream?*

The realization was too much, and I collapsed to the floor of my cell in shock as I replayed every nightmare from this place over and over in my head, realizing each of them had been real events and not dreams after all.

I'd been used.

I'd been used to kill, rob, and injure. My powers had been used—my very body—to commit the kinds of acts I'd sworn to spend my life trying to stop.

And the visions. Whoever had used me must have done something similar to what Henry does to allow me to see during those events. Had they wanted me to see or had it been a byproduct? An unforeseen side effect?

Only once before in my life had I ever felt as angry as this realization made me. It was just after I learned that Finch had killed my mother on purpose, just to force-fulfill a prophesy that he thought would make me an all-powerful custodian. And back then the anger had caused me to smash Finch into a concrete wall a few times, reducing his bones to putty and nearly killing him.

Somehow someone had developed or spawned some kind of puppeteer ability. I'd heard some fairy tales about ancient custodians with powers like these, but most of those stories were considered folklore, not history.

And yet I was sure of it. Those dreams that had haunted me and caused me to wake up sweating bullets were 100 percent real. And I was suddenly just done. Over it. Mind made up. Pain be damned. This puppeteer ability would also explain the physical confrontations I'd had with my father, making him blameless for his actions.

I lifted my right hand into the air and hovered it twelve inches above my left hand. For a moment, I paused and took a couple deep breaths.

I had to move quickly. The amount of pain the chip would be able to apply to me would depend on how long it remained connected to my nerves. If I moved fast enough, I could minimize the effect.

With a solemn nod, I made the move.

The pain chip wiggled for a nanosecond before popping off a piece of my flesh and flying up into the palm of my right hand.

Sadly, that nanosecond had been enough for some serious pain messaging to be sent to my receptors. I felt the full pain sent out by the chip. I was surprised the pain wasn't localized to my left hand, where the chip had been implanted, but was instead felt body-wide all at once.

And it was even more intense than I'd feared. In fact, while I was in its pulsating grasp, I wanted to retract my decision and go back to being a prisoner. It was too late at that point, of course, but I wanted to take it back and undo that choice. That's how massive the pain was.

Concurrent with all this action, my vocal cords had also decided to register their reaction to the pain, and it was loud and vaguely Wookiee-like. I bellowed so hard some of it snuck out the microcracks in the prison door's design and reverberated down the sterile hallway.

It was the kind of pain you need a few days to recover from; unfortunately, I had only seconds. Guards would be here any minute. And I needed reinforcements if I was going to get out of here.

I blew my cell door off with a simple finger wave, stepped into the hallway, and screamed at the top of my lungs. The cry raced down the hallway in both directions, allowing my superior hearing skills to use basic sonar principles to calculate the number of other cell doors in the hallway. There were thirty total cells, including mine.

"Everyone back away from the door!" I wasn't even thinking at this point. I was just acting. Adrenaline had bum-rushed my brain and was calling all the shots.

I snap-flew to the far end of the hallway in half a second and then began my deliberate walk, air-punching each cell door open as I passed it. Soon enough, twenty-nine other custodial prisoners stood in the hallway with me.

"Phillip Sallinger here. Anyone know me?"

"Yeah, over here," came a voice from the back. "Brandt Crittendon. My little brother Bentley is your buddy, right?"

"Yes!" I replied enthusiastically. "Anyone else?"

I waited only a few seconds, but the lack of another reply saddened me. Where was my father or Haywood? But I didn't have time to dwell.

"Look, I'm a strong-ass telekinetic, but I'm blind. If someone can take the lead and tell me how to help, I think we can break out of here. Agreed?"

The consensus was clear from the responses.

"Awesome," I shouted. "Just one more step before we take off, and this is going to hurt. Everyone put your left hand in."

Moments later, all thirty of us emerged from the elevator at ground level, each clutching the left hand and holding a bandage over it to stop the bleeding.

After removing twenty-nine pain chips in one fell swoop, I'd orchestrated our ascent to the surface and subsequent escape. Everyone was bleeding and no one was happy, but at least we were finally all free from that internment camp.

My friends and I had been on the right track all along. The secret we'd been searching for had been the prison, and I'd just escaped it. I allowed myself a small smile.

Our victory was short-lived, though, as we were immediately confronted by a legion of armed guards between us and a four-story-tall perimeter fence.

"We're screwed," Brandt informed me. "Dead to rights. They were waiting for us, Phillip."

"You know," I said in response, "I'd almost rather die fighting right now than go back in that cell. In fact, I'd *definitely* rather die fighting than go back in that cell. I'll give fifteen seconds for anyone who wants to surrender, then I'm gonna start putting the hurt on these assholes."

I waited a beat but heard no footsteps.

"I'm with you," came a timid voice.

"Me too," said another.

"Form a circle, facing out, side to side, let's go," I barked.

"This is suicide," Brandt said quietly, hoping I could be persuaded privately.

"I don't care. I'm done. I'm nobody's lab rat." I adopted a defensive pose and shouted out, "Ready?"

Most of the rest of the escapees repeated the "Ready" cry back to me. The din grew as the horde approached. Suddenly, a familiar noise.

*Ooph!*

"Honestly, I thought you'd *never* call me." It was Emmaline, in full-throated sarcasm mode as she placed her hand on my shoulder.

*The beacon*! I only now remembered Bentley had placed one of his teleporter-friendly electro-homing devices on my mask. They must have just been waiting anxiously, for weeks, for that beacon to go off. Or even just hoping that it would. For all they'd known, I had been killed.

"Everyone grab onto the person next to you!"

I felt two more hands on my shoulders and then—

*Ooph!*

Silence. Quiet. No more violent horde of prison guards. No more sirens and horns. No more shouting.

We were back in Charles Field; I could smell it.

And I was overwhelmed instantly. All the pent-up stress and anger from the weeks in the prison finally came rushing on all at once, and it was too much. My brain short-circuited, and I blacked out.

# 24

# MOVING DAY

Freddie had pretty good eyesight, so he stood guard outside while Patrick and I scrambled to pack up as much as we could.

"Only the essentials, buddy."

"I know," he said as he entered his room.

We knew that I was on a list—*the* list. The list the DHS had of known custodians.

We knew they were behind the kidnappings and rogue custodian missions and that they were very familiar with Freepoint, Goodspeed, and all the other custodian safe towns.

They'd be angry after the escape I'd mounted. Thirty of their captives were now loose out there in the wild, and we figured they'd want them back.

And we knew they had found the key to identifying us by our DNA.

All of which meant that we couldn't stay here. Our home was no longer safe.

It was probably exceedingly stupid for us to be here now, even if only for a few moments. But I felt some part of me needed to say goodbye to this place. I guess I wasn't sure we would definitely get to come back some day. Everything was so messed up right now. I decided Patrick and I—and all the Ables, really—deserved a chance to grab a few personal items of importance to carry with them to our new home. Even if it came with a small risk.

But I doubted the DHS was going to be doing full sweeps yet. They'd be scrambling, sure. And mad as hell, yeah. But logistically there'd be too much for them to deal with regarding the breakout and the missing inmates.

I walked to my room. We'd already stopped by Henry's house—his family was safely out of town already—so he was in the living room, giving me sight. He hardly knew it, since he was playing a handheld video game he'd desperately wanted to rescue from home before we went into hiding.

I looked around my room. I spent so little time here these days. I was doing most of my sleeping outside and really came in here only to change clothes.

On my nightstand was a photo that had been there for a little over three years. It was a small three-by-five picture of the family. Mom and Dad were in the back, sitting on the top step of the front porch, and Patrick and I sat in front of them. It had been our Christmas card photo the year before she died.

I grabbed the frame and placed the photo in the small box I held under my left arm.

I walked around the room looking at the toys and trophies and posters. I sighed at how little value any of it seemed to hold for me now, in this situation. Poster of my favorite movie? Not very useful to a band of teenage vigilantes living in the woods. Science fair awards? Just worthless paper now, even though they had once been cherished and beloved symbols of my worth as a person.

There was some useful stuff in here too. I found my phone and charger. I figured a blanket and a pillow couldn't hurt.

I pulled a few changes of clothes from the dresser drawers and stuffed them in the box too and then went back out into the kitchen.

I thought for a minute, wondering if I needed anything from the kitchen. I finally grabbed a small metal pot and a couple ceramic bowls, placed them in the box, and shrugged. Off to Dad's room.

I hadn't spent much time in Dad's room since he'd gone away. And even before that I didn't venture in very much. It was still "Mom and Dad's room" in my mind, so it was a constant reminder of her persistent absence.

I poked around, mostly just looking at first. Then I started opening cabinets and drawers. I guess I thought I might find something useful like cash or, you know, instructions on what to do if he ever got kidnapped and somehow used for evil.

I checked the closet and was almost offended not to find any of Mom's clothes still hanging there. It was only Dad's stuff. Suits, jackets, button shirts, khakis—not a single shrine or memorial in sight. Maybe I'd seen too many movies.

It certainly wasn't my place to decide what Dad should or shouldn't have done with Mom's clothes or other belongings after she died. She'd been my mother, sure, and I had loved her. But his relationship to her was something more. More than familial love alone, it was also romantic love. And it carried years and years of weight and history.

It was probably too difficult for Dad to see Mom's clothes in the closet every day as he went to get dressed. It probably wouldn't have been good for his overall mental health to keep that stuff around either.

For some reason I had expected to see something of hers. A skirt or a blouse. A single dress—perhaps her wedding dress.

But there was nothing.

I rifled through a few boxes that were on the floor in the closet, but it was all old books and other keepsakes. One of the boxes was full of photo albums.

I should have just gone straight to the main dresser, because everything interesting was in there. The third drawer down on the left took my breath away.

He did have a shrine.

The drawer was full of various things that had belonged to my mother. Some T-shirts and other clothing. A jewelry box with rings and necklaces inside. There were photographs—almost exclusively of her or the two of them, many from back when they had been dating.

And he'd kept her old ballet slippers. She had worn them in her youth. She'd danced right up until she had me. And she'd always kept her favorite ballet shoes in a shadow box she mounted on the wall. Now here they were.

I was both greatly warmed and heavily saddened at the sight of these items and the discovery of Dad's shrine. I closed my eyes and took a few deep breaths.

As it turns out, I did find something else in the dresser that might be useful. It's very presence in this house alarmed me, but I still took it. I put it around my back and out of my vision, dropping it gently into the box. I waited a beat to make sure Henry hadn't noticed, but he appeared to still be consumed by the video game.

I made my way through the house and outside, where Freddie was looking up and down the street anxiously. He was a good kid. Kid—he was my age, just a little shorter than the rest of us, and yet I saw him as a kid.

Sometimes I saw all the Ables members as kids . . . like they were all my little siblings. I guess I knew that they needed looking out for a little extra. Or maybe I just made that up because the real issue was that I needed to be needed?

I folded the flaps of my box together to close it and lifted it up into the back of my father's Jeep. It was four-wheel drive, and at least two of the Ables coming with us had a driver's license. A vehicle might come in handy. I didn't know; I was just guessing. Shoot, I'd been just guessing for a good couple of years now.

"You alright?" I asked.

"Sure, boss," Freddie said with a smile. "I'll feel better when we all get out of here."

"Me too." I turned to head back toward the house and heard a familiar noise behind me.

*Ooph!*

"Hey, friends," Emmaline called in a singsongy way.

I turned around to see she hadn't arrived alone. Penelope and Greta were with her.

"Now how did three women get packed faster than you men did?" Emmaline teased.

"I blame Patrick," I said, just as Patrick zipped up with his box.

"I heard that," he said, smiling.

I looked at him a second and cocked my head. "I said only the essentials, Patrick."

He held out the small box he'd packed as evidence he hadn't overpacked. "I know, look!"

"Is the dog not coming with us?" I said.

"Oh man!" Patrick took off into the garage, which had become the dog's room since we didn't really need to keep a car in there these days anyway.

"Alright," I said, turning to the others. "Who are we missing?"

"Bentley and Brandt are meeting us here," Penelope said.

"Awesome." I hadn't known if Brandt was going to come with us. He had his own friends, I supposed, but I guess he felt a desire to keep an eye on Bentley firsthand. They were the only two Crittendons we could account for right now.

"Lead Foot and Limbs are coming too," Freddie called back. Limbs was the new nickname for Porter, and getting the group to start calling him that instead of "Leper" was one of my finest leadership accomplishments thus far in my young life.

"Anyone else coming?"

No one spoke up quickly, which wasn't a good sign.

"I called around to a bunch of the other kids from the roster," Greta offered. "No one answered."

Penelope weighed in with an explanation. "Phillip, a lot of folks have already left town. Families have been quietly slipping away ever since you got yourself captured and became famous."

"Infamous," Henry corrected her as he rolled up. "We have to let the rest of these kids go right out of our minds. We can only protect the ones we can protect, Phillip."

"I know," I sighed. "Still wish there were more."

Suddenly Sherpa came bounding down the sidewalk and started trying to jump into everyone's arms at once. He was an affectionate puppy, and cute enough that he never had to ask for attention when people were around.

"Sherpa!" Emmaline had helped name the dog, but she'd also been checking in on Patrick a lot in my absence, and she'd come to bond with the animal. He raced directly to her as soon as he heard her voice. They clearly adored each other.

Patrick came out the front door just then, a bag of dog food under his arm. "Hey, Pat," I called, "go ahead and lock up, will you?"

Just then Brandt and Bentley pulled up in Brandt's jet-black sports car.

"Did anyone order pizza?" Bentley called out from the driver's side of the car.

Brandt opened his door and stood up, showing off three pizza boxes from Jack's. Everyone ran to him immediately, because that is the correct social response when someone appears with unexpected pizza. It's just what you do. It's only polite.

Lead Foot and Limbs stepped out of the back, having been picked up by Bentley on his way over.

"I can't even believe they're still open," I said before chomping down on a slice.

"They closed just now," Bentley said, walking around the front of the car. "We got the last three pies. They're going out west, they said, to hide out for a bit until things blow over."

I looked over and saw Freddie grabbing a slice, and I suddenly remembered we were supposed to be hurrying. It had taken only a short few minutes for us to let our guard down completely and just start carrying on like we were at Ables practice.

"You know what?" I said, ending the good vibes. "I don't want to be a downer here, but we really shouldn't linger any longer than we have to. It's not safe for us to be here at my house or even in Freepoint."

"He's right," Henry agreed. "Let's get out of here."

"Bentley, you got the spot?"

"Yep." He unfurled his map and conferred with Emmaline briefly. She looked at me and nodded.

"Alright ladies and gentlemen. Bring it in."

Everyone moved in to form a tight network of hands and shoulders. Patrick scooped up the dog and put a hand on my arm.

"Ooh," I alerted Emmaline, "don't forget the Jeep. All our boxes are in there."

She reached her left leg out behind her and tapped the Jeep's bumper with her tennis shoe. "Everyone set?"

We all nodded.

I said a quiet personal goodbye to my home and my life, desperately hoping I would have another chance to say hello one day to both.

# 25

# UTOPIA

I walked through the campsite carrying a bottle of water, observing how we'd come to do life out here together.

We were in the Smoky Mountains, at least forty minutes from any kind of town. Penelope and Emmaline had found this spot while doing some light location scouting before I'd escaped the internment camp and been rescued.

We had two large caves for shelter and had built a firepit in each.

Outside the caves, we'd set up a handful of tents into a makeshift village.

As it turned out, 80 percent of what we'd brought with us was useless out here in the woods. I'd brought my phone and my charger, but not only did I not get a signal this far out, I didn't have anywhere to plug in and charge up!

Emm had graciously used her teleportation ability to ferry us all back and forth for a few follow-up supply runs, and then we'd scrounged enough cash to send Limbs and Lead Foot to a big-box store for food and the tents. We had to send them because everyone else on the squad had been at least first-stepped by Ettinger's DHS goons at some point along the way, so their faces on camera would be a bad thing.

Those two idiots brought back more potato chips than real food, but that was what we got for sending the two youngest members of our group for groceries.

We'd been here four days, and if it weren't for the reason we were out here and the overall fog of anxiety hanging over us, it might have even been fun—like camp.

Everyone had a job, and for the most part we'd managed to avoid devolving into killing each other.

I spotted Bentley on a log down by the creek and walked over for my daily dose of news from the outside world. Bentley had become rather consumed with news of the outside world and spent most of his time huddled in various spots around the camp listening to news radio broadcasts.

"They hit Freepoint today," he said in a monotone manner. He was staring off into the woods across the creek. "They're really doing the whole thing up, Phillip. Cameras and news crews. They're just . . . going through peoples' houses and businesses as they please. Like they're sets from a movie and not our homes!"

I sighed. "You know, it doesn't have to be you always listening to this stuff. We can take turns. I'm worried about you, buddy. You take all this so hard, and it's starting to mount up."

He shook his head and shook my hand off his shoulder, then he immediately changed the subject back to the news. "You know what they have now? They have commercials. They're recruiting people to help turn us in." He took on a false baritone voice, imitating the spot's narrator. "If you see something, say something. Do *you* know a custodian?" He quieted down again and went back to his distant stare. I could faintly hear the chirping of the radio in his headphones.

I stood up to leave, but he spoke again.

"They can do whatever they want, Phillip. Public support is totally on their side. Every day another custodian commits some terrible act. There's so much evidence."

I started walking away. I had only so much bandwidth available for this "rambling prophet" version of Bentley.

"They're still using your dad . . . The public is really fascinated by him. They call him the Manipulator in the newspapers."

I turned around in anger. "Well what would you have me do about it, Bentley?"

He was ready for it. In fact, he had intentionally provoked it just so he could have a chance to speak his mind.

"Anything, for starters! But this hiding out in the woods is the very definition of doing nothing, and I don't know how much longer I can watch."

"Why does it have to be me that takes such initiative? If you feel this strongly about it, why don't you just—"

"Because I can't!" he shouted, cutting me off and silencing the entire camp with his outburst. "My powers aren't strength or anything physical. What, am I going to go out there and think the enemy to death? You're the strongest custodian I've ever met, and you're just roasting marshmallows and singing campfire songs while the world burns!"

"There's an army of suddenly evil custodians out there doing awful things. How in the world do you think I should go about stopping them?"

"Not them—the source!"

"What?"

I could tell everyone in the group was listening now, and a few had even moved closer to our position as we bickered.

"It's never more than one, Phillip. Never more than one at a time. Your dad does a crime, Haywood does a crime, a custodian I don't recognize does a crime . . . all individually."

"What's your point, Bent?"

"I think we have a puppeteer."

Everyone seemed to react to that statement, some with a gasp and others with just a lack of breathing of any kind for a second or two.

I'd already suspected this, but I hadn't told anyone in the group yet. Not even Henry or Emmaline. Especially not Patrick.

"I . . ." I started. "I know we do."

What followed was a kind of combination of an anxiety attack and a confession, as I explained my experiences while at the prison. Tears rolled forth as I talked about the nightmares I'd had . . . visions of me doing reprehensible things. And I was full-on sobbing by the time I got to the revelation that those visions hadn't been dreams at all, but real actions my body had performed while some demented devil took control of my powers.

It was as cathartic to finally get it all out there as it was emotionally upsetting to relive all those memories.

It would be difficult for everyone to process. I decided to go for a walk and clear my head while the others worked with the new information I'd given them.

"Wait," Emmaline called after me. "I'll come with you."

*You want me to step out so you can have some alone time?* Henry asked silently, mind to mind.

I smiled. *Sure*, I thought back. *Thanks.*

The air was chilly. Winter was definitely here, though there wasn't any snow on the ground yet. At least not in this location. Instead the ground was beginning to harden and the fallen leaves were changing from crunchy to soggy from all the Tennessee December rain.

"I just wonder sometimes if I'm the only one who cares about protecting these kids," I said, defending myself as we walked along the edge of the creek away from the camp. It took about seven steps before I tripped and fell to the ground with a thud. "Shoot," I exclaimed.

"Whoa, are you okay?" Emmaline said, helping me up. "I thought . . . I thought you could see when Henry was around. Did we go too far away?"

"Usually I can. He asked me if I wanted him to sit this one out." I brushed myself off, though I wasn't certain I had any debris on my clothing that needed brushing off. It just felt like the right thing to do in the moment.

"I guess I don't understand how it all works."

I sighed. "Sometimes I don't either."

She grabbed my hand. For a split second I thought things were about to get flirty, but she merely lifted my hand up to her shoulder so she could guide me. Which was plenty nice as well.

"So why would he sit this one out?" she asked, innocently enough.

"Well"—I found myself strangely compelled to tell her the truth— "everyone around here knows that I like you, so, I'm guessing it's that."

"Ah," she said with pretend profundity. "So this is why you tripped and showed up at my front door gushing blood, then?"

"That would be a yes."

"Short step up here as we go over a log," she warned before continuing the main conversation. "Why didn't you just use your cane? I've seen you use that thing a bunch of times."

"I was trying to impress you, I guess." I hated admitting embarrassing things, but this girl brought a rare blunt honesty from me; it was one of the reasons I liked her. "It sometimes feels like the cane is just a symbol of weakness. One more obvious 'Hey, everyone, I'm disabled' visual aid."

She scoffed. "Whatever."

She had an odd way of saying one word as a response and then going silent for a while. It was difficult to get a read on.

"What do you mean 'whatever'?"

"Do you think Bentley walking with his leg braces makes him look weaker?"

"Well . . . no," I stammered.

"Because Bentley has a disability. His braces help him manage that disability. I don't see why your cane wouldn't be the same thing. Another log," she said as I felt her rise, leading my hand and arm along the path. "The only difference is that it's you. You're just being harder on yourself than you would be on anyone else. And, if I'm honest, harder than anyone else would be on you as well."

I grunted, hoping to sound like I neither agreed nor disagreed with her but that I had, indeed, understood her meaning.

"I agree with him, by the way," she added. "Bentley, I mean."

"Oh yeah?" I was surprised, but not offended.

She elaborated. "We're not doing any good for anyone out here. I mean, sure, yeah, we're protecting the younger ones. But what from?"

I just let her keep talking without interrupting, partly because I wanted to hear what she had to say and partly because I had a huge crush on her.

"If things out there keep going this direction, then the threat's going to be so enormous by the time it reaches us here that we'll stand no chance and we'll all die. Which will suck, by the way," she tacked onto the end, as though I didn't already know that dying would suck.

Again I said nothing in response.

She wasn't done. "If we're all going to die or get captured in the end, what's the point of prolonging it?" She stopped walking and turned to face me, so I stopped as well. "Especially if the odds are better now than they will be at literally any point in the future."

"We're just kids. And the younger ones . . ."

"I think every single one of those kids back there would rather die fighting than die a sitting duck. I'm not saying we're all gonna die for sure, but . . . we're all gonna die for sure. Soon—if we do nothing. I know you're worried about Bentley listening to too much news, but maybe you should be listening to more of it. Or even some of it. A tiny bit even. Because it kind of seems like you're avoiding it because you don't want to know how bad it's getting out there."

"I can't take it, Emmaline. My heart, my anxiety, my panic attacks . . . I can take only so much bad news," I said, my voice rising in passion of my pain and not out of anger.

"I know." She meant it. She knew all about the mental health stuff I was dealing with. "But ignoring it doesn't make it go away. It's still there. For all the rest of us . . . it's still there. You're the only one who is benefiting from you not keeping up with the news."

She was throwing word bombs of logic with pinpoint accuracy. And yet, even as she openly told me to my face how wrong she thought I was, it never felt like an attack. It never felt like she hated my guts or anything, like it sometimes felt when I argued with some of my other friends.

"You think it's your job to protect the younger custodians in your care, right? The little Ables?"

I nodded.

"Maybe hiding isn't the best way to do that right now . . . if you're trying to protect them in the long term."

I opened my mouth to retort but was startled by the sound of a twig snapping around fifty feet off to our north.

She whirled her head around.

"Who is it?" I whispered.

My mind raced over the last few minutes of conversation and then played out possible reactions of any of the folks who might have been listening would have to it.

"Bear," she whispered back.

*Bear? We don't have anyone on our team named Bear.* Then it hit me. "Oh shit! Why aren't we running away?"

"First of all, that would only attract its attention more. Second of all, what are you afraid of, you superhero?"

"I'm still blind, you know."

"And I'm still a teleporter. Now will you please shut up," she breathed.

I heard the animal grunting as it rooted around the forest floor. According to Emmaline, the bear never looked at us. So either it hadn't seen and smelled us, or it just straight up didn't care.

Just a few minutes later, I heard it move away.

Emmaline's hand went to my shoulder as she leaned in close to my ear and whispered again, even though the bear was long gone, "That was amazing." I could hear in her words the crooked smile on her face as she said it.

# 26

# BREAKOUT

We know where to go because Bentley had, as usual, done some homework. What I had thought was just a mindless catatonic stare into the woods had in fact been his brain overworking, drawing up ideas and plans and chasing down every lead and possible nugget of useful information.

From my recollection, and Brandt's, Bentley was able to pinpoint the location of the elevator leading to the prison. It was on the third floor of an open parking garage. Only there was no way to get a car up on the third floor, not for regular citizens. The garage was advertised as having only two levels. But up on the supposed roof was an entire level perfect for parking two hundred more cars that was going completely unused.

Because that's where the secret elevator into the underground prison was. Of course you wouldn't want average Joes up there parking and finding the thing on accident!

We assumed there were cameras up there, so we'd planned as stealthy an entry as possible.

"I'd just like to state for the record one more time my desire that no one get squished," Henry said, for about the ninth time.

"Jesus, Henry, no one's going to get squished," I barked. "Unless you keep talking about getting squished in the elevator shaft, and in that case I'm ready to let Freddie power up and give you a good squeeze. And you're not even going in the elevator shaft, so why do you even care so much?"

In addition to the cameras, the elevator had all kinds of security measures to keep people out, such as a keypad and a retinal scanner.

We intended to bypass all that crap and just have Emmaline teleport us straight into the elevator shaft.

But if the elevator happened to be rising to the top when we jumped in—squish. That's what Henry was worried about. "Why can't we just wait until someone goes in, thereby ensuring the elevator is going down right after that and the shaft is empty?"

"That's fine if we want to wait forever. Who knows how regularly that elevator is even used!" I was done with this discussion, in part because I felt Henry was continuing it mostly to bug me. "Besides, you act like you're not friends with a telekinetic who can control heavy objects."

The girls had brought Gretalope out of forced retirement, using their radar/sonar device to give everyone a good feel for the layout of the underground facility. After Emmaline jumped it from the woods to Chicago, we'd driven Dad's Jeep into the lower level of the garage, Gretalope inside, and gotten our readings from there.

So we knew that the prison had nine floors, with thirty cells per floor, and a total of four elevators—two on each end of the prison.

Security inside was minimal. I had told everyone about my time there and how flimsy the construction was. This was a place where they assumed no custodial superpowers would be used, because of those chips. So they didn't plan for it. Only a couple guards on each floor, and they were unarmed. A few other personnel here and there.

"This is going to be so easy," I said. They were never going to see us coming.

It would be so easy, in fact, that we weren't even bringing everyone inside. Henry, for instance, would remain on a nearby rooftop. He could get my camera's feed in his glasses from that distance, and there was no reason to put him at risk physically if we didn't have to. His power was so important to helping me use mine, I wanted him protected.

Bentley remained as well, both because he didn't have a physical power we could use in a brute force attack and because he had unique computer abilities like hacking that he could employ from a short distance away, and those abilities might help us avoid needing to use that much brute force after all was said and done. He was already typing, trying to hack the prison's mainframe, which was much more prepared for security concerns than the physical prison itself.

Greta would stay behind and help Bentley. Her coding was pretty great—even Bentley admired it—and she had the same inventor's brain as him.

Penelope could also use her abilities from this distance. And while I had every intention of taking advantage of them on this mission, I didn't need them to start. And again, I wasn't putting anyone's physical well-being at risk if it wasn't necessary.

Limbs, God love him, I wasn't able to think of a good use for, so I told him to stand guard on the roof and protect everyone else.

Brandt was standing by on the roof. Because of his age and experience, we'd all decided he should be the one to take the point on dealing with all the newly released prisoners we were about to spring—helping them escape, helping them get de-chipped, though through more traditional surgical means than I'd used personally. He would also find the able-bodied ones who could go with us to the other prisons to stage similar breakouts.

Inside, I expected to find two things: an unused pain chip and details about the locations of the other prisons. We were here, first and foremost, to mount a rescue. Every custodian with a chip in his or her hand was a victim of more than just incarceration. But the chip and the prison data were just as important in my eyes.

We also hoped to find Ettinger here. We weren't positive, but she had been here near the time of my escape, and I had some words I wanted to share with her. We also had some questions. If Bentley and Greta couldn't hack from the servers the locations of the other custodian prisons and I was unable to find it physically inside this prison, we were going to lean hard on Ettinger for that information, even if we had to get ugly.

That left Patrick, Lead Foot, Freddie, Emmaline, and me for the physical in-person attack crew.

"Alright, guys," I said to them. "Hands in. Emm?"

We were all standing on a pallet. Emmaline put her hand in first, and we all piled ours on top like athletes before a big game.

"Everyone remember the plan, right? Floor by floor. Together. Listen to commands, and keep the radios open." Everyone nodded.

I took a deep breath and then used my powers to lift the pallet up off the ground a few inches, hovering it in place. "Let's go," I said.

*Ooph!*

We were inside the elevator shaft, still all standing on the wooden pallet, which was still hovering.

I could see the elevator below us a few floors. "Bentley, you into the elevator system yet?"

"Not yet, give us thirty seconds," he replied. I could hear two sets of hands clicking away on keyboards in the background.

The elevator jostled, made a whirring noise, and started to move upward . . . toward us.

"Relax," I told the crew. "I got this if we need to stop that thing."

The car stopped after climbing only one floor. We all breathed a sigh of relief.

I heard the radio crackle in my ear. "I'm into the elevators," Bentley barked.

"Okay, great," I said. "When the elevator doors close, keep them closed, and we're all going to hop inside it."

There was a moment of pause and no response. Then finally he replied, "It's empty. Go for it."

Emmaline popped us all inside.

"We're in position," I said, and the elevator began to move. We were going to start at the floor closest to the ground level and work our way down, cornering any of our potential foes as we pushed downward floor by floor.

*Ding.*

The elevator doors opened. Before us lay a long hall, cell doors on either side. There were two uniformed guards, one at each end of the hallway.

The guard nearest us was asleep in a chair right next to the elevator doors. The other guard turned to look at us when the elevator opened and was so shocked to see a bunch of teens in street clothes that he just stood there agape and didn't say or do anything.

"Emm?" I whispered.

She sprung into action. Honestly, it was difficult to hear people talk about how powerful a custodian I was after seeing what she was capable of. She put me to shame, and almost never took credit for it or even sought credit for it.

*Ooph!*

She was standing behind the stunned guard at the other end of the hall.

*Ooph!*

They both disappeared.

*Ooph!*

She appeared in front of us in the hallway and then reached down and touched the hand of the sleeping guard.

*Ooph!*

They both disappeared.

*Ooph!*

She reappeared before us in the hallway with a prisoner. She'd stuffed both guards into his cell and brought him into the hallway in a matter of about two seconds.

She smiled devilishly and then held out her hand and opened her fist, revealing the master key to the cells in the prison.

"Patrick," I barked. "Rescue time."

Patrick turned on his jets and had the other twenty-nine cells unlocked in under ten seconds, as confused custodians stumbled out into the hall.

"Everyone! Everyone, listen!" I yelled. "I know you're confused, but time is of the essence. You're being rescued. My associate Emmaline is going to teleport you to a rooftop two blocks away, where my associate Brandt will give you all the details. But we have to hurry because we have eight other floors in this prison full of wrongfully jailed custodians, and we need to get them out as well. So please push your shock to the side for ten seconds and just grab hands with the person next to you."

There was a little resistance, but it faded quickly as most of them instinctively did what they were told and held hands with those around them.

*Ooph!*

Emmaline disappeared and popped back up among them.

"Bentley, close the doors and take us down a floor," I said into the radio. "Emm, we'll see you there."

On it went like this for all the remaining floors.

We tried some variations that let Freddie and Lead Foot take out some guards while working out some aggression, but at the end of the day this place just wasn't ready for an assault like this, and we easily subdued all the guards and personnel and got all the prisoners out.

On the bottommost floor, there was a large office off the main hallway. While Emmaline and the others emptied the final floor of cells of their prisoners, I went after the other two objectives.

I'd been hoping to find Ettinger inside the office, so I was disappointed to discover it was deserted. But there was a safe in it, which I dismantled like it was made of LEGOs. It contained an entire fleet of unused pain chips. Activation required just a bit of code, and I was certain my friends Bentley and Greta could help with that. I put a few in my pocket.

And just as I began to tear through file cabinets and personal notebooks of the medical staff for information on the other prisons, Bentley radioed with a breakthrough. "We found the other sites, Phillip. Come on back up, and let's get out of here."

I smiled. The mission had been a complete success. We'd done everything we set out to do. But even in my euphoria I couldn't shake the feeling that we'd merely been allowed to win—that we were still misunderstanding the facts around us.

And while that wasn't exactly the case, we definitely hadn't won anything yet.

# 27

# WOUNDING FATHERS

My father stood in front of the Capitol building, just about a mile away on the far side of the National Mall, arms outstretched, daring me to attack. Smithsonian buildings and museums beloved to me lined the grassy stretch between us.

Bentley had discovered files on the prison computer detailing all the other prisons, including the first and largest custodian prison, which was in Washington, DC, built underneath the US Capitol.

And Dad had shown up about thirty seconds after we had.

Round three was about to begin. I would have preferred a different battle ground, but it hadn't been my choice. Dad—and whoever was behind him in the shadows—had home field advantage.

He'd won the first two, but something told me fate was about to swing my way for once.

The snowfall was heavy; there was already two or three inches of snow on the ground, with much more to come. Despite the blizzard conditions, it wasn't really that cold. Maybe that was just my adrenaline kicking in.

I knew it wasn't my father calling the shots—even if it *was* his physical body on the line—so I was able to enter the battle without worrying about guilt or family obligations, focusing solely on the strategy of the battle itself. I mean, I didn't want to kill him, of course, but I knew he wouldn't be angry with me tomorrow for what happened here tonight.

I had a dozen Ables backing me up. Penelope was actually using her powers in reverse for once, taking her weather-controlling ability and using it to make it *not* snow right where we were standing, giving us a nice bubble free of snow and whipping wind.

Freddie'd busted his insta-breather open and grown to full giant size, seemingly ready for anything that might happen.

Limbs had pulled off his arms and grown them back a few times over, stacking them neatly in front of us in case we needed some projectiles. Emmaline leaned over and whispered to me privately, "While maybe useful in some weird way, that is possibly the most disgusting thing I've ever watched a person do."

I couldn't disagree. If push came to shove, sure, I'd probably consider tossing those icy suckers at whoever I had to. But severed arms weren't exactly my preferred projectile.

It honestly seemed foolish that my father's controller thought he should be boasting. Whoever was puppeteering my father and forcing his actions had only seen me take him on one on one. But they were underestimating the powers of the kids all around me—or more importantly, what their powers could do when combined.

I felt invincible given the current matchup. So I decided to get dramatic.

Pretending to use a giant invisible lasso, I hooked the US Capitol building and ripped the dome clean off, intending to give him a bit of his own medicine and sew him into a trap, the way he'd done to me in the train yard.

As soon as he jerked his head back to see what was causing the commotion behind him and got concentrated on the dome, I doubled down my attack. I spun and kicked into the air. A wave of pulsing telekinetic energy flew across the mall, taking out trees and streetlights without slowing down, and struck the Ulysses S. Grant memorial—a large metal sculpture of the Civil War general on his horse.

As a result of that wave, the statue came loose and hurtled rapidly toward my father's position. I smiled in anticipation of the mayhem.

But without even turning his head, my father's right arm shot out and easily deflected the statue off into the Potomac.

*How'd he do that?* I wondered to myself.

Henry could hear me, of course, and he responded with a thought of his own. *Maybe whoever is controlling him, the puppet master if you will, isn't watching this battle from your father's eyeballs, or even from his perspective? Maybe they're watching from above? Or to the side? Or on multiple video monitors? No way your father knew that statue was coming. Someone is controlling everything he does, Phillip.*

*I know. It's almost as if this isn't a level playing field.*

As the dome toppled and spun toward Dad, I saw him using both arms to slow its progress, but he was too slow or too late, or the dome was too heavy. It landed on his position, sealing him underneath.

I flew instantly up into the air one hundred yards and whooped in victory. "Woo-hoo! How do you like being on the receiving end?" I was taunting him. It was never a good sign if I was taunting anyone during battle—even a simulated fight or video game battle. Me taunting almost always meant I'd taken my eyes off the goal and was about to get a nasty surprise.

This time was no different. I looked down midcelebration to see the Capitol dome coming at me from the ground faster than a rocket. I literally only had time to wince and turn my body slightly.

Thankfully, my friends below hadn't just come along to watch.

A colossal crunching sound erupted behind me, so close I thought it was the sound of my own death. Instead, I turned to see that Emmaline had zapped up here at the last second, with Lead Foot in tow, and he'd kicked the shit out of the US Capitol dome. The spire careened off to the northeast and ultimately pierced an office window in the West Wing of the White House. The rest of the dome's debris fell to the Mall below in chunks and pieces.

And yes, this battle on the Mall provided evening talk show hosts with a few weeks of punch lines, chief among them all the "even the custodians hate the president" jabs.

"We can't fly, so . . . bye," Emmaline said, rhyming on accident before she disappeared to carry her and her helper back to ground level. Better that than both of them falling.

"Thanks, Owen," I bellowed at them from the air.

I really needed to call him Owen more often, at the very least so he didn't think I thought his real name was actually Lead Foot. I'd taken so much care to craft Porter's nickname from Leper into Limbs, but I'd just kept right on calling Owen by his nickname. And while "Lead Foot" wasn't as openly derogatory as "Leper," it still probably served to diminish Owen's persona or at least caused the rest of us to label him according to his ability and not any other criteria.

I gently floated back down to the ground for now, wondering what my father's next attack would be.

*Maybe you shouldn't react to his actions, but do some of your own aggressive stuff*, Henry chimed in silently in my head. He'd been listening in on my internal monologue again, but he was also making a good point, so it was hard to be mad at him.

One of my biggest flaws was the desire for spectacle and grandeur. We'd made no attempt to hide ourselves, and the emergency forces and news personnel had shown up and started staking out the best vantage points. They began to pile up at the street level around us, and news vans and choppers were everywhere. This moment would be immortalized on the evening news, regardless of the outcome. I wanted to leave peoples' mouths gaping open, even if all the situation called for was to make them turn their heads for just a brief moment.

So instead of getting proactive in attacking my father in a way that made sense or was convenient, I leaned hard into "making a statement" territory and tried to do things that would impress anyone and everyone watching this now and for all time.

God, when I stopped to think about it, I was pretty insufferable. For the last four months I'd done nothing but follow my own selfish impulses, often at the peril of my friends and loved ones, all because I wanted to be a showman more than I wanted to be a hero. For a few seconds, I sickened myself. Fortunately I remembered there were current life-or-death stakes and quickly decided my self-reflection could be shelved for another day. Plus I was basically asking for Henry to weigh in the longer I thought about things this way.

I saw my next move. Like an angel had emerged from heaven to shine a light on my righteous path, a swath of moonlight washed over the Washington Monument. After rocking it back and forth a bit, I pulled the monument from the ground, lifted it above my head by several yards, and reared back . . . only to drive it forward like an arrow fired directly at the Capitol.

The monument jumped away from my hands as I tossed it, accelerating at an unreasonable rate as it sped toward the target. By all rights, it should have smashed into the main rotunda of the Capitol

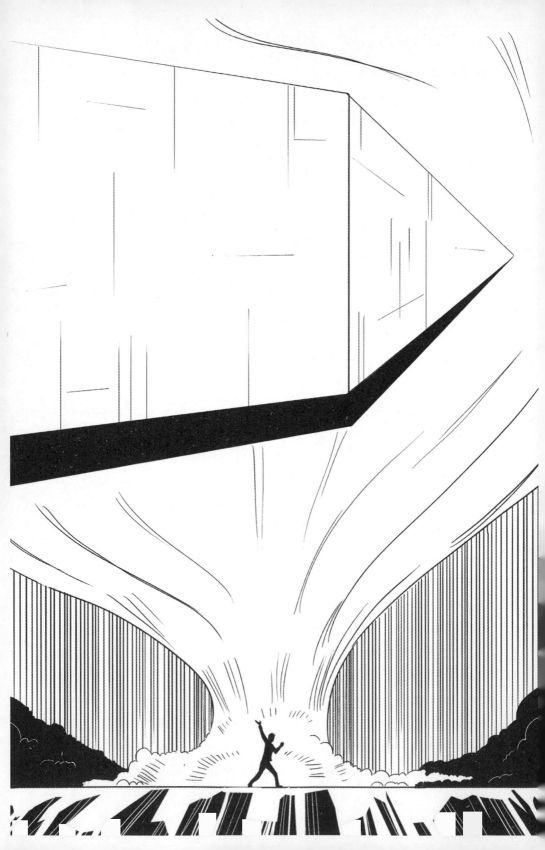

building. But it didn't. Instead it stopped in midair, spun in a semicircle, and raced back toward me with astonishing speed.

I lifted a nearby piece of sidewalk into the air to create a makeshift ramp just in front of my position, and the monument grazed it on the top edge. Giant Freddie did the rest by uppercutting it, punching the memorial projectile into a trajectory even farther over our heads.

The Washington Monument took out the Lincoln Memorial in an explosion of busted stone, and I'd like it on the record that this was the fault of someone other than me. Granted, I did originally toss the Washington Monument, but when it comes to the Lincoln Memorial's destruction, I am *not* having that on my resume.

Another thing I was not having on my resume was "lost to his father."

I knew Dad wasn't in control of his actions right now, and I wouldn't hold anything he did today against him, but he still had to be stopped. And I knew on some level that I was strong enough to do it.

It was time to pull out all the stops.

Without even knowing for sure that I was capable, I began trying to lift the entire Capitol building off the ground. I mean, I knew I was capable of lifting more than I had lifted previously—even the Washington Monument had ultimately been more weight than I'd ever controlled prior to tonight—but I still didn't know for certain that I could do it.

But as the ground below my father began to shake, and he along with it, I knew. I knew I had the power. Even more than enough power, I realized. *I really am stronger than most telekinetics.*

While I continued rocking the Capitol out of the ground, I carved out 20 percent of my brain to focus on a new task: defensive capabilities.

Like most cities in America post 9/11, Washington, DC, was covered in waist-high concrete poles designed to prevent a suicide bomber from driving a vehicle into a building or sacred area.

Hundreds of them leaped into the air at once, ready to serve as my own personal bullets to fire at anyone who tried to stop me.

And yet, my father still tried to stop me. He used one hand to try and keep the Capitol on the ground and the other to punch away inbound concrete missiles.

"I see how you are," I muttered. "Still trying to hold me back after all these years." I knew it wasn't really him; I just had some stuff to work out, and this seemed like a good time. "How's that working out for you now?"

I needed to distract him, get him off his plan. But most of my mental energy was already consumed by the two-pronged attack I was mounting. Which is why Dad's next move hit me when I least expected it, and it was a doozy.

Suddenly a video monitor appeared, hovering in the air two hundred feet off the ground, and I was the one who was distracted. I don't know where he stole it from or how he was holding it in place while still appearing to have full use of his abilities.

A video began to play on the screen. A video of my mother. She was bent over my crib, singing to me. It was an old home video.

Mom sang like an angel. "You are my sunshine, my only sunshine." Like a lot of modern mothers, she didn't understand the morbid origins of the song she was singing and simply took the words of the chorus at face value.

"You make me happy, when skies are gray," she continued.

The Capitol building lowered to the ground, now under the telekinetic power of my father and his puppet master, while dozens of the concrete barriers I'd planned to use as bullets fell back to earth like duds.

The imperfections and impurities of Mom's singing voice were ultimately the very qualities that made her voice so aurally attractive, especially to a blind person like me, even if I was biased on account of being her son.

I certainly felt the tug and chased after it even while ignoring the implications. The video monitor was here for a reason: to show that video clip to me in order to elicit an emotional response in me.

For a reason: to cause me to lower my guard or otherwise push my emotions to the top of the responsibility list and devalue logic, math, and science.

And I nearly fell for it hook, line and sinker.

*Ooph!*

I smelled Emmaline's fabric softener before I heard her whisper. "Phillip. You don't have to do this alone. Stop trying to fight him by yourself and use us. We are all capable. Able, even. Lead us."

*Ooph!*

She was right, and I didn't have time to be properly ashamed, because we had to move.

*Henry, can you help me here? I need you to fog him up hard, like, I need thirty seconds or so to lay out an idea for the rest of the gang, and I can't do that if I'm still fighting him physically.*

*I can try, Phillip. You know I've never been able to do it for very long. I'm not as strong as you think I am.*

*Just try.*

*Will do. Fogging now.*

"Alright, everyone on me. Here's the plan. We're going to distract and pummel. Distract and pummel. And hopefully one of us will find a window to use this." I pulled out the Taser I had found in my dad's bedroom.

"I was wondering when you were going to bring that out," Henry said with a smile. It figured he'd somehow seen me take it.

"Superpowers are great, but we're all still just human. My dad's not a gun guy, so this is what he used to carry on the job, and it's a massive dose. He'll go down like a tranquilized rhino. But if he sees it coming or is able to stop the person wielding it, it's worthless."

"Two teams. Team Distract, on my left. That'll be Henry, Penelope, and Limbs." They moved to the spot I had motioned toward. "You guys use your powers to distract my dad. Keep him off guard. So Penelope, lots of wind and snow and ice, and Limbs maybe you just confuse him by doing something weird with your ability. I mean, let's be honest, your ability is pretty weird just when you demonstrate it. Henry, I want you to fog like you've never fogged before, and keep his mind in a state of chaos, okay?"

"Team Pummel," I barked, "on my right. Patrick, Freddie, and Lead Foot. As he's being distracted, you guys beat the crap out of him. Freddie, you're huge, so just keep moving and boxing. Patty, you pick up Owen and run in random-pattern circles around Dad, letting Owen literally kick him every time you go by."

"Which team are you on?" Henry asked.

"I'm on both teams," I said. "I'm going to try and distract him with a little help from above. But I'll also pummel him with my other hand. I'm thinking flagpoles maybe." I looked around the area. "Lots of flagpoles around here."

"What about me?" Emmaline asked, knowing as well as we all did that hers was truly the most useful and powerful ability among us. Which is why I'd saved the most important task for her.

I placed the Taser in her hand and closed her fingers over it. "I need you to electrocute my dad."

We all put our hands in, and I attempted another of my signature pep talks.

"We can do this, guys. Together. Whoever is behind my dad's actions right now is the key to everything. We stop my father, we are one step closer to stopping all of this. Now are you with me?"

There was the usual variety of affirmative responses, but they all were genuine and enthusiastic.

"Um, I'm totally with you, but you haven't given me anything to do in this plan." It was Greta's voice.

I looked at her for a moment and tried to bring forward memories that simply didn't exist. Then I played over the Chicago attacks and our other escapades the last couple months. And I came to an embarrassing realization.

"You know, Greta, I have no idea what your power is," I admitted, hoping honesty would be charming, as I really only had time to be bluntly honest anyway.

"I figured," she said wryly. "It's okay, I'm not offended. I guess you guys thought that I'm just a nerdy coder girl who makes inventions. But I do live in Freepoint for a reason, you know."

"Well, what's your power? Which team should we put you on, Pummel or Distract?"

She giggled.

So did Penelope.

"So you know her power, but the rest of us don't?" I asked.

"I know it too," Bentley admitted.

"You never asked," Greta sniped.

"It's been kind of a busy couple of months for most of us," I shot back.

"You'd better put me with Team Distract."

"Distraction team it is."

"Oh, and you should be ready to close your eyes when I say so."

# 28

# THE PUPPET MASTER

Penelope went first, drawing up a tornado of snow around my father, hoping to hinder his vision and disorient him.

Henry could, under normal circumstances, fog someone for longer if he did so at a lighter level. The harder he tried to drive a mind into chaos, the faster his abilities dissipated. And tonight he'd just used the full beam at Dad for almost a minute. Even so, he went to work throwing mental distractions at my father's brain.

Young Limbs really embraced the assignment. He raced to a position about one hundred feet from my dad and started pulling off limbs and regenerating them. Then he loaded them up into a slingshot he'd started carrying around a few weeks ago and shot them at my dad. It was easily the most absurd thing I'd ever witnessed, and that's saying something.

My own distraction was, per my tendencies, more dramatic.

I was very familiar with the National Air and Space Museum. I'd been there at least half a dozen times in my life. It was on my right, about halfway between my position and my father's.

*Perfect.*

I knew the layout by heart, and not just because I'd walked the museum before; I'd also *heard* the museum before. A sighted child walks into the Air and Space Museum and marvels at the look of the planes and space capsules. The sleek curves and pointed ends. The thin wings and bulbous engines. A blind kid like me walks in and experiences the shapes of those aircraft by sound, by letting the ambient noise of the room—the customers, the tour guides, the window cleaners, the cafeteria workers—bounce off them and dance about.

Battlefield decisions are easy to second guess from the future. Hindsight always makes some moves seem questionable. And if I had to do it all over again, with the wisdom of age, I would not have wrecked all those planes.

But I was fifteen, fighting for my life, and desperate. And I'd seen way too many movies, so I always thought cinematically. And I hadn't lived long enough to develop a strong enough sense of history . . . or respect for history.

So out came the planes, all controlled by my brain, every one of them probably priceless.

The Wright Flyer (the plane the Wright brothers flew), SpaceShip-One, even the Spirit of St. Louis. A dozen aircraft in all, some replicas and some originals. Some jets, some rockets, some capsules. I used half of them to fly tight circles around and above my father, dive-bombing every now and then. The other half I used as projectiles, forcing Dad to try and dodge them in the midst of all the other stuff coming at him.

I walked toward him as I used one hand to play amateur air traffic controller and the other to drop artifact bombs.

Patrick was moving so quickly you could almost see a trail behind him like a tracer round. He made oblong oval shapes, allowing Lead Foot to repeatedly whack Dad with his iron boot, and cheerily saying hello to me every time he passed me on the outer edges of his circles.

"Hey, Phillip." "How's it going, Phillip?" "Man, this is more fun—" "—than it should be." I tuned him out, which is something I'd learned to do ages ago.

Freddie towered over my father, slamming his fists into the ground like a game of Whac-A-Mole.

Everything we had set out to do was working. We were distracting him, which limited his ability to send attacks our way and also allowed us to land a few blows, further weakening him.

"I'm losing him," Henry blurted out suddenly.

"What!" I panicked.

I was out of projectile aircraft from the museum. I looked around for something else to throw at him, but it was too late. We'd wavered just long enough to give him a foothold.

Dad's right arm shot out straight, grabbing Patrick by the throat and stopping my brother in his tracks. In the same motion, he swung the arm back and used my brother and Lead Foot as a hammer, pulverizing Freddie in the stomach. It sucked all Freddie's wind, and he instantly returned to his normal size.

"I'm out of juice, Phillip. I'm sorry," Henry cried.

Dad's other arm came up, and he did something I didn't even know was possible. Like a beam of heat or energy, he caused a telekinetic laser of sorts to emanate from his palm. It was a destructive wave of pure force.

He swung it right to left. Buildings along the edge of the National Mall began to crumble, including the National Gallery of Art—works by da Vinci, Rubens, and van Gogh torn to bits by my zombie father's magic energy ray. One thing custodians proved this evening was that we had little comprehension of the importance of artifacts and even less regard for their well-being.

He blasted Limbs into the air, and Penelope joined him seconds later.

I lowered my head in shame, awaiting my own turn hurtling through the air in defeat and probably also a great deal of pain.

"Close your eyes, now!" Greta yelled.

I'd honestly forgotten all about Greta. I'd accepted defeat. I assumed we were all toast, destined to die on this battlefield or end up incarcerated for life.

Being blind, I didn't feel the need to obey her command, but thankfully everyone else did.

Later, when we watched the video, we were able to clearly see Greta's unique power in action. She bent over, and the outer edges of her body seemed to pull slightly inward. She grunted, and all her muscles seemed to flex at once as an incredible rushing sound grew from nothing to a roar in seconds and a bright light began to glow from her center of gravity.

Then, in a whoosh of visuals and sound, she appeared to transform her entire body into pure raw light, the brightest light I'd ever seen. Then that light exploded and covered the entire area.

Her ability was sort of an EMP of light. She could temporarily blind anyone in a certain radius by briefly turning into light itself. Even the cameras that had been rolling at the time of the incident struggled to process the light she emitted, resulting in a lot of eyewitness videos from journalists and citizens where swaths of pixels appeared to seize or flash.

I saw the window we needed . . . the only one we were going to get. And I pounced on it. "Emmaline," I barked into the radio, "now!"

My father had been blinded by Greta's unexpected light show. Neither he nor his puppeteer had expected that attack, and Dad fell to the ground. It would wear off, but not anytime soon.

Emmaline teleported directly into my father's path. "Please don't hold this against me, Mr. Sallinger," she said before plunging the Taser into my father's neck, just beneath his chin, and firing the device's electric discharge.

My father had been through a lot, physically and mentally, and the Taser was just too much. He passed out right away and slumped onto the ground with a quiet thud.

Finally I'd defeated my father. Well, we had, collectively. The Ables had done it together.

Ultimately, the credit wasn't as important as the outcome. The point was this puppet master was going to have to face us now—or at least commandeer a new puppet. My father wasn't going to be used for nefarious purposes any longer, of that I was certain.

Everyone who'd been watching this battle was now as blind as my father had been. Or me. Anyone even tangentially looking in this direction, in fact. All the newspersons, citizens, and gawkers. All those living in condos and apartments and homes close enough to just look out the window. All the cops, firefighters, and EMTs. All now blind, even if the cameras some of them had been operating continued to record. Greta's power had unexpectedly given us privacy out here in one of the most public places imaginable.

And then I heard the footsteps.

They were high heels, by the sound of it. Echoing as the steps grew clearer.

Then I remembered there was a large subway station underneath the National Mall. And I realized our villain—the puppeteer, our true evil foe—had been just underneath us this entire fight, watching from the relative safety of the earth's interior, probably using multiple cameras feeding into one mainframe or central hub.

The footsteps finally lost that muted echo that accompanied most sounds rising up out of the subway stairwell, and out from behind the wall stepped Marian Ettinger.

She walked deliberately and rapidly. Her confidence was not in question. She left the sidewalk and strode through the grass. Her high heels defied the snow that lay on the ground beneath her; she simply refused to acknowledge it, and while that didn't erase it from existence it definitely erased it from *her* existence.

"Just a complete waste of time, Phillip," she said in that same confident manner I remembered from my interrogation. "All you've done here tonight is waste time. And money. And resources. And nearly get your father killed. And destroy some priceless art."

"Did more than that," I said in defiance. "Got you to finally reveal yourself. And took out your greatest weapon."

"Sure, you cost me my favorite puppet," she spat, referring to my father. "But now I have an even more powerful puppet to put to use."

"You did all this to get to me?" I knew I was stronger than my father. And adults had been telling me for years that I had more power than I realized or that I was uniquely strong. But still, I didn't think of myself as terribly important.

As it turns out, neither did Marian Ettinger.

"You! You think I did all this to get to you?" She was incredulous. "Ha ha ha ha ha ha. Oh, child. You're powerful, sure. Maybe even stronger than your dad. But you're icing, not cake. I didn't do any of this to get to your pathetic ass. No"—her gaze shifted to my right, where Henry sat—"I did all this to get to *him*."

I tried to engage her with my powers, but nothing happened. And I had a sick and sinking feeling.

"Who do you think tried to crash your plane and get you all first-stepped in the first place?" She said this matter-of-factly, but it was new information for us and she knew it. She was trying to knock us off our game, and it was working.

"You've spent so much time pondering your own superpower," she spat, "how uniquely strong you might be, that you never considered if anyone else around you might be extraordinarily powerful—like Henry. Imagine if instead of puppeteering a single custodian's powers, I was able to multiply that ability via the massive brainpower of one Henry Gardner. Why . . . that would make me nearly limitless, wouldn't it?"

I felt my spine tingle as my body floated up off the ground.

"And I was able to get to him thanks to someone you all know very well." She gestured with her hand, and suddenly Jurrious Crittendon appeared beside her. "My right-hand man, really. I definitely needed someone inside the custodial community."

Bentley's father saluted us all with false ceremony.

"And all I had to do was promise to make him a senator. Granted, he'll be the first US senator born of custodian blood, but no one has to know that until after he's elected. And he'll also be my puppet, figuratively and literally, eternally loyal to me—as all of you soon will be as well, once you've undergone Homeland Security's Patriotic Conversion Therapy." She winked, in the creepiest way possible. "I know it sounds dramatic, but trust me . . . it's basically a day spa."

"There are cameras all around us that are recording right now," I taunted, still unable to truly see the entire field.

"Sure," she said, "that's true. There are. But I could still manipulate things in my favor. I could make it look like you tried to hurt me," she snarled.

I felt my arms go up in front of me, in attack position, as Ettinger pretended to be choked and lifted herself into the air violently.

"Like you threatened me," she continued, forcing me to drive her rapidly toward the ground and stop just short of impact. "And even while the cameras record images that suggest you are going to kill me on the spot, I can still control all of you at once, with the power of Henry's mind."

I could see via peripheral vison that all the Ables were currently floating in midair out of their own control. Then, right when I thought things couldn't get any worse, they got exponentially worse, as Ettinger began forcing each of us to turn our powers toward the innocent by-standers nearby.

Henry lifted off his wheelchair and hovered in the air, convulsing like an epileptic during a seizure, as she maximized his mental abilities beyond levels he'd ever thought possible in order to control the abilities of all of us at once.

Freddie ran off into the nearby streets, knocking down apartment buildings and offices.

Penelope flew up into the sky, the snowfall quadrupling in volume and speed as she disappeared into it.

Patrick was sent off running toward the west, and I had no idea where he went or if I'd ever see him again.

As for me, I was forced to stand and then fly over to the White House, where my powers were used to grab the building and lift it into the air hundreds of feet.

I tried to pretend it wasn't real.

We had lost. And being forced to sit through the enemy's victory dance seemed like more than I could bear, so I wished for it to not exist.

Smithsonian buildings exploded like popcorn. Large pieces of rubble became smaller pieces of rubble. Sirens & alarms rang out.

The earth rumbled from the battle as though an earthquake was happening, and nearly all hope was lost.

*Hey, buddy.* It was Henry.

*Henry! How are you—*

*Just listen. I don't have much time. I've carved out enough of my brain to send you this message. You need to end me, buddy.*

*What? I can't do that. I can't—*

*I do not have time, Phillip. It's not a movie. I can't give you a rousing speech to change your mind. I'm losing this window a bit at a time the longer we talk. Listen—with my brain, maximizing the power as she's done—she is unstoppable. With her controlling our powers, there is no way to use them against her. It all ends with her. She's an epidemic, Phil, and the only cure is for you to kill me.*

*I can't do it. Why is this the only way?*

*Right now. Throw something sharp at me. Do it. Don't think about it.*

*Henry, I don't think I can—*

*Stop thinking! Act! You are almost out of time.*

I devolved into tears and sobs. I was literally incapable of intentionally killing my friend, even if I knew logically that it meant I was likely to die as well, along with more of my friends.

Most of the rest of the Ables were already commandeered, tumbling off to some evil act they'd been forced into by Ettinger's wrath.

Only Bentley remained. He stood still and silent, head down, leaning hard on his cane.

I looked at Bentley, knowing he was clueless as to my current situation and argument with Henry. I wondered how I would explain to him that I had killed our friend on purpose because that friend begged me to and swore it was the only way.

In the end, I wasn't strong enough. I couldn't do it. I couldn't kill my best friend. No matter what we'd been through the last year or so . . . no matter what the logic or math of the situation might be calling for . . . I couldn't do it.

All of civilization might fall because of my inaction, but I still couldn't do it.

I began to bawl.

But Henry was stronger than I was. He'd always been stronger than I was.

He knew the true stakes we faced, and he was able to place his own importance in a proper place along the timeline of events.

*I was afraid of this*, he thought. *I just want you to know that it's okay. It's kind of endearing, actually, that you don't want to kill me, even though it's the only way. I'm flattered.*

Only too late did I realize that Henry was about to use my own abilities against himself, and I didn't have time left to even try to stop it.

My right arm went up at Henry's bidding, and with it a huge, jagged chunk of stone from a nearby demolished building, a rock easily several tons in weight. With a flick of my wrist, the stone raced over to hover just a few stories above Henry's head.

"Nooooo!" I cried.

In the corner of my left eye, I saw Bentley look up from his slumped position. He stared at me, boring into my soul with his gaze.

If Ettinger was using Henry's expanded brainpowers to control multiple custodians at once, then we had to remove that threat as soon and as rapidly as we could. Even as Henry commandeered my right arm, my left arm was still doing Ettinger's bidding, tossing the White House into the Potomac and laying waste to more nearby monuments and buildings.

She fought me even on the right arm, and instinctively I found myself fighting back against her.

*Good man*, Henry thought.

And my right hand flew open with no input from me, dropping the massive piece of museum wall on top of my friend, crushing him.

His final thought had been to congratulate me on killing him. That's how much he'd placed the lives of others above his own. I would spend the rest of my life trying to comprehend his sacrifice.

With his death, Ettinger's reign was also brought to an end.

She lost control of all the Ables, and in her disorientation she was helpless enough that Emmaline hit her with the same Taser we'd used on Dad.

$$\lightning$$

Even though the news cameras had glitched momentarily during Greta's "brightening" moment, the audio mics had recorded everything just fine. This helped fill in the gaps for everyone who had merely witnessed these events without truly understanding who was doing what and when.

By the time Ettinger woke up, she'd already been implanted with one of her own pain chips and tossed into jail, ensuring her puppeteering days were over. My only denied wish was to implant the chip inside her hand myself.

# 29

# AFTERMATH

Being allowed into my father's hospital room was euphoric.

We hadn't spoken since he'd been kidnapped. Since then, we'd had three fights and a whole hell of a lot had changed for custodians on the political spectrum and around the globe.

He was still asleep, so I stayed at the foot of his bed and tried to keep as quiet as possible. I fell asleep myself, still exhausted from the whole ordeal.

At some point I cried out in reaction to a vivid nightmare, and Dad awoke. I heard a great sigh as I turned toward him.

"Hello? Phillip?" His voice was weak and scratchy.

"Yeah, Dad," I replied. "It's me."

"Are you okay? Is Patty okay?"

I definitely loved hearing him ask about our well-being. I loved even more hearing him call Patrick by a nickname out of pure instinct. That was my dad there in that bed, for sure. And I'd had enough encounters with fake dads lately to earn the right to be emotional about it.

"We're good," I called back. "All good."

"Where is Patrick?"

"He's okay. He broke his leg, so he's getting a cast and crutches and all that jazz."

"Oh, my," he groaned.

"Nah, he's fine. He could use a few weeks of going slow."

I heard him smile ever so slightly as he exhaled again, then wince in pain. "Boy," he said softly. "You really kicked my ass, didn't you, son?"

I laughed out loud at that.

"Well," I replied, "you didn't give me much choice. Especially given how badly you'd kicked my ass in the first two encounters."

He sighed. "I still can't see," he revealed. "They told me it might take a few days for my vision to come back. Some crew you're working with," he acknowledged. "This blindness isn't easy. I've taken my eyesight so much for granted all my life. I don't know how you do it."

*I'd taken my own eyesight, such as it was, for granted as well. It was so smooth, Henry sending images without effort. It became my normal. I'd forgotten what life had been like for me before Henry. And now I would mourn my friendship with him more than the lost vision.*

"So . . . how much do you remember?" I asked.

"Just bits and pieces. Flashes. Like a dream."

"Yeah, me too."

"You were . . . she got you too?" He was suddenly concerned.

"Yeah, for a time. About three weeks, give or take."

"How'd you get away?"

"Plenty of time for that later, Dad. There's a lot to catch you up on, and we need to take it slow according to the doctors."

"Why do I have the feeling I'm going to have to be all proud of you again?" he said, sounding proud already.

"I doubt it," I said truthfully.

"How do you mean? All anyone can say about you is good things. They talk about you like you are a true hero—you know that, right?"

I did.

"But I'm not, Dad. I destroyed so much property. So many museums and artifacts and monuments . . . I just treated it all like it was my own personal armory."

"Well, it's just stuff, Phillip. No one's going to blame a kid in that situation for using things near him in battle."

"That's not all."

"Son, you are being too hard on yourself, as usual. I'm sure you made some choices along the way you'd take back, but I'm also sure your good decisions outweigh your bad ones, whether you believe it or not."

"We got a dog."

"What!" His volume had increased dramatically. "You did what?"

"We got a dog."

"Of all the irresponsible—"

"There's more," I said.

He seemed annoyed but paused for me to continue.

"We quit going to school for two months, we stole from NASA, the Jeep is destroyed—"

"Phillip, Phillip, stop. Stop. Shhhh. I'll tell you what—we'll talk about it later. We can talk about the mistakes later. Let's just spend some time being excited and happy about the good things you did out there. I am so, so proud of you, boy." He meant it, and that made me lose it completely . . . the purity of his parental pride.

I hung my head and started crying.

"Henry's dead, Dad," I sobbed.

"Oh, son," he said in sorrow. He pulled me to the edge of the bed, and I laid my head on his chest.

"Henry's dead, and it's my fault."

"Phillip. I'm sure it's not—"

"It's my fault because it was my powers. My hand, my energy. Henry asked me to do it and I couldn't do it so then he did it, but it was still me." I just let loose, and the emotion came flowing out of me.

"She was after Henry all along because she could use his mind to puppeteer more than one custodian at once. And she did, she controlled all of us at the same time, Dad. And Henry knew. He knew it was the only way to stop her." I cried some more and then a bit more.

Dad just held me close and told me it was going to be okay. I knew that it would be, but also that it would never be the same.

⚡

I wasn't about to go home by myself that night, not with my father and brother in the hospital.

But I also couldn't sleep. Big surprise.

I decided to make late-night walks a regular tradition for me in this place.

Dad was in intensive care, and Patrick was down in one of the ER beds sleeping off a painful leg injury with the help of some good meds. After checking on Pat, I tapped my cane along the ground floor hallway toward the waiting room, because I could hear that there was a television on in there. I could at least listen to something.

I hadn't been in the ER waiting room since the remodel, so I used my cane a little extra and just sat in the first open seat I could find.

The television was playing a game show of some kind. They were calling it *The Baffler*, but it seemed like an ordinary trivia game. I wasn't a trivia buff, so I lifted my hand up ever so slightly from the armrest, grabbed "control" of the television, and flipped through channels one at a time.

Sports. Sports. Wall Street. Sitcom. Medical drama. Sports. Another medical drama. Then finally—news. I stopped on news. I was too curious.

It'd been about twenty-four hours since everything had gone down at the National Mall, and surely the world would be talking about it.

"You cannot look at footage like this and be a custodian denier any longer," the lady pundit argued. "This is the final proof we need for us all to accept that they are here. They are everywhere. And there's nothing we can do about it. Some of them are good, and some of them are bad . . . just like the rest of us humans."

*Oh, I like this lady,* I thought to myself.

I flipped to the next channel; another news station. Why did they always seem to cluster all the news channels together on the dial?

The male speaking on this channel was in full sermon mode. "Look at the disregard. Look at the disrespect for our history, our culture, our ancestors and their memories! These so-called custodians are un-American. They are only looking out for themselves. Look at all this senseless carnage caused by custodian-on-custodian crime!"

I flipped again. More news, this time an interview with an eyewitness. "And then all the sudden that thing just went zooming by my window. I thought I was dreaming . . ."

I flipped again, this time landing on an infomercial. You know, one of those long commercials that play late at night, where they hype up a few dollars' worth of plastic as a miracle time-saver or life-changing invention? This one was for a two-in-one device that combined a pocketknife with a computer storage drive. I lingered more out of confusion than interest. And that's when I learned I wasn't alone in the waiting room.

"There's nothing on, believe me. I've flipped through all the channels three times myself." The voice was that of a young boy—younger than me, at least—but it still startled me.

"Holy crap! You scared the crap out of me!" I blurted out instinctively.

"Oh, oh, sorry. Sorry," he repeated. "I thought you knew I was here."

I panted a bit. "I'm blind," I informed him—or so I thought.

"I know. I know who you are."

"Oh," I said, suddenly self-conscious. What shirt am I even wearing? "I see."

"I'm Morris."

"Hi, Morris." I was still coming down from a miniature panic attack, my breaths gradually growing longer and more even. "Do you have a family member in the hospital?"

"Yeah, my dad."

"I'm sorry to hear that," I said, truthfully. "Is he a custodian?"

"Nah, I'm not that lucky," he replied. He sounded about nine or ten years old. "We're human support. My dad's one of the drivers. He helps you custodians get around whenever there aren't enough teleporters or there isn't an urgent need for speed."

I thought about our trip home from the airport in Chicago back before all this started. We'd been driven by someone exactly like Morris's dad. It may have even been him.

"Got caught up in the invasion trying to help get people out. He's in a coma."

I felt awful. A pit in my stomach. I hadn't caused his father's injuries; that was all Ettinger. But I couldn't even think of anything helpful to say.

This man, this father without special abilities, believed in us so much he moved his family here to drive us around because that was how he could pitch in and help the cause. And it had nearly killed him.

We don't think about the people behind the scenes until we're forced to. And it shouldn't be that way. I'd gotten a free ride from someone like Morris's father and then had promptly forgotten that man and his entire existence. I wasn't even sure I'd thanked him.

"Morris," I said, "I hope your dad's okay. I've gotten rides like that before, and it really means a lot to have people like you and your dad helping us." I stood up and started to head back out to walk around some more. "I'll be here for at least a couple days with my dad upstairs. I'll come check on you tomorrow and say hi."

# 30

# WHERE WE STAND

One night about a month later, I snuck out of my bedroom at around one o'clock and tiptoed through the kitchen and the living room. I slid the glass patio door open as quietly as possible, stepped outside, and walked into the grass of the backyard.

It was cold. Too cold to sleep out here, but I still needed a moment as part of my new routine. So I laid the pillow and blanket down, lay down on my back, and started my breathing exercises.

A few moments in, I heard the sliding door open and close. I thought maybe Patrick had come out to join me, perhaps having his own trouble sleeping after everything we'd been through.

Instead, it was my father. He'd heard me and had followed me outside. He placed his own pillow down on the ground next to mine, and lay down on his back beside me.

"So," he finally said, "you wanna tell me what all this sleeping outside stuff is about?"

"I wasn't going to sleep out here tonight," I countered.

"Well, duh," he responded. "It's freezing out here. But Patrick says you've been sleeping out here a lot, and I wanted to know what you had to say about that."

Finally I found the words. "I don't feel safe in my own bed."

He seemed to pull back just a few inches as he pondered this thing that confused him.

"But you feel safe outside in the backyard?"

"Yes," I said, finally understanding it myself. "Because out here . . . on my back, under all the stars . . . I can finally be insignificant. There's an entire universe out there. And only here, in this one . . . on this one planet . . . are my actions important. Only here do I matter. Everywhere else? I'm nothing. I'm space dust."

"And you take comfort in that?" He didn't get it.

"I do, yeah," I said, just being honest.

Freepoint was finally beginning to look like a city on the mend. Debris was being cleared, and homes and other structures were receiving repairs as needed.

The air was cool, but we hadn't had snow in a few weeks. Sherpa and I were out for a Saturday morning walk. I would be following my usual route of late, which took me out west of town, deftly avoiding taking me anywhere near Bentley's house.

He still wasn't talking to me. And neither was Penelope, though that might have been because she also was mad at me or out of simple loyalty to her boyfriend.

As for the rest of the Ables, it was hit or miss. Greta had been distant—again, probably out of loyalty to Penelope. Freddie was still coming around and being friendly, as were Owen and Porter.

I'd told them all what had happened, even Bentley and the others who were angry at me. I guess some of them just didn't believe me. It was hard to blame them. No one had heard our conversation there at the end because Henry and I had been thinking, not speaking. The only proof I had was my own word, and it just wasn't enough for some people.

I didn't know what Henry's family thought of all of it; they'd never returned to Freepoint after the evacuation.

I wasn't doing too well with all this. I hated it, in fact. But I was trying to focus on the positives.

Patrick and I had never been closer. The time alone without Dad had, in a weird way, been good for our sibling relationship. We picked at each other less, and we were being courteous to each other at a much higher than normal rate.

Talking through the battles and our mutual abductions had started to bring Dad and I closer than I would have thought possible. Though there were still some issues.

He had not been happy at all about the dog, and he'd been straight up angry about the Jeep. But ultimately he realized we had feared or assumed he might never come back to us. So because of that, and the fact that we'd saved the world, we escaped any formal punishment for our misdeeds. After all, the Jeep had been destroyed by debris during the battle in D.C., and wasn't really my fault. Though Dad kept saying he was more angry about me taking it in the first place than its ultimate destruction.

And I had been able to spend more time with Emmaline. We'd even finally gotten our first date, and not a drop of blood was spilled.

Hilariously, our first date took place in France. She made a joke about being able to teleport so our date options were unlimited, and I came back immediately with a gag about Paris and french fries, and that became a thing. So she teleported us to Paris, the city of food—and lights, I hear—and we ate American french fries at McDonald's on a balcony overlooking the Seine River.

She then took us to Antarctica for snow cones. And if you're not charmed by that, then your heart is made of stone. Regardless, I was charmed, and our first date became—as we joked about first dates—the most memorable and exciting first date in history.

Sherpa and I passed Charles Field, the Ables practice grounds and the site of a great many memories for me personally. Sherpa smelled something interesting on a nearby tree, but he gave up quickly and we continued north.

I had one ear listening to the radio as I walked, with the other ear open to the ambient noise. Never a good idea for a blind person to cover up both ears while walking in public.

I was catching up with the news, because folks here in Freepoint weren't all that interested in talking politics and current events lately. Something about a government agency leveling the town in the name of imprisoning its residents tended to turn a city against the elected officials.

In the wake of the events in DC, a bunch of corruption had come to light, and it went a lot further than just Ettinger and her own personal agenda.

Bentley's father was facing charges, of course, for conspiring with Ettinger to corral custodians into internment camps in exchange for political power. But he hadn't been alone on the custodian end of the affair. A dozen others, all from Freepoint, were indicted as part of a sweeping crackdown, including one of Bentley's older brothers, Branson.

Half the staff at DHS were arrested or fired, and the division set up to investigate custodians was shut down in full.

A lot of video evidence ultimately helped turn the tide of public opinion in the custodians' favor—videos basically of the torture we received in those prisons, and many of us were minors. The video that seemed to be viewed the most and played most frequently in news broadcasts happened to be of me ripping my pain chip out of my hand.

Fear can be a powerful motivator. It can whip entire nations into a fervor before the facts have even come to light. And there would still be plenty of skepticism directed at custodians. But the public had drawn the line at child torture and false imprisonment.

There were lots of things that had changed that didn't yet seem good or bad. I was a flash-in-the-pan celebrity. My name had been in all the news stories. I would never be a secret custodian again. And it would be a while before my story moved far enough to the backs of peoples' minds for me to be anonymous again.

Of course, being one of the faces of the absolution of custodians in the real world meant I became less liked here at home, where many of the other custodians didn't think I was all that special or worthy of such attention. But it's not like I asked for these things to happen to me. I just . . . found myself in circumstances that became famous. I hadn't wanted it.

But there was nothing I could do about what other people thought about me. All I could do was what I thought was the right thing to do in each moment. And if I wasn't able to do that, I would at least own my mistakes. Beyond that, it was out of my control.

I wasn't going to go door to door pleading my case with all the citizens of Freepoint, trying to win back friends or positive opinions. There were really only a few opinions that mattered to me. And those people—the ones I wanted to plead my case to—well, they wouldn't let me have an audience just yet.

Which was getting awkward now that we were all back in school together every day. I didn't mind the school part. I'd had fun skipping for those two months and pretending like I was ready to make adult decisions, but I knew now that I was not. I still needed school, for more than just the knowledge itself—for the relationships, the interactions, the growing up.

Maybe I just wasn't ready to grow up. And maybe I was realizing I shouldn't have to be ready to grow up at this age.

We walked by Jack's Pizza. The family had been working hard to get the restaurant back up and running. I'll admit, I was anxious for them to open. I hadn't had a slice in six weeks!

DHS had really done a number on the city when they invaded. It didn't make the news because they hadn't wanted it to. But when Ettinger convinced the Senate to give her temporary emergency authority to deploy the National Guard, she used it to cause as much damage as possible. She had told the Senate we were living in secret moving camps, like Robin Hood or something, defending ourselves with heavy artillery, motion sensors, and superpowers.

It wasn't the first time someone with too much power lied to their superiors to do some evil shit. It wouldn't be the last either.

Tanks, heavy machine guns, grenades—they'd all been used. The mayor said 70 percent of the city's structures had at least some level of damage.

So much destruction. She must have had one hell of a grudge against custodians. Which was weird, given that she was one.

Maybe she just wanted power. It was always possible the motivation was simple power. People who'd tasted it seemed to really love it.

I admit that I enjoyed the feeling I got from using my abilities to move enormous objects. I didn't enjoy that power enough to want to hurt other people just so I could get more. But the world appeared to be full of people who did.

Sure, we'd defeated this one. But there would be another. And another.

It was the reason custodians were needed and why we had an obligation to use our powers to help other people. The world was always going to be unfair, and the rich were always going to keep getting richer at the expense of the poor.

The face may look different from time to time, but there was still always going to be a powerful hand reaching into the pockets of those without power.

And I couldn't fix it all. Or fight it all. I couldn't even right all the wrongs I would personally witness or experience in just my own life.

But I was damn sure going to try.

# THE END.

# ACKNOWLEDGMENTS

This book would not have been possible if not for the work and support of the great people at Turner Publishing, my friends at MadeIn, my CinemaSins family, my business partner Chris, my editor, artist Callie Lawson, my friends, my family, and most importantly my wife—who pushed me to write these stories down. And finally, the readers who supported *The Ables* through an original publishing, a reissue, and now a sequel . . . there are too many of you to name, but I'm humbled you would care to spend time with my characters and their adventures.